THE
POSSESSION
OF
DELIA
SUTHERLAND

THE
POSSESSION
OF
DELIA
SUTHERLAND

BARBARA
NEIL

NAN A. TALESE

DOUBLEDAY

New York
London
Toronto
Sydney
Auckland

PUBLISHED BY NAN A. TALESE
an imprint of Doubleday
a division of Bantam Doubleday Dell Publishing Group, Inc.
1540 Broadway, New York, New York 10036

DOUBLEDAY is a trademark of Doubleday, a division of
Bantam Doubleday Dell Publishing Group, Inc.

Library of Congress Cataloging-in-Publication Data

Neil, Barbara.
The possession of Delia Sutherland/Barbara Neil.—
1st ed. in U.S.A.
p.   cm.
1. Women—Fiction. 2. Marriage—Fiction.
3. Illegitimate children—Fiction. I. Title.
PR6064.E426P67   1994
823'.914—dc20   93-34160
CIP

ISBN 0-385-47215-3

Printed in the United States of America
April 1994
First Edition in the United States of America

1   3   5   7   9   10   8   6   4   2

For my daughters,
Charlotte, Rebecca and Victoria,
with love and gratitude

PART ONE

Prologue

IT WAS A FOOLISH THING to fall in love with a dead man. This would never have happened had I not been asleep. Asleep, impervious, for forty-five years.

I'm all right now; secure in my rootlessness as I never was with property, ownership, responsibility. I remain peculiar, remote. The difference is that I'm aware of it. Take the lady at the next table who's here every day as I am, except when it rains. She watches me, pretending not to, trembles segments of Croque Monsieur down into the mouth of the fluff of poodle on her lap, then wipes her greasy fingers on always the same silk flowers pinned to her lapel. Their real purpose, it would seem. She's certain I'm mad, my thoughts animating me the way they do. She's seen those tears, I expect, those damned tears. And I laugh, I do laugh. I don't mind. But she would like to know me, just the same. I can't let her because there'd be no end to it. However, it's already autumn and soon the weather will drive everyone inside the café. She'll be one of the first because she's old and already feeling a chill in the sunshine, less comfortable watching the crowd flowing, joining, leaving. When she does go in for the winter I'll give her one of the smiles she's already tried to share and say, *"Bonjour, Madame."* But that'll be the end of it because I'll stay outside not minding the cold, never have.

The first thing she would ask me about, if I let her, would be the postcard. My postcard propped against the thick china saucer of my coffee cup, the way it always is while I write in this exercise book and others like it, sorting things out, making sure I've missed no point, no signal; then I'll collect them together for you, so you'll really know me at last and, in your knowledge of me, regardless of

3

judgment, I'll find the greatest peace short of, well, dying. Surely when pretense is done with, that is what we seek, to be known?

The postcard: the waiter whisked it off the table with the cups and wineglasses I'd accumulated during the course of a morning. I didn't see it happen but realized almost immediately the card was gone, must have showed panic by standing to shake out the pleats of my long skirt, scraping aside my chair, searching under the table. The old lady was watching me do all this. When the brisk young waiter passed her on his way back into the café, I noticed the red nails on her buckled fingers scratch his sleeve. Maintaining his tray aloft he reluctantly inclined sideways to catch her words, swiveled his torso around to look at me while she was still speaking. He came over, reached his left hand high to pluck from his tray my card, and drop it on my table with a disdainful shrug.

I pretended I didn't know what had happened, that she saved my card. I will thank her. Soon I'll buy her some new silk flowers for her lapel.

The waiter might well have thought my card was litter. I received it three months ago and it's been so handled, so read, reread and examined, it's as limp as cloth. White lines of paper are breaking through from the back into the glossy-colored picture of a fish market. The cheap printed colors are bleary, so the heaps of orange crabs are stained with the black of a pile of mussels beside them on one stall; a great fish on another haloed with its own ghost. The water in the crowded harbor behind them is a dishonest blue. I know that because the blotchy postmark reads "Marseille" and it's the scene I have in front of me. Across the busy road there are the stalls, the harbor, all less bright, but there just the same. The message on the back reads, "There you are, Mrs. Sutherland." That's all, no greeting, no signature. Does it mean, "There you are, that's where you should be?" Or, "There you are, I told you so?" Or is the first word stressed on a sigh of relief, "*There* you are, Mrs. Sutherland?"

Have I been found?

One

DELIA SUTHERLAND was driving at twenty miles an hour, the speed limit she had imposed on the eight miles of private road within her own estate; a demesne uncut by any public route other than footpaths, and sealed with a gate at each of the four entrances. Something lay motionless blocking the way ahead. Drawing closer she found it was a roe buck. Leaving the car's engine running, she crouched to examine the hardening dribble of blood running from the nose, the paralyzed alarm in the eyes. With her foot against the creature's belly she rocked it to estimate the weight before gripping the rough fur and hefting it into the back of her dust-caked pickup.

"Leave. I said *leave.*" The two Labradors riding with her withdrew to separate corners, panting uneasily. She drove on cursing, "Damned maniacs, lunatic drivers . . ."

A house came into view, away there through the trees, across that field and the next, at the top of the park. She saw it as anyone does who has been born in a place, loves it, and has lived nowhere else. In other words, she did not see it at all, merely assimilated the security its presence gave her with the other sensations of the moment like fatigue, like hunger, like the smuts and smell from stubble burning earlier in the day still clinging to her skin.

It was a gray stone Georgian building. Nine long windows on the first floor reflected the advancing sky; eight more on the ground floor, separated by double front doors, threw back a dark outline of trees. The length of the windows, the front doors with their dropped jaw of steps, the arched pediment at roof level, gave the building the appearance of being perpetually aghast at some shocking secret whispered by the countryside. The graceful architecture

5

on the east side regressed to a lower, Victorian wing, partially ob-
scured by a yew hedge the same age as the wing itself. A planting
which proved that, even on completion, the ugliness of the addi-
tion had been conceded.

Delia Sutherland drove on and, when the house was blocked
from view by an avenue of beech and lime, she stopped again.
Reaching behind her for the gun supported by brackets on the dog
guard, she pulled it down and broke it open, all without lowering
her eyes from something outside. The dogs came close to the bars,
alert, swallowing whines of excitement. "Hush, boys, shh." The
fingers of her right hand felt blindly about the dashboard—a packet
of mints, a biro, some greasy rags, a glass straw of bull semen—until
they encircled the smooth, firm body of a cartridge. She slotted
that into the gun, nosed the barrel through the open passenger
window, brought one leg beneath her and twisted in her seat. As
she lifted the gun and took aim, the dogs groaned in their throats.
"Steady, babies, steady." She laid her cheek against the stock and
raised her right index finger in a sloppy salute before squeezing the
trigger. From a nearby lime tree a spinning tumble of black and
white feathers hit the ground, tossed and was still. "Gotcha, you
little bugger." The dogs began barking at the dead magpie and she
let them.

Minutes later the house was in closer view. Now its dilapidation
was visible. Stains, tracks of green tears, spread from windowsills.
The balustrade around the parapet was broken in places and
through one of these a tuft of grass swayed in an upper breeze, a
paper hat on a high-court judge.

As she turned into the drive leading to the house the knob came
off the gearstick. "Bloody foreign cars." She shoved it back on.
The dogs jostled at her feet as she ascended the five chipped steps
to the front doors, turned one of the bronze handles and, leaving
the lustrous evening behind, entered Sleet House.

The hall smelled of slow-passing time and of another, fetid, odor
that made its own way in the stillness. An odor of which Delia
Sutherland had never been aware. Across the hall was a wide
wooden staircase that broke halfway up, left and right, into two
narrower flights where a window let through some shy light. In the
hall fireplace, logs were blackened from an attempted fire during a
cold spell in May.

She shut the front door and said, "Brrr," to the dogs when it was not chilly at all. She often said that. It was a draft that chilled her, only for a second, as it chilled most who entered Sleet House.

The dogs pushed past her into the gunroom. It used to be the library but, the books having been sold thirty years before, the sensible thing had been to make the room useful. The oak shelves lining the walls were now cluttered with a multitude of accessories for sports no longer pursued at Sleet—tennis, croquet, fishing—as well as countless gumboots, a pile of flaking leather puttees and outer clothing dating back years. Shotguns and rifles stood in a space where the shelves had been removed.

From their sofa covered with a muddy sheet the dogs' attention was riveted on their mistress cleaning her gun at the central table, until she threw them two bones from a bowl there. Back in the hall she reexamined her unopened mail lying among newspapers and rejected the unpromising envelopes for the second day running. It was Saturday's mail, this was Sunday.

She heard the sift-sift of slippers coming from the kitchen passage in the Victorian wing through an archway to the left of the stairs.

"Evening, Curtis," she said without looking up from unknotting the dog's lead she had meant to leave in the gunroom.

The old man was stooped. When he spoke, his head remained lowered, leaving his eyebrows to do the lifting. "Evening, Miss Delia."

She had been "Miss Delia" to him ever since she was born and he had just arrived at Sleet House as footman. Back in the days when there was a real staff, real work, back in the days when life had vigor. Back in the days. There had been a brief period of "madam" when she was first married but it did not last. He raised an exquisite hand to his blue-white hair, swept back from long-lidded eyes that blinked disappointment, blinked resignation. The high-cut nostrils of his supercilious nose were, to the few who knew him, the barometer of his mood.

"There's the beefbone for the dogs in the gunroom, Miss. I've cut it in two. Kidneys in the dining room for yourself."

"Thanks, Curtis, can't wait."

"Quite so, Miss." Both suspected the other's sarcasm but kidneys it always had been on Sundays and kidneys it always would be, so long as he cooked, as he did on that night only because Mrs. Files was off.

"Good night then, Miss," shuffling towards the dining room.

"Night, Curtis," she called, possibly too late because he was already in there closing the curtains. She heard the door on the far side of it open and close as he made his way to the back stairs and his own flat on the first floor of the wing.

Head back in concentration, Delia Sutherland felt in the pockets of her army-surplus trousers to retrieve keys and loose change which she threw on the table. As she crossed to the stairs the echo of her steps walked the walls and ceiling.

"Bung, Ho. C'mon, boys." The dogs skidded after her; the clicking of their claws made the two of them sound like ten.

The hall remained empty for a few minutes until a woman entered through the front door which she shut again behind her. She leaned something bulkily wrapped in black plastic against one of the chairs, removed her jacket, then hissed, briskly rubbing her arms and shoulders through the sleeves of her cotton dress. It was that draft again. If anyone had bothered to trace the source of it they would have found a skylight propped open and forgotten at the end of an upstairs corridor in the Victorian wing. The cold walls beckoned down the air to guide it past seven unoccupied rooms—a long time ago chambermaids had slept in them—along to a swing door that opened into the main house. Here the draft nosed and whimpered, disconsolate until the front door was opened again, which made the swing door shudder enough to allow the draft to escape and sail above the tattered carpet of the passage, sway the corn in the numerous gold-framed pastoral scenes hung between the entrances to eight guest bedrooms, and undulate down the stairs. In the hall, avoiding the blast of heat bowling through the arch leading to the kitchen on the ground floor of the wing, it rattled the dining-room door and the doors of the unused ballroom, it fluttered newspapers on the onyx-topped letter table, curled around the palm-tree hatstand bearing dusty fedoras, old cricket caps and deerstalkers, and whistled at the front door before racing to its penultimate destination: the morning room. Here it rested in the depths of the sofa before blowing on Dorelia's ankles in the Augustus John drawing, sifting papers on the mahogany partners desk, and scanning the remainder of the Caldwell library in the glass-paned Chippendale bookcase. Its last mischievous act was to billow the robes and ice the sandaled toes of a group of ten-inch-high, K'ang Hai porcelain figures, their heads meekly inclined to the vase each held, containing a single tulip. That done, the draft was sucked up the scorching flue of the morning-room fire, which burned throughout the day, the year, and was left to die down at night so the perpetually hot ashes were enough to ignite the first log of the morning.

Delia Sutherland's own west-facing bedroom, high, cold-feeling, even in summer, brimmed with light. The pink-and-gray curtains and covers were the same ones that had witnessed her mother's long, fatal illness there thirty-seven years before. Dead organza hung from a tester above the wide bed and more of it skirted the dressing table to hide a kneehole and drawers. That dressing table was a memorial to a very feminine woman with a different view on life from her daughter, Delia, who, with eyes tight-shut to concentrate, had pinned her hair up, and out of the way, since she was seventeen. The little attention she did give herself was quickly dealt with in the bathroom. So the dressing table, the silver-backed brushes, crystal jars containing old cotton wool, an amethyst pillbox with three white pills powdering away inside, remained untouched.

Delia Sutherland undressed, wrapped herself in a toweling robe and, pulling pins from her no-nonsense wedge of hair, gazed from one of the three windows over fields and trees set in a silence three thousand acres deep; an August silence.

There was a knock and Muriel Fuller poked her head round the door. "Thought I'd find you here." She lugged her package over to the armchair where she sank down.

Muriel was fair-skinned, pale-haired, pretty. But when, as now, she was tired or depressed, her neat, well-arranged features lay like sediment on a drained dish.

"Hope I'm not disturbing you," she said, peering inside her shoe, shaking out a pea of gravel.

"No. Lovely to see you. What have you got there?"

Muriel, about to answer, was silenced by the appearance of her old friend. It was not the six feet one of angular womanhood that surprised her, she was used to that, it was the volume of Delia's gunmetal-gray hair, a thundercloud swallowing her face. "Your hair," she said.

"What about it?"

"I've never seen it loose before. Isn't that odd? In all this time? And, well, it's extraordinary. Wonderful, really."

"Good thing you didn't come earlier; I've only just arrived in."

"Harvest?"

"No, I'll go out to that later. School governors."

"On a Sunday?"

"The head walked out. Sent her resignation right in the middle of the summer holidays, won't come back. We were talking about stand-ins, replacements."

"You enjoy your school bit, don't you?"

"Yes, I do. Twenty years nearly, it must be. What's in that bag, Muriel?"

"My excuse to come over. Honestly, Delia, there are times when, if I couldn't escape to you, I really don't know what I'd do. It's not that Tom's unsympathetic but he won't talk things through as much as I'd like to."

"I won't be long and we can have a drink downstairs. What things?"

"Melinda again, I'm afraid."

"I was thinking about her only the other night. Do you know, I don't think I've seen Melinda since she was fifteen or so."

"Don't worry, I feel the same sometimes. But she was home this weekend, for once. She's so unhappy with that boyfriend I told you about. I swear he's hit her. There's a mark on her face. She can't seem to break away. He's got her into debt now. You see, she comes home, I mop up her misery, she waltzes off restored and I'm left feeling utterly shitty. So, a drink and a moan with you would be lovely."

The telephone rang; Delia Sutherland sat on the edge of the bed to answer it in her usual fashion, impelling the caller, by silence, to speak first.

"Delia?" It was a man's voice.

She had her hand over the mouthpiece. "Go on, open it, Muriel. Yes, David?" It was David Rosen, her solicitor. Solicitor, trustee and friend.

"Listen, Delia, I have some sad news."

She noted the "sad" rather than "bad." "What is it?"

Muriel had begun to unwrap the black plastic. "I told you, it's my excuse for coming. You know how Tom hates me leaving him, even for half an hour, during the weekends."

"It's about Francis." Rosen paused, allowing her to prepare herself.

10

"Well, go on," Delia Sutherland persisted.

"It's that strimmer I borrowed from you a couple of months back."

"Well, the thing is . . ." Rosen opened.

"Yes?"

"He's dead."

She pushed the receiver into her lap with the voice still talking, until there was a click and the dialing tone.

"Delia, what's the matter?" Muriel sat beside her on the bed.

Rosen must have been calling from home so that is where she rang. He answered instantly. "Sorry about that," she said.

"Not at all. You okay, Delia?"

"Yes. Thank you. So he's dead? Really dead?"

Disconcerted by the thoroughness of her inquiry he protested, "Well, yes. Yes, he is," before returning to the conventional, "I'm so sorry."

"How?" Last doubts might have been cleared by knowing the manner of it.

"It seems he drowned in his swimming pool. It happened last night. Are you there?"

A moment or two, then she said, "I suppose you want me to come up and sort things out. Legal aspects and all."

"No hurry. You know how tidy he was about his arrangements. Give yourself time to get over the shock."

"Eleven tomorrow suit you?"

"Only if you're sure."

"Eleven, then. Good-bye."

Muriel placed her arm tentatively around Delia Sutherland's shoulders. "Who's dead?"

"Francis."

Muriel withdrew her arm. "Oh."

"Yes. Quite. That's what I thought."

"No, my dear, I'm sorry. I didn't mean to sound, well, like that. It's awful. Just awful. How?"

"Do you think, actually, I might be alone? No offense."

"Of course, of course. I'm so sorry." Flushed with embarrassment, confusion, Muriel reached for the strimmer. "What about . . . ?"

"Oh. Right. Leave it in the gunroom, would you?"

When Delia Sutherland was alone one of the dogs came whining at her feet. "Get away, boy. *Place.*" The animal sloped back to the corner shared with his brother who had remained, head on paws, as he ought, and was thudding his tail to draw attention to the fact.

She saw nothing from the window this time because the tears in her eyes triplicated the trees, sending them skywards. She touched her face, rubbed her fingers and said aloud, "Tears," as though the phenomenon, having been discovered, should be named.

Two

THAT'S HOW CLEARLY I can see her. I know how she moved, what she saw, what she thought. But I can't say "I" because I am no longer she, that woman, that Delia Sutherland who, even when alone, pretended astonishment at tears.

See me. See me in the sunshine now. It was never like that before. If you could—and soon I will be conspicuous among the empty chairs and tables—you'd stop so we could absorb the changes in each other, and allow the selves we used to be to surface. Those first impressions that are stronger than anything time can do. You will be there one day, coming towards me from the crowd. I'll look up from all of this and I'll see your face. Of that I'm certain.

The postcard again: the waiter whisked it off my table the other day with all the cups and wineglasses I'd accumulated during the course of a morning. I didn't see it happen but realized almost immediately the card was gone, must have showed panic by standing to shake out the pleats of my long skirt, scraping aside my chair, searching under the table. The old lady was watching me do all this. When the brisk young waiter passed her on his way back into the café, I noticed the red nails on her buckled fingers scratch his sleeve. Maintaining his tray aloft he reluctantly inclined sideways to catch her words, swiveled his torso around to look at me while she was still speaking. He came over, reached his left hand high to pluck from his tray my card, and drop it on my table with a disdainful shrug.

I pretended I didn't know what had happened, that she saved my card. I will thank her. Soon I'll buy her some new silk flowers for her lapel.

All right, why tears, then, as I stood at my window? Were they angry tears? Or were they duty tears? I never thought Francis would go first. Wild, lavish, a joker, the sort that survives against the odds. I'd pictured him so well as an elderly man, still vain though diminished, pulling unresisting young women to him; flattering, charming, twinkling on into senility. It was me, big-boned, stay-at-home Delia, who might have been expected to contract some galloping cancer. Hurt wives frequently do.

People were surprised when we married. Over-tall, gangling Miss Caldwell, dark-browed, reserved, cold even, who lived alone with her widowed father, another odd sort.

The things people say that they think you can't hear—you know them, they hang in the atmosphere to enlighten and hurt when you're alone. "Fancy that girl nabbing Francis Sutherland who was seriously rich, handsome, someone who brought *l'air de fête* to the simplest gathering." Perhaps a clue lay in the isolating phrase, "He could have had anyone he wanted."

We met at a local dance. I was nineteen. I hadn't wanted to go but my father made me. I'd been to dances before and come home disappointed, reminded of an unspecified emptiness. I was outstanding, as always. What girl wouldn't be at six feet one in a dress that had been such a success when her mother wore it, now with a line where the hem had been let down? I spent most of the evening with an orange juice, was danced with twice; once for a dare. I was with him when he collected, made jolly sure they paid up. We all knew when Francis and his crowd arrived. There was a scintillation in their part of the room which was nowhere else. They were Londoners who'd arrived due to a combination of accident and curiosity. They'd left what they'd thought was a dull affair, lost themselves in the country lanes and found ours, which was duller. We'd thought it was glamorous until they arrived. They stayed apart commenting loudly until, one by one, they broke in to dance with the prettiest girls.

I knew he was looking at me, then turning his back, laughing with his friends. It was his bad luck that, in one of those cups of silence when the band stops and the conversation ceases to flow, I should hear him say, ". . . and chat up that bloody great obelisk."

He came over to me. I leaned against the wall, crossed my arms, pretended to watch the dancing while he spoke to me. Then I answered.

He did not like it. He blushed, stepped back, walked away adjusting his bow tie. They left soon after.

I went home with my emptiness unspecified no longer. I'd been waiting, all my life, apparently, for that rude stranger.

Even in those days I walked the crops, escorted the vet to a sick cow, worked in the estate office filing and making calf records. I'd enjoyed it all until that party. Running the place for my father had given me satisfaction. I would try to be authoritative with the red-headed cook, Mrs. Files, who was always cooking something of her own, interminably pregnant. Now I couldn't concentrate. During hours of walking I talked to him, to Francis, told him things inexpressible in words. At night, I held my old Labrador, Gertie, close in bed. She was given to me as a pup when Mummy died. Even Gertie I would have relinquished to have Francis approach once more; to have another chance. What was it he had said to me? Distanced by humiliation I never heard. Had it not been for a single gesture, when he touched his eye with the back of his hand, that swift movement he made when I said what I said—what that was I've forgotten—had it not been for that I could have loathed him for a day and dismissed him from existence. The way I'd done with others. As it was, he was sharing my head, laughing then retreating, touching his eye with the back of his hand, feeling for where my words had entered him.

Some days after the dance there was a letter on the hall table addressed to me. When I saw my name spilling off it in a fluent, arrogant hand, I knew it was from him. That he should write to me was the most unlikely thing because it was what I had most wanted. His letter remained in my pocket, unopened, until late in the afternoon when Gertie and I walked to the lake. I sat on the bank to read while she harassed the Canada geese.

Friday afternoon
It has taken me six telephone calls, two promises and a favor to have the pleasure of writing the words:

Dear Delia,
You see, I didn't even learn your name? I have counted every hour since we met. I'm the man who tried to speak to you at the Harveys' dance. This doubtless makes me one of many that evening, and every other day of your life. Which of my flaws shall I describe to jolt your memory? But I don't really want you to

15

remember because if you do you'll surely reject me again even before I can see you once more. That's what I want more than anything in the world. Don't be frightened by my writing so boldly. I'm frightened enough for the two of us and it makes me very shy and safe to be with. Would you write to me, Delia? Write to tell me you'll see me once more? I wait for that.

Francis Sutherland

How could he have known, unless by instinct, a letter would have been the only way to approach me? I did write and invited him to tea at Sleet. If it was all a joke he couldn't laugh at me there, couldn't hurt me again. If he was going to do that it would be later; after he had gone, and I wouldn't know.

Francis Sutherland arrived at Sleet House on a wet afternoon in August. Delia Caldwell opened the front door. "I suppose you'd better come in," was how she greeted the man who had unpegged the base of her existence for the past two hundred and fifty-six hours.

She had her hand raised to accept the rose he was holding towards her, when, frowning, he withdrew it to sniff into the cone of cellophane. "Hope it's okay."

"Thank you."

"And I've brought this for you too." He handed her a flat package and watched, excited, while she began to open it. "It's a scarf," he told her before she had finished. "I hope you like it."

"Yes, I do. It's beautiful." She tied it around her neck.

He opened the front door, reshut it.

"What are you doing?" she asked.

"I felt a draft, that's all. Thought maybe I hadn't closed it properly. Hey, no, look. It's better like this." He retied the scarf on her.

She leaned towards the glass above the letter table. Before seeing herself she was reminded of the first sight of his letter. "Why did you write?"

"Did you mind?"

"No. But why? I mean, everybody telephones these days, don't they?"

"Maybe, but not me. Not when something really matters. I'm so pleased you asked me to your home and didn't suggest some other place."

16

"Why?"

"I've never . . ." He slumped, inarticulate, into a chair by the wall.

She did not go to him but bent over to see what she could of his expression in the gloom of the hall. "What's the matter?"

"I was thinking how we have feelings that seem unique to us, then we try to express them and what comes out isn't unique at all but dull cliché. I was going to say, I've never met anyone like you. Think of all the men and women who must have said that to each other. I'd like to do better." He launched himself to his feet, ramming his hands together. "Never mind, the point is I wanted to see you in your own setting, and that's where you asked me. And it's great. Okay?"

A fat Labrador pressed its nose into his crotch. He was going to redirect it under the guise of stroking, which he knew would be welcome to both dog and mistress, when he noticed a sore on the old head which stopped him.

"Well. I'll show you round, then."

"I'd love it. Thank you."

His enthusiasm made her glad. Perhaps it was not all a joke and he was not going to laugh later. She was in front of him and he enjoyed her walk, an unconcessionary walk. She was owned by nothing. And he liked the neutral way she guided him, indicating any interesting paintings by raising her arm without looking, yet it was clear she knew them well. "Nice light in that one, the way it comes round the cloud and, oh well, I can't explain."

They were in the ballroom. Flaking gold plasterwork and eau-de-Nil walls nursed two fireplaces and four sets of french windows. Her grandmother had created this space by knocking together two rooms. This ruined one façade of the house but in those days entertaining large numbers was the thing. The cold, in this room, meant business. Francis Sutherland tucked his hands in his armpits as he picked a path through the clutter of furniture. Tapestry-covered chairs and sofas with seats five feet deep were arranged around the fireplaces. High lacquered screens, inlaid with mother-of-pearl, protected the seating areas from drafts. The numerous side tables were crowded with enameled boxes, pewter figurines, miniature clocks and sewing sets in ivory cases. On a long stool pushed up to the back of a sofa were piles of photograph albums bound in red calf, browned with age. The echo amplified and dis-

torted even the sound of breath; the sensitive became self-conscious.

"I like this very much," Francis Sutherland whispered, pointing
to a dark painting hanging beside the fireplace.

"Yes. Me too. It's an oil sketch. My favorite thing in the house."
She opened a set of shutters. "Can you see it better? When I was
little, well, young," as though for her the word "little" had been
disallowed, "I'd come in here, open the shutters like this and look
at it, pretending I was the figure there. Do you see her? Just below
the trees? Still, doesn't do to get attached to things, to objects."

Except you are, he thought, you are. And why do you move me
so much, you strange, fellowless girl?

Throughout the ground floor of Sleet House she passed, without
explanation, blanks on the walls. Shapes where furniture had stood
were impressed into the carpets, marked by ineradicable dustlines
on the floorboards. There were so many that Francis Sutherland
joked, "Burgled, were you?" Her expression made him add,
"Sorry. Doesn't matter. I'm not serious."

She faced him as though he were a task to be tackled. "Sold,
Francis. All right? Sold to pay debts."

"I'm sorry. I wasn't trying to pry. I had no idea." He slapped his
hands on his thighs. "Debts, debts, that's okay. Nothing wrong
with paying debts."

She saw his embarrassment, how he was trying to pass it off.
"You're not English, are you? Your voice isn't."

"Bahamian."

"Bohemian?"

"Bahamas, right?" He had been through that one too often.

"I thought they were all black over there?"

"No. Not everyone. Not everyone, by any means," and that too.

"How old are you?"

"Twenty-nine?" as though if she wanted he could improve on it.

"God," she said.

He found the best improvement he could make was, "Well, only
last week."

She looked away.

He had never met anyone so aggressively shy, wished he had
listened to some of the gossip offered with her address. Except he
had wanted to discover for himself; did not want to spoil this new

feeling, wanted to make it last. Why did it never last? Why were all those beautiful women so, so knowable?

She was ahead of him at the foot of the stairs calling, "Well, come on, then." So he did, hands in pockets, whistling.

He asked polite questions. "When was the house built?"

"Seventeen-thirties."

"Was the architect anyone famous?"

"Don't know. They say it could be Hawksmoor or Vanbrugh. No records."

"Why?"

"Some gambler owned the place. Had to sell up to pay debts. He was so bitter he burned all the papers to do with the house. The bore is we have no plans of the flues so, when a fire smokes, it's nearly impossible to trace the block. Same with the drains."

"Ah, drains." So that was the smell in the hall, the one he had thought might be coming from the rose. Now it was trailing with them up the stairs.

"What?"

"Nothing. How awkward. About the drains."

"Not really."

Faced with the dreary passage and dull paintings he said, "Let's go outside. Show me round the garden." He took her hand as though it had always belonged to him and had come into her possession by mistake. She seemed not to want him to do it but he didn't mind, he wasn't scared of her. "Come on," he said.

"But it's raining."

"So what? You're English and don't mind. I'm mad, so I don't mind either."

There, she nearly laughed. She let him keep her hand until, on the gravel path at the back of the house, he pointed to the sky. "Look at those bloody great clouds, Delia, aren't they something? So vast, so gray but . . ." She withdrew her hand, repossessed it even after the tacit decision that it was his. He did not understand.

"You shouldn't say that. 'Bloody great.' "

"You mind my swearing? Really?"

"No. It's just that no one should say 'bloody' anything unless they're English. It never works. Makes them sound like second-rate mimics."

"But I am half English. I was educated at Radley like my father and uncle and grandfather. I went to Oxford. Dammit, my mother was English. From Norfolk, and what's more I've kept a British passport." She had not stayed to listen so he caught up with her for his last sentence, "I said we were from Norfolk."

"I heard, you know."

"You were so far ahead I thought maybe you didn't."

"I mean about 'bloody great obelisk.' I heard what you said to your friends about me at the dance."

"I really don't remember. I can't think what I would be trying to mean by saying that."

It was the truth. But he did remember what she had said to him when he had approached her, complimented her. He would never forget it.

She walked him round the once-was garden and the silences between their exchanges grew longer.

"Nice dog," he said as it tripped him on leaving a greenhouse.

"I was given her when I was eight. When Mummy died. Old now, though. Warts and things, sore places, you know."

"Yes, yes. I saw them."

No area of the garden had been maintained. The topiary had twisted into wild contortions; gravel paths were lost beneath pasture grass blown from the fields. Stone urns, decayed by yellow lichen, marked the points of what had once been a fleur-de-lis sculpted in turf. Now it was a mirage in weed. A ladder had been left so long against a high, cone-shaped cypress tree the branches embraced it.

"It's sad," Francis Sutherland said. "You could make it all so wonderful."

"That takes money."

He walked more and more slowly, hands in pockets, not whistling now. There had been so much he wanted to tell her, wanted her to know about, and be impressed by. His background, the daredevil blood in his veins. He wanted to tell her about his father and uncle, Scott and Barclay, twins born at the end of the last century and sent to England to be educated. After school they wanted, not to go to university, but to return home and help old Wallace Sutherland make more money speculating on real estate. Prices were rising then, the Americans having seen the Caribbean's potential as a playground. And the twins missed the fishing. That was what they were doing when Scott was caught by a sixteen-foot hammerhead shark. He had been diving for conch while his brother stayed aboard playing the line. When Barclay saw the blood and commotion, he reached for his rifle and killed the shark with one shot. Scott's forehead resembled the top story of a Venetian palace after the seventy-six stitches had been removed.

Francis Sutherland wanted to tell Delia Caldwell how, when the First World War broke, the twins raced back to England to enlist, only to be informed, "We don't want you colonials in our war." So they consoled themselves by making more money and having fun. Before long the British attitude altered and they were allowed to fight in that war that had little bearing on them.

They were posted to Belgium where Wallace sent generous money orders so his sons need not live too badly. The result was that they lived with a flamboyance quite repellent to the English.

Their periods of leave were legendary. In town they would buy a car, surround themselves with an entourage of whores, and the party began. When leave was over they would return to the barracks in the car—once there were as many as eight women in the back—throw the keys in the air, "All yours, girls." Next time: new car, new girls.

Barclay was killed at Passchendaele and Scott returned to the Bahamas missing his right arm. But times were still good. In fact times were even better. Prohibition had begun in the States. That was when Scott Sutherland made real money. He began with a single schooner, which he would moor five miles off shore of Nassau, to meet English ships laden with spirits. Then he sailed to Long Island Sound where the liquor was distributed onto lighters and carried to the mainland. Easy.

During one of those operations, off the Biminis, one of Scott's black crew fell in. He couldn't swim and was quickly swept away. Scott plunged after him, pounding the waves with his single arm. Soon he too was lost. Two days later a turtle fisher in the Gulf Stream was about to launch his spear when he saw his quarry was a man snoozing on a piece of driftwood. It was Scott.

There was the time hijackers came alongside his boat and he threatened to shoot. They laughed at the one-armed man with the weird forehead, until he drew a pistol from his belt, aimed at a seagull on top of the mast, shot it dead. They left.

That was his own father, Scott. He did all those things. They weren't his, Francis Sutherland's, stories, no, but his history; his stock. He'd have done the same had there been wars to fight; had there been money to make. But there weren't wars and there was money, an awful lot of it to spend. His only work was developing property and making more money.

He had not told these stories to other women. He never shot them as a line because you don't shoot the truth. Besides, there was enough glamour about him with his wealth, his looks, and his softly-softly American accent to create rumor that worked in his favor. Delia Caldwell was different. He wanted her to know everything about him. He had never had such a longing to talk, but when had this begun, this silence? What had he said?

He had given up trying to keep pace, and stopped in the deep grass wondering about her raincoat. This was the sixties: that was more like something her mother would have worn.

Delia Caldwell was waiting for Francis Sutherland to catch up. Soon it would be all over. Nothing for it but tea then he would go. That was that. She realized it was going to be the same again: that new missing, that new loss. And hadn't he tried with his flower and his scarf? With his talk? His following her round in the drizzle? She wanted to say something leading back to where friendship might have been possible. Countless minutes had passed without a word. She would speak. Something would come if she made herself turn. And she did, so abruptly that he stumbled. When he had straightened, she said, "It's been jolly good fun. I mean, you coming and all."

She waited for an answer. None came, and slowly the scene assembled: a sodden garden and the sky clearing too late. His feet were lost in unmown grass, his trouser legs wet to the knee. There were dark patches on his shoulders where the rain had penetrated, and the collar of his jacket was turned up. There was a bluish shade around his lips and his hair was stuck to his forehead. Fun? Had she said fun? Delia Caldwell dropped her head, but as if that strange shape into which she wound her thick hair had been grabbed, her head fell back and she laughed. Without excuse or explanation she laughed.

Francis Sutherland watched her laughing. He understood it was not at him. You're wonderful, he wanted to say, and different and strange, and he wanted to say, I love you. He couldn't possibly because she did not like him, not very much, not yet. I love you, I want to get those words out of me because they hurt unsaid, inside me like this.

She ushered her laughter back to its source with, "Oh dear, oh dear, sorry, oh dear." Now he was watching her. She did not mind in the way she usually did. Your hair's black like mine, your skin's olive, your eyes are, what color? His expression was so fierce, so urgent. She had laughed at him, he hated her, and she fell from that high plain of laughter, past his face and the brightening afternoon, past any possibility of happiness. It wasn't far to the house. It would be all right, safe again inside.

Something occurred to Francis Sutherland when she was ahead of him on the steps to the morning room. "Delia?"

"Yes." She did not stop.

"Wait." So she did, inclining her head to him on the step below. "I'm sorry. For the dance. For how I was."

She looked away reliving the shame and how her sweat had left damp patches under the arms in the stiff silk of her dress. She felt the same desire to hurt back, had even crossed her arms. When she did look at him he was just completing that gesture with the back of his hand to his eye.

The path from "Sorry" to marriage was short. The path back to "Sorry" was shorter.

When certain old friends of Sutherland's were asked the frequent question, "Why the hell did he marry her?" they replied that, on the night of the dance, after Delia Caldwell had issued her curt response, whatever it was, Sutherland had returned to his group with the statement, "I could make that woman beautiful."

Three

MY CAFÉ—I regard it as mine, I've been sitting in it a good part of every day for nearly three months—is called the New York. Hardly very French but its style is, maroon awning and paintwork, bentwood chairs. There are tables right outside on the pavement. That's where I am. Behind me is a semiprotected section open to the street, yet inside the building. It is from there the old lady with the silk flowers sits to watch me, and anyone else who amuses her. We both arrive early enough each morning to take up our usual seats. Her problem is going to be that, last night after closing time, which was in the early hours, they inserted the glass panes in front of her section, and they are still there this morning. They've made it into winter quarters. I watched them putting the glass in, as I often do on returning from my walk down the Quai de Rive Neuve, around the flyover, along the Boulevard Charles Livon. This takes me past the recruitment center for the Légion Étrangère. Not a busy place. Even in daytime, if I walk that way, I don't see much coming and going through those gates.

So we're separated, the old lady and I; she won't have to move indoors with the cold weather after all, only she can't see me so well. I think they'll remove the pavement tables any day now. I'll arrive one morning to find they won't have set them outside, so I'll have to be inside, whether I mind the cold or not. I must buy those flowers for her lapel. The thank-you flowers.

You dead ones. The power you have, leaving us with our questions and truncated hopes. I am thinking now of my mother and father who loved each other with passion. What it would have come to over the years, within the rails of matrimony, who knows? She was vibrant, vivacious, beautiful and, of course, having died young, remains so. My father was gentle, quiet and gave her his adoration for the world to see. There was a time when I was part of the passion, held my place as the product, the proof of it. That state. My memory of it is powerfully abstract.

I was four when my brother was born. No sooner was he born than he died. My parents' grief threw them into each other and left me alone with mine. And I wanted him too, my brother, I had my love ready.

When my parents recovered, if that is what people do, I found myself no longer one of a trinity. Perhaps it was not safe to love me anymore. After all, I might die too. But I didn't die. I preferred to believe it was that that made them withdraw, or hide, their love—it comes to the same thing—rather than that I was ugly. She was very fair, very fine, my mother. She was life and light. I was none of those things and knew it even then.

The house was filled with activity and joy when she was alive. The music she loved to listen to, Ben Webster, Coleman Hawkins, always jazz, was played on her record player in the ballroom throughout the days and evenings, loudly so everyone in the house could hear. There were all kinds of visitors, all kinds of parties until Quiet came to settle in the ballroom first. After that I heard jazz on occasional afternoons coming from the morning room. Soon Quiet arrived there too. It rested for weeks on the stairs, along the passage outside my mother's bedroom. Inside, raised on pillows, she still laughed, talked and played her music. Then, Quiet.

I pushed the door, let it swing wide, saw Mummy lying flat, not moving, and Daddy sprawled across her crying in a way I had thought only children did.

I went to look at her face but she was covered. I put my hand over Daddy's and right away his convulsions stopped and he held his breath.

The glory of that moment, that I could give him comfort, that he would take reassurance from me.

He lifted his head towards Mummy's profile in relief under the sheet. His puzzled eyes turned to his own hand where mine covered it, and followed up my arm to my shoulder, to my own face.

"No," he said, "no," removing his hand from under mine, returning to his business of weeping.

He'd thought my hand was hers. It was never easy after that to reach out to another. Easy? Easy? I never had the courage to try, in case again I should be the cause of, and meet, such terrible disappointment.

Few people worked inside Sleet House after Julia Caldwell died. There was little to do anymore, and no one to notice anyway. Daily cleaners came and, having satisfied their curiosity about the widower and his daughter, left again from boredom. Mrs. Files was always there diligently overcooking her usual dishes. Curtis became butler. There would be no more footmen.

It was Curtis who suggested to the tall Miss Delia that she might find something to fit among her mother's clothing. There were cupboards of it, still uncleared, four years after her death. Uncleared but not uncared for because Curtis aired the coats, suits and dresses, brushed and pressed them. Whatever else there was to do in the house, these lovely things could not be left to ruin. That was how, in Form 3b at the age of twelve, Delia Caldwell came to be wearing Hartnell tweeds and Dior blouses. No one knew what they were, not even Delia, only that they looked intangibly familiar and wholly ridiculous.

It was Curtis who drove her to and from school before returning to his cottage, which he did in any free moment, because his sick brother was there. At seven he returned to the house, bringing supper trays from the kitchen to father and daughter in the morning room. That done, he was free. He could shut his door on the world, be at peace with Maurice.

The morning room was where George Caldwell spent most of his time, gruffing his way there mid-morning with his crowd of damp-smelling dogs. This was the room whose french windows led onto the steps where some years later Francis Sutherland would say "Sorry," a room where the past dawdled to tell and retell old stories.

On returning from school Delia headed to the morning room. Those porcelain figures in the corner were the first thing she touched. She stroked their robes and sandaled feet even before greeting her father who would be sitting at his desk.

"Ah, there you are, old thing," he always said. It made her feel she had been lost to herself and was found.

He remained at his desk and usually did not speak again. His expression was concentrated, his eyes busy wasps searching for an

26

exit, lips bunched in consideration under his scrap of mustache. Delia never disturbed him.

At nine-thirty she would say, "Good night, Daddy."

Startled, he would look up. "What?"

"Good night."

"I say. That time already? Good night, then," reluctantly, as though sorry to conclude a dialogue that had been long and rewarding.

George Caldwell's grief never diminished. He drew on a blanket of age, allowed his responsibilities to slide. The studied bag and shab of his kind of Englishman became the real thing. He was a sad old man at forty. If he could make do with barks and grunts, rather than speak a full sentence, he would, even to his daughter.

"Why did she die, Daddy?"

"What? What?"

"Why . . . ?"

He only needed half the question to be repeated. "Oh, some sort of thing growing inside her. You know." No harm, he thought, in soft-truthing life. She would continue to watch him, waiting for more of an answer, which he was not going to give. She wanted something else from him too, something other than answers. He did not want to know what that was. He was too tired. It was all too tiring. There were moments when she looked like her mother, more so as she grew. Sometimes, when she was playing with her dog, her face screwed up, laughing away from its licking tongue, particularly, then, she was like Julia.

Julia. He had not spoken the name since she died, nor had anyone else. Not to him. The funeral was the last time he heard it spoken.

When he played his saxophone and Delia sat listening, tapping her feet, loving his music, her whole demeanor reminded him of Julia. Once the illusion was so powerful he stopped playing to see her better. Even then her frustrated pleasure—"Don't do that, you can't stop like that. Go on"—was so like Julia. And, and yes, it was Julia. She'd come back, just as she'd promised she would. He set down his saxophone, went to her there on the sofa, took her into his arms. "Oh, darling, I've missed you."

This? This big girl? All bones and shoulders? "I say. There, there. Too big for cuddles now, what?" He had hardly held her before he released her.

He changed the subject to deflect their mutual embarrassment. "What are those shoes you've got on? Funny-looking things."

"They're yours. Curtis took me to the shop but ladies' shoes don't fit me anymore. He said I should talk to you about it. I'm size eleven now, the same size as you."

"Nothing to be proud of. How old are you?"

"Fifteen."

"So you are. So you are. Just checking. Well, we'll have to go shopping, won't we? Bound to be somewhere in London for big feet. Fats Waller, eh? 'Feet's Too Big.' I think I can play that."

He jigged back to his saxophone, snapping his fingers, singing, ". . . don't want ya 'cause ya feet's too big, don't need ya 'cause ya feet's too big . . ." and took up the instrument. After two pips on the mouthpiece to warm up, he began to play.

For all she tried, Delia could not catch the tune.

That saxophone. He had not played a great deal when Julia was alive.

The only time Delia invited a schoolfriend to stay she found herself being shaken awake during the night. "Delia, can I get in with you? I'm scared. I can hear noises. Listen."

Delia listened, clasped her friend's hand. "Come on, Sarah, nothing to be scared of."

They barefooted down the stairs, across the hall, to peer through a taut stretch of light at the morning-room door. The glass panes of the bookcase reflected a disjointed collage of George Caldwell, knees bent, leaning back, saxophone slung against his body. He was playing for all he was worth in his balding corduroys and flapping cardigan, a pipe bulging from one pocket, a handkerchief from the other, which he frequently released to wipe his mouth.

"Who's Sorry Now," "After You've Gone," "Misty"—he played a few bars of each. Like Mrs. Files and her cooking, he always played the same tunes.

When the notes grew fuzzy he pulled the saxophone from his mouth, detached the mouthpiece, sucked and spat into the fire. After that he played some of "The Isle of Capri," before pausing to duck his head, smiling in a bashful, appreciative way, with the glaze of dream in his eye, acknowledging applause from his glory days in the thirties. As a student at Cambridge he had formed a small combo called the Turn Ups. There was Jimmy Hartley on trumpet, Pete Weaver on clarinet, Richie Redman on piano, Benji Bowman on string bass and himself on tenor sax. Penny Weaver, sister to Pete, sang with them. It billed well in the summer of '35 at May balls, parties and dances: "Bad Penny and the Turn Ups."

Ah yes, Bad Penny. Bad Penny crossing Magdalene Bridge on her bicycle; Bad Penny on a Sunday in Grantchester; Bad Penny, naked in Byron's Pool: "You're the only one, George, the only one . . ." Bad, bad Penny.

What an odd noise that was, outside the door, a snorting. Was it the dogs? Had he forgotten to shut the kennel door? He looked into the hall and saw the pajamaed legs of Delia, and that pretty friend of hers, disappearing round the top of the stairs.

After choir the next day—choir during which Delia Caldwell mimed the words rather than let that strange sound from her mouth so different from the sound in her head—Marcia Gostwick grabbed her elbow. "I hear your Dad's as rotten at music as you are."

Now Delia Caldwell believed she understood why her father turned all those kind offers away. Invitations to go to stay, to come and stay, to take Delia on holiday. Invitations that had dwindled over the years since her mother's death. And he was right, the price of friendship was exposure and ridicule. They had needed Julia to bring them into social life.

Delia lived in the present. Everything would be all right if nothing changed. George lived in the past. In the morning room he hung every portrait, both painted and photographic, he had ever commissioned of his wife—eighteen in all. So many. Perhaps he had had a premonition. Perhaps he sensed he was furnishing a future of reminiscence. Under the many eyes of Julia gazing at, away, all round him, the tempera Annigoni, the Cecil Beaton study on his desk, George Caldwell worked his way into casts of time: photograph albums, scores of theater programs, outdated address books, hotel-room keys with elaborate attachments to discourage theft—and stolen just the same.

On an afternoon in 1963, when Julia had been dead eight years, George Caldwell returned from a day trip to London.

"I say, D? Where are you?"

"In here," she called from the gunroom where she had her shotgun in pieces to oil it.

"Look what I found on the train." He unrolled a magazine, *What's On in London.* "Here. Right here at the back. I'll read it out: 'Richie Redman and his Turn Ups, one night only at the Dog and Duck, Barnes.' What do you think about that, then, eh? The boys are still together. Got to see them. Once a Turn Up always a Turn Up, that's what we used to say."

Two nights later Delia saw him at the head of the stairs, illuminated by electric light draining from the upper passage. Pinching the lapels of his red-and-orange striped blazer, its single button straining, white flannels mildewed at the hems, he performed an unsteady pirouette. "This is what we wear, you know, the Turn Ups."

"Are you sure? They might have updated."

"Bollocks, old thing." He lifted a straw boater from the hat-stand. "Shall I? Or shan't I?"

"I don't think so."

"Maybe not. We used to," replacing it among the other hats.

When Delia came downstairs the following morning she found her father dressed as he had been the night before, dozing beside the fire in the morning room. He must have caught the first train back. She sat down ready for him to wake; and when he did he pretended he was still asleep.

"Daddy?" He grunted. "Come on, tell me about it. How it all went." She waited. There was no answer. "How was Richie? Were the others there? Pete, Jimmy, the ones you told me about? How are they all?"

"All right," without opening his eyes.

"Do they play a lot together?"

"It's only Richie and Benji. No sign of Penny. Didn't like to ask. Jimmy's gone. They've got a young'un now. No Penny."

"Will you join them sometimes, have it be like the old days?"

He stood up, crossed to the window, jingling change in his pocket. "No such thing as old days, D. Don't make my mistake and think there is. There's only each day. That's all. What they do is play now and again, for fun, you know."

"But you'd like to do that too."

"Well, they said they'd call."

Later that day he was practicing. Day and night, after that, he practiced the saxophone so as to be ready for the call to rejoin the Turn Ups. His bottom lip was sore from where his teeth pressed into it, and his speech became distorted until his aching cheek muscles toned up. Nestling with a book, Delia would come across

30

slips of bamboo in the creases of the morning-room sofa—her father's discarded reeds, stained yellow with nicotine.

One morning she arrived downstairs, aware her father had been playing most of the night. Notes were still easing through from the morning room into the hall, where Curtis mopped, clashing a metal bucket.

"Curtis. Keep it down, please. My father's playing."

"Playing, Miss Delia?"

"Practicing his saxophone. Surely you can hear?"

Curtis screwed the mop against the drain in the bucket. His cheeks were mottled and trembling. "Surely I can, Miss Delia. Wish I couldn't. 'Who's Sorry Now?' I am, that's who. Thought he'd given all that up years ago. Fact is, your father can't play. Never could. If you don't know that you've got no ear."

The affronted authority of his anger shocked her. "Really, Curtis," she managed, then walked on through to breakfast.

No ear? Was it possible?

It became rare to see George Caldwell sit at his desk. When he did he passed papers from left to right, to left, selected a letter, read it, slipped it back, lost it again within the rest of the pile, which was stained from where he had spilled his tea, and muddied from the time he dropped the whole lot and the dogs came over to see what had happened.

If Delia sat opposite him he placed his glasses on his nose, bowing his head to scrutinize a document. Through the window behind him was a view of grazing Friesians, a hunched shoulder of young firs bordering the Wild Garden, a glint of the lake lying below the half-mile furl of Old Carrots Field. The light fell so Delia could not see he was snoozing. If a snore gave him away, woke him, he readdressed himself to whatever was in his hand. Once, when that happened, Delia pointed to the stack of unanswered letters. "Would you like me to see to those?"

"What?"

"Those?"

"Ah. These?"

"Yes."

"Good idea. Good idea."

There were inquiries about cottages, about the renting of a field for the annual plowing competition; there were applications for permits to walk or ride through the estate; applications for jobs.

31

A week later Delia reached for the other tray, the one containing yellowing bills. "Shall I?"

"Those?"

"Yes."

"Do, old thing." He looked away as he said it, disassociating himself from whatever she found there. He rose from his chair, patting his pockets, and said, "So, well, I'll be off, then."

He left the room to reappear in that forlorn blazer, those sad flannels. "Don't wait up," he said.

Delia followed him into the hall, watched him toy with the boater and hesitantly reject it, as he had on the night of the Dog and Duck. She had no idea where he was going. Could not guess, but then: she had no ear.

Long before her eighteenth birthday Delia Caldwell had taken over the running of Sleet Park and discovered massive debts. On the occasions she considered selling a picture, or some piece of silver, she usually discovered it was already gone.

Four

FRANCIS AND I were married within five months of his first visit to Sleet. I did not visit him in London; he came to me at Sleet. That was how it was. Long before he proposed he would arrive there unannounced with the excuse, "I woke up this morning and had to be with you. If I'd stopped to ring I might have died."

I don't think he knew what to make of me. As a woman, that is. He didn't know how to approach me. Seven weeks passed before he ventured further than taking my hand. I was believing he only wanted me as a friend on whom to practice his passionate phrases.

One day he arrived to find I was away at a cattle auction until late in the afternoon. He was with Daddy in the morning room when I returned. Before I could sit down he said, "Come and see what I've done."

Daddy rushed me along with, "Off you go, D, there's a good girl."

Francis had spent the day hacking a path through hazel bushes growing under an oak forest. It was autumn. The colors of the trees and coppice burned all around us. There was no room to walk side by side and he went ahead, brashing at stray undergrowth with a billhook.

"I did this sort of thing when I was a boy, back in the Abacos, in a place we call the Yamacraw."

"You're always going on about the Abacos."

"And why not? They're beautiful."

"I'm sure. But, actually, what are they?"

He threw down the billhook, swung around. "Jesus, Delia, they're islands, for Pete's sake. The most beautiful in the whole of the Bahamas. Coral islands with pink sand and pine trees. You'll see. You'll come there soon." I'd have challenged his arrogance then, just for fun, had he not added, softly, "But first, darling, come to me now, won't you?"

He pulled me close, pinioning my arms while he kissed me for the first time. A kiss I'd planned, dramatized so often; now I was not allowed to move. Not at first, until he felt my response and knew I wasn't going to run or resist. His hands caressed my face before setting the weight of my hair free to shelter us. He raised me from the ground. My surprise at being lifted at all—women my height are rarely lifted—gave way to amazement at his strength. Our faces were lost in my hair, my mouth pressed down on his, when I heard movement in the hazel bushes ahead of us, and two soft steps, heartbeats in the earth. I knew, without looking, a deer was our witness.

My thigh was cold, where, holding me with one hand, he'd pushed away my skirt to grasp my leg so it circled him. I felt precarious. "Trust me. Relax," he breathed. So I did. And I knew he wouldn't let go then, because he was inside me. That one late kiss became the complete act of love.

Our bodies must have reached the ground at some point because I remember the feeling of hazel switches digging into my back, and seeing a strip of bronze evening sky between astonished branches, when he asked, "So now will you marry me?" as though he had been refused a hundred times already.

He showed me to the end of his track and there was a whole new perspective on the lake. Any two people whose overture to sex could be so acrobatic and mutually satisfying were bound to be together. Francis's way, I thought.

We were based in London in his own large house. During our short courtship I hadn't grasped his necessity for mass companionship, a flow of people through his days and long nights. Exotic, energetic, they were Francis's people and he theirs. They materialized when we were on our honeymoon at the house in the Abacos, where he was born and grew up. It was a changing crowd that eddied around us, glossy, loose, easy from life under the sun. Their tireless grace demanded display and competition in diving, swimming, water-skiing, dancing, until one by one they plunged into extravagant sleeps anywhere at all, a vacant bed, the floor, the sofa, or the warm wooden dock, in heaps or alone, limbs this way and that like so much gorgeous debris.

When we were at Sleet together I still left our bed shortly after dawn, as I had always done, to walk the dogs and catch up in the estate office.

Coming in for breakfast I'd find him already in the dining room, standing near the window, tilting the newspaper at an angle to catch the light. Resting his weight on one leg, he was unconsciously sensuous. The light contrasted his features, his hollow cheeks, his black eyebrows with a ladder of concentration between them, which would become his first permanent lines, and his eyes—the only place I've ever seen a color remotely resembling his eyes was inside a mussel shell. There was already a dissolution going on in his face which, for a few years, would heighten his beauty. From the doorway I would enjoy him, unable to believe we were together. He would pretend to be oblivious to me until, still reading, he'd set his head in my direction and mime a kiss, lift his arm, inviting me to him.

I remember that scene so clearly because it happened every day for a period. Probably not a long one, but, in what was to become a peripatetic existence, it felt like permanence. For me, those few moments were union. We were drawing something imperative from each other. For years after Francis stopped coming to Sleet I would enter the dining room and find myself looking for him, there by the window.

Evenings at Sleet. When Daddy had left early for bed, we stretched out on cushions in front of the morning-room fire, making love, reading, watching television. Sometimes Francis would undress me. I would lie back naked trying to pull his shirt free, only he restrained me.

"So I'm to be the only one unclothed?" I'd ask.

"Yes. For now. Look how beautiful you are. I'm going to honor your beauty."

So he did, for a long time, with his hands and his lips, before allowing me to undress him.

That is what we had been doing when he cradled his head in my shoulder and said, in the voice he used for urgent matters, the voice he'd used when he'd said, "Come to me now," that day in the hazel coppice, "Your father's not well, is he?"

"He's fine. A bit eccentric, that's all."

"But he's tired too, he's told me so. He's told me how things are with him. They're not good, honey. I mean Sleet. He can't cope much longer. The place is a mess financially. You must know that, you're practically running it."

"I don't know everything. I don't know about his investments."

"There are none. They've all gone."

In truth I never thought beyond the following month. And there was always the picture in the ballroom to sell. There was always that.

"Listen," Francis was saying. "Are you listening? I'm buying the place from your pa. I'm going to put in good accountants and lawyers, otherwise nothing changes. He'll be here, you'll run it. Okay? Say it's okay? Say I've done the right thing?"

Right thing? Well he'd done it. I'd thought I'd make everything all right once Sleet was mine. The inadequacy of that was as plain to me then as it is now. "Darling," Francis was saying, "together we can make this place wonderful. It only takes money."

It only takes money. And this was my husband speaking. Actually, though, could there have been a more generous gesture from a man in love?

Those friends of his were everywhere we went. They were in Kenya where we watched big game; in Norway, where we fished for salmon. They turned up in Paris, where I thought we'd gone to be alone. Then to Switzerland, they came, their arrivals undiscussed, delivered by clouds. From the nursery slopes below, I watched them up there, swallows against the steel-gray mountains. And we raced in a pack in London too, Francis, his friends and I; to go-cart tracks, and roller-skating, and dancing, dancing, dancing. Only at Sleet were they as disoriented as hummingbirds in the Hebrides.

What happened to me that I couldn't do those things, fly like they did? Some shock at birth, some tiny unobserved trauma which left me taking corners a little too wide and no balance for a bicycle? Impediments easily disguised until you're with those to whom they matter.

They were jealous of their lost bachelor, didn't share their conversation and humor with me. I lacked the social dexterity to help myself. Was I gauche? Was I inept? There's no doubt. They all had names for each other. When I was christened Big Black Dee, I thought it meant I belonged.

36

I'd married a community when I believed I'd married a man, a community that worshiped athletic elegance and good times. Nothing in my own nature or the shadows of Sleet had prepared me. But sometimes, on the increasingly few occasions we were alone, Francis laid his head against me and said, "I'm a weak man, don't leave me when you learn it." Francis weak? He was the swiftest, the strongest, the best.

I asked once why he hardly used my name. He called me "honey," "baby," "darling." The only time I heard "Delia" from him would be in a crowded place, calling me formally.

"Don't I?" he said, shaving, not giving me full attention. "Maybe not. I don't think I like it very much. I see you more as a Helen, Catherine or a Sophia. Sophia's a lovely name. You're not a Delia."

He might as well have said he loathed my nose. After that all of his alternative endearments only reminded me of my defaulting name. The nonsense of torment.

When things he'd made me swear never to change ceased to charm him—"Why don't you cut your hair, it's so frowsy like that?" "Couldn't you wear just some makeup?"—I knew I was losing my footing and retreated more frequently to Sleet.

"There you are, old thing," Daddy would say from his chair by the fire, simply as though I had been mislaid for a moment or two.

There was a day, mid-week, at Sleet. I suppose I'd been married ten months and my excuse for being there this time was to prepare for Francis and a dozen friends arriving at the weekend. I was going up the stairs when Daddy came out of the morning room very excited.

"D, stop a minute. Something amazing . . ."

"What?"

"Come in and I'll tell you. Very odd. Very nice."

He beckoned and shuffled, impatient while I settled my load of towels and soaps for the guest rooms on the top stair.

"Do come on, quickly."

Was it the call from the Turn Ups at last?

Stepping back and forth he pointed at the floor. "I was here, right here in front of the fire like this. No, I tell a lie. Like this, actually." He sat in his chair. "Wait. It's got to be right. Let's think. I was definitely standing." So he did, palms up, carefully reconstructing the scene.

"And, Daddy? What?"

"Think I'd been putting a log on, like this"—he went through the motions—"then I turned round, like this. And I saw her. She was there, almost where you are now."

"Who?"

"Julia. Right there, I tell you."

"Oh. Well. Good."

"As young and fresh . . . Wearing her WRAF uniform like when we first met."

I said an extraordinarily silly thing—embarrassment, perhaps confusion, "It still fitted, then?"

"What? What?"

But as he wasn't really talking to me, my response didn't matter. "Did she say anything?"

"She spoke, you know. She held something out to me, a white envelope, I think. She said, 'I've got tickets to the theater, Porgy, and I'm not going without you.' "

After a while, when he was comfortable, calm again, murmuring to himself, "Right there, she was . . .'not going without you' . . ." I knelt beside him.

"Daddy? You all right now? You are, aren't you?"

He blinked at me and said, "There, there. There, there."

Later, emptying a chest of drawers in our bedroom to replace it with a larger one, I found a flat box among the pullovers Francis wore at Sleet. Inside, in layers of tissue, was a scarf. Like all the scarves Francis gave me it was lovely. I pressed it to my face, glad he was soon arriving, and carefully refolded it so he wouldn't know, and I could be surprised.

It was sometime during that period Muriel and Tom moved into a perfect Queen Anne house nearby. I'd met her at the school where I had taken over from Daddy as a governor. Muriel had been visiting with a view to sending her newborn daughter there when she was five. That's how popular St. Mary's was then. She and Tom were probably dinner guests that weekend, because I nearly always asked them when Francis invited his own friends. I liked Muriel from the beginning, I trusted her, and my feelings never changed.

Among those who arrived with him was someone I didn't know, a frail-looking girl with black hair and even younger than I. She was shy, nervous of me, and I was moved. She even called me Mrs. Sutherland, which made me laugh. The two of us went for a walk before dinner and she told me how she went to art school, lived in a rented room because her family were in Cornwall, and she was lonely, didn't eat properly because she couldn't afford to. Patricia. Her name was Patricia. At a party the night before, Francis had caught her pushing canapés into her handbag and teased her before buying her dinner. She was very grateful, he was very kind, very generous. We talked again after dinner, sitting together on a sofa in the ballroom, which we used, even though Francis said it was a cold, hostile room, because there were so many of us. I liked her very much. We looked alike, I knew it. When I went up to bed and left them, she was much happier and talking to the others.

The next morning, coming to breakfast after my usual routine— the dogs, the estate office—they were all there, Francis, the friends and Patricia. She was wearing the scarf. The box was empty in the bedroom waste bin.

All morning I watched the bend to his neck as he listened to her speaking, his hand near but never touching her, wanting to. In the afternoon they all went for a walk. I wonder what their names were; suppose I knew them once, must have. Before they left for that walk she tied the scarf around her head, Patricia did, and Francis untied it, arranged it on her in a different way. "That's better," he said and she thanked him, saw herself in the glass above the letter table, told him he was right. I didn't go with them but stayed in the house searching from room to room for the girl I thought I was, for the one I wanted to be, saving the morning room until last.

Daddy was there, fast asleep, and I sat opposite, hoping he'd wake so I'd hear, when he saw me, the restoring "There you are, old thing." Perhaps, if I heard that, I could start again better when the others came in.

Dear old man, there he was, head slumped left, mouth wide, his snippet of pipe-gingered mustache, a few tenacious strands of coarse hair diligently parted and combed across his head just as it was in all the old school photographs hanging in the downstairs lavatory. I knew what he was going to do if I woke him: glance around, wet his lips, parched from their gaping, feel for the pipe in cardigan pocket, then, pretending he hadn't been asleep at all but waiting for me, he'd say it.

I couldn't wait and went over, put my hand on his shoulder, shaking him but not hard. I did not shake him hard.

After that there was nowhere else in the house. So Gertie and I went into the garden and the potting shed, a long, brick-built lean-to running the length of the kitchen-garden wall. We walked down its narrow alley, pushing aside the mower, on past the wooden shelves of secateurs and baling twine and sieves, biscuit tins of nuts and bolts, stacks of newspapers, an empty champagne bottle; past the hoes and rakes and shovels lined against the wall, all the shears hanging on it, and we collapsed in the corner at the far end, Gertie and I, onto a heap of crumbling tennis net. I held her close, breathing in the smell of dog, creosote and loam.

I heard Francis's voice at the same time as he backed into the potting shed, drawing Patricia after him by the wrists and kicking the door shut.

"It's so run-down everywhere, Francis—dilapidated. Why do you keep it like this?"

"I haven't had time yet. You'll see, I'll make it beautiful. Come here."

He snatched her so close I could only see her forearms on his back. The tin winter light falling through a pane in the roof gave them away, while they kissed and circled, and his hands pressed her breasts. I saw him bend, still with his mouth on hers, reaching for her hem, his hand sliding past the long woolen socks she'd borrowed from me, to her thigh which was almost green in that dimness. He lifted her and raised her leg around him. She gripped it high while he supported her.

How couldn't they hear the blood in my head? My rush of sweat? This, then, was how he did it every time, the first time. His way. It was like watching myself with him, was strange, exciting and terrible. Terrible. So like me and not.

Gertie pulled away, plodded through the implements and sacks of seed potatoes to snuffle Francis's ankles and wag her tail, jaws wide and panting, laughing, the way dogs do. Humans making love was a recent novelty in her long life; it always amused her, made her want to join in.

"Goddamn it, Gertie. What are you doing here?" Francis said, adding in a different voice, "That means Delia's around."

"But she came from that way." Patricia pointed out of their dusk into my dark.

Francis came near, straining to see if it was really me and studied hard when he knew, to see if I had seen, which wasn't certain, low as I was and yards away. He crouched. "Jesus, Delia. What are you doing there? What is it?"

"I think Daddy's dead."

I never told him I'd seen, that I knew. It didn't matter. The ease of his deceit proved she wasn't the first and certainly not the last. But her name is the only one I remember. Trust was gone and there was nowhere for it to return to. My love hadn't died, understand, it was cauterized, the race of it stopped. Security would lie in sustaining the past as I'd known it with the routines and reassuring inconveniences of Sleet. And he let me do that, Francis, never called in his ownership, remained respectful of Sleet's true tenure. He was graceful in matters of finance.

The heating became an issue and the broaching of it a dinner-time routine. Pushing his plate away he'd turn sideways in his chair towards me, cross his legs, link his hands behind his head and stretch back as though settling to a familiar performance, which it was, because nothing ever changed. Although I knew what was coming I loved to see him move that way. He was so physically disencumbered. He'd open with, "It's just not human living in this kind of temperature." At this point we'd argue, I more than he. He never had his wish, not with the heating, the double glazing or the redecoration. He wasn't vehement about any of it, it was just one of the few remaining channels for communication. He used the time to study me, try to make out what I really meant, how much I really knew. His mouth was drawn, tired of his lie, our lie, pleading for the cue to say, "Sorry." Only he remained uncertain of whether I knew there was anything he should be sorry for. A mature woman would have allowed that apology so he could unburden his stale guilt, make room for a fresh one. I know it, but I was not a mature woman.

We continued to share a bed. On occasions I felt him beside me listening to my wakefulness, wondering where I'd gone. What if I'd leaned over and said, It's all right, Francis, I'm back, we'll start again. What if?

After some time he began to make comments about a family, babies. Why wasn't I pregnant? It was not always in private he suggested I get myself "checked out," his words. Despite resenting his assumption the problem was mine, secretly I made appointments, to see a gynecologist. Somehow it happened that each time an appointment was due I was confronted by another clue, another scarf, as it were, giving Francis away in new lies. Pretend as I did I never made myself cold enough, or far enough, not to feel. From fear, and spite, I would cancel the appointment.

In the summer of '67 I went to the Royal Show as usual. The Royal Agricultural Society had invited me to dinner as a courtesy to acknowledge Daddy's term as Vice President during his days as an active farmer, days which had ended long before his death. I booked a hotel room in Leamington Spa for two nights; the dinner was on the first night in the Society's tent at the showground. It was pleasant to meet a few old buffers who spoke kindly of him, of how he'd contributed his efforts to the farming community before, as they put it, "his bad times." "Never quite the same after your mother's death." Well, no, I believe not, but never knew him otherwise. They told me what a joker he was too, a hilarious imitator of Groucho Marx. This, Daddy? My father? Yes, it was pleasant to be among them.

The next day at the show I dealt with business early, ordered a Massey Ferguson combine harvester for ten thousand pounds, walked round the utterly modern herringbone dairy units and watched the Friesian judging, which was when the rain began to fall. Within an hour the showground was a mudbath and I left to drive home rather than spend another night in Leamington Spa.

Francis, who was alone at Sleet, a rare thing, would be as excited as I about the combine. Anything that eased Sleet into the twentieth century pleased him. Driving back I imagined us dining together, a team with a common aim? Friends? Brothers? No. It hadn't come to that. I was hoping yet the conjurer's spring would be located, released, and we could be transformed back into the lovers we had been.

Well, I arrived at the house and of course Francis wasn't alone. There was a woman with him. Memory superimposes Patricia's face and name, which is wrong. Only that is what she was, just another Patricia: slender, dark, vulnerable. Always the same type.

He had taken her to our bedroom, our bed, and clearly intended to that night as well. Francis was beside me when I opened the door, had kept pace with me up the stairs, talking all sorts of nonsense, presumably to divert me. There were her shoes by my chair, a Ginger Rogers nightdress on my bed, her hairbrush and makeup on my dressing table. All of it was outstanding in its guilty presence, blocking everything else from sight.

"Darling? Delia?" Francis repeated, nothing else; catching my eye whenever he could, asking, in truth: Well, what do you make of this? What have you got to say, now you can no longer pretend?

At the same time he was gathering those items, carrying them to the door in his arms like an overburdened lady's maid, assuring me all the time, "She's going now, darling." I passed him what must have been her overnight case, hung it from a spare one of his fingers, and he went.

To our bedroom he took her, when there were any number of guest rooms. But he was a lazy man who liked his comforts.

When he returned moments later—I heard a car driving away: that poor girl—I said, "Do you want a divorce?"

"No, Delia, please. Don't leave me. That was nothing. I'm sorry."

"Nothing," I screamed, trying to decide where to throw a diaphragm I'd found in the bathroom. I could think of nowhere better than at him.

"Darling, darling, forgive me . . ." He caught the missile mid-air and, still speaking, peered at it. When he realized what it was he flung it away as though it were one of the dog's turds. "You're everything to me."

"Someone's got to pick it up," I said, pointing at the corner where it landed. I distinctly remember wanting to laugh then.

"I couldn't be the man I am without you."

"An unfaithful one? No, I see you couldn't be that, very well, without me."

"Please, Delia. I warned you I was weak. But I love you. I'd try to change if I thought I could. Darling, please forgive me and I'll try." His face was awful to see.

No, we had no child. He was our child.

Since the very first letter, the one he wrote after the dance, there had been a number of them. He wrote letters of conciliation: to apologize if he had been in the wrong; to help me through my pride if I had been. I always knew if one was due. He sent one after that, sweet words, elegant ones; something for me to keep, and to make the memory of him finer than his presence had become.

Nevertheless, this time I moved into my mother's bedroom. Hers was the lightest with the finest views, it was the best in the house. I wanted something of the best right then. Or was I seeking security in an incomplete past? Me, a ghost, dwelling on the sets of finished lives?

Francis's visits to Sleet became rare. He began to stay away from England for long periods, living in his house in the Abacos. I learned the manner of his existence through rumor and the gossip pages; his face occasionally loomed from them, startled into an incomplete expression.

Because he had sold his house in London we met from time to time at Brown's, which had always been his favorite hotel. We would dine while I talked about Sleet which, he having bought it, cost him nothing under my management. It seemed imperative to me that that was how it should be. He never questioned beyond what I told him.

The periods between these meetings became longer, sometimes months, a year or more, so I saw the changes in him. His body thickened in an unhealthy way as he progressed through his forties. That shouldn't be a bad decade for a man, poised as it is between the desperation of youth and desperation at the loss of it. He began to lose his fluent movement and care less about his appearance. Worst of all I knew that, despite his efforts to hide it from me, his enthusiasm, the true source of his charm, was dying away in cynicism and boredom.

"So how are you?" I'd ask him. "How's life?"

And he'd answer, "Wonderful. Really great. Why wouldn't it be?" wanting me to supply a reason and have it be the right one.

His visits to Sleet, they happened. Sometimes he came with hordes of people as well as caterers and florists and I would tell Curtis and Mrs. Files to steer clear until they'd all gone. These strangers would transform my home as though it were a stage, which is accurate because nothing that took place or any word spoken during the ensuing, protracted party was sincere or even very real. Other times he came alone, unannounced, the way anyone would to his own home.

The last time Francis Sutherland came to Sleet, Delia Sutherland was dozing, feet up, by the fire in the morning room. The minutes of the last Parish Council meeting had slid to her lap. She opened her eyes to see the muted television concluding the *Nine O'clock News,* and shut them again to concentrate on the skein of sound:

flapping flames, window frames chittering at the wind, the rain and, yes, there it was again, the doorbell. With no haste she and her two Labrador puppies moved from the girdle of fire warmth into the immediate chill beyond and out to the unlighted hall.

The dogs, embarrassed at having failed to hear the bell, compensated by growling into the cracks between the front doors. Beneath the outside light was a man in yellow oilskin and sou'wester.

"From the Water Board," he said and told her, above the noise of the now-barking dogs whom she did not trouble to quieten, that effluent had been leaking into the river for forty-eight hours; that they had finally traced it to her slurry lagoon at Home Dairy and she would have to act immediately.

Seating him among the shadows of the hall, Delia Sutherland rang her cowman telling him to meet her. She shut the dogs in the gunroom and dressed against the weather. For an hour the three of them inhaled the stench as they walked the banks of the lagoon in darkness and their torches stroked beams of light across a pulsing vapor. They had all slipped a few times, ankle-deep, into the liquid drained from the dung of two hundred and fifty cows, before the breach was found. Then Mr. Water Board left, still clutching his handkerchief to his nose.

The cowman filled the ditches leading from the field to the river with straw to soak up the seepage while Delia Sutherland drove to the tractor shed three miles away and returned on a JCB digger. For three hours she pushed earth from the adjacent field up against the weakening bank, backwards, forwards, back again in deepening ruts. The headlights reflected off the wall of freezing rain, so it was mostly guesswork and the digger eventually stuck, reared, at the top of the bank, its shovel half-sunk into the lagoon.

She jumped down, was joined by the cowman and they stood shouting suggestions as to how they'd release it. Suddenly Delia Sutherland waded waist-deep into the putrid fluid. The cowman yelled at her to stop. "It's only shit, Mike," her voice came back through the noisy weather.

It was after one when she returned to the morning room still wearing waterproof trousers and raincoat. She walked directly to the drinks tray, poured a whisky, tossed it back, poured another.

"You stink." The voice came from behind her.

She paused, tasting the whisky, before turning to Francis who was tipped into the chair she had left nearly four hours before.

"Nice to see you, Francis. How long have you been here?"

He gazed into the brandy balloon cradled against his belly. "Since ten. Looked for you. Thought you must have gone to a party." Tacking against the following silence, he added, "Late-night joke, Delia, that's all. Been frolicking in the dung? Good for insomnia, is it?"

She saw that slime slithered from her trousers. "Slurry lagoon's leaking. It'll mean a fine. Second time this year. Factories seep tons of foul effluent polluting miles of river and get away with it. Me? Just a trickle and that's all it was. You can bet I'll be forking out five thousand."

"Sleet can handle that."

"Maybe. But not if we go on as we are. Bad harvest. Milk quotas. Now they're talking about wheat quotas."

"Farmers. Always miserable. Don't understand a word anyway when you talk shop." Lolling his head against the back of the chair he flicked ash from his cigarette at the fire and missed.

"I'll go and change," she said. She returned twenty minutes later wearing tartan slippers, and a gray dressing gown tied with a cord over striped pajamas. She hunched onto the club fender, hands shoved in pockets, and Francis Sutherland parted two of the fingers covering his eyes.

"Christ, what have you come as? A bloody great prep-school boy?" He closed his fingers against the sight.

"Not an obelisk, then?"

He uncovered his eyes. "What did you say? Obelisk? Do you never forgive and forget, Delia?"

"The former, one's forgiven much, everything even. Not the latter. It's not in one's nature. One can't."

" 'One,' all of a sudden, is it? Why don't you say 'I can't?' Scared it's too intimate?"

She suddenly wanted to be another kind of woman. The kind who knew how to approach a man, her own husband, hold his face in her hands and say, Darling, what happened to you? Come here, come here. But it required something to do that, something she had never been given, or learned, and would not know how to begin. Instead she said, "So how's life? You don't seem wildly happy."

"Should I be? I arrive back home—"

"After eighteen months."

46

"Seeking the companionship of my wife who finally appears at one in the morning, posing first as a sewage engineer then as dorm prefect. I've no family as such and only fair-weather friends . . ."

"We've been married twenty years, Francis—"

"Twenty-one."

"All right. And you've never before complained about your life. Is something wrong?" He remained staring into the fire, arms flung over the sides of the chair. Apart from a noncommittal movement of his head, he was not going to answer, so she went on, "I thought things between us were how you wanted them to be. I thought it was your choice. I've drawn a degree of reassurance from that."

"We haven't slept together for sixteen years."

"I'm surprised you have time for such calculations."

"All the time in the world."

"Reassurance because it's helped me believe, in the odd moments when I feel down, that I'm not such a bad old stick. You know, not making a fuss and so on, the way some wives would. From a man's point of view it would seem you've had everything. You've lived precisely as you chose; you've had money, sunshine, a background wife to protect you from commitment, and you've made a lot of other women very unhappy. What more can a man ask?"

"A lot."

"Like?"

He mumbled something.

The whites of his eyes were a broth, his slack mouth pared away and damp at the corners. The vitality had been blotted from his face by sun and liquor. It was webbed with lines.

"Did you say what I think you said?"

Their eyes tangled. "I said 'love,' dammit."

"Ah. That. I thought you said that." She stood to rewrap her dressing gown, as though "that" were caught in its folds and causing bother. "A little sudden, isn't it? Arriving here after all this time and talking about 'love.' Well, I don't know what to say to comfort you. It seems many women have fallen in love with you over the years."

"Did you?"

"Good heavens. What a thing to ask. I can remember how it was between us at first, if that's what you mean."

"But were you? Why can't you say it? You haven't said you love me since the first year of our marriage."

"Haven't I?"

"I was in love with you. It wasn't a game. There'd been beautiful women in my life for well over ten years before we met and I thought I'd loved some of them. But you. Remote, defiant, eccentric, you affected me. All I'd wanted was to marry you. I still do love you." He lurched towards her, toppled from the chair. To make his fall appear intentional he approached her on his knees and would have buried his head in her lap, had she not backed away. She cleared her throat to speak but left it at that.

"You're cold," he said.

"You're drunk."

"You're shutting me out like you shut me out then. I never knew why." Propping his elbows on the fender he craned his head over his shoulder, judging the distance back to his chair.

"You never asked," she said.

He gave up any possibility of the chair, gazed into the fire instead. "So there was a reason? I knew it wasn't just that girl, the one I brought here. You did it before that. Shut me out. Something I did wrong? Or didn't do?"

"There was a reason once. That turned into two or three. They, over the years, dissolved into silence between us, and I suppose that became the reason."

Very slowly he faced her. His expression was the threatened, pained and downright irritated one of any man confronting an articulate woman he has wronged. "I'm trying to talk to you, Delia, really talk, and you're making it so hard. I'm not good at this and you say these things. Why can't you give me something simple? Say it in a word, for pity's sake. Something a man can understand."

She leaned over her lap, hands clasped, sashaying her tartan-toed feet. "Patricia."

They had had conversations, one drunk, the other tired, but never so near, so raw, and never, never had she mentioned Patricia, or any of the others she knew of.

"Who's Patricia?" he said.

Then she did it. Her head fell back and she laughed and laughed. Smiling, he watched her, said, "Oh, Delia, you could have been so beautiful. We could have had such fun."

"You really don't remember her, do you? I knew you wouldn't at

48

the time but it didn't stop the . . . well, I couldn't help minding."

"If it weren't for Sleet things'd be different."

"Oh yes. If it weren't for Sleet. It's been everything to me. Thank God for it. Thank *you*, actually, I suppose. I don't forget, as you remarked, so it works for the good as well."

"You're wrong. If it weren't for Sleet we'd have made something together. But you ran back here as soon as the going was hard. Sleet's the "other man" as far as I'm concerned and I'll never forgive myself for inviting him in. I should have left it the way it was when I met you, rotting. And here you remain, where you've always been, separate, aloof, self-sufficient. Aren't you ever lonely?"

"Funny, someone else asked me that once."

"But in the night? In bed? Alone? Always alone. How can you bear it? Doesn't your body want more? You weren't a frigid woman."

"Good night, Francis."

"I'm sorry. That sounded wrong. It wasn't what I wanted to say."

"I must go to . . . to sleep now."

"Listen, listen. Wait. Please talk."

"Good night, again. I'll see you in the morning," and she said that as gently as practice allowed her.

"What's a little while longer, Delia? Stay with me. Don't go. Don't leave me alone this time."

She went. She did wait a moment outside the door. Perhaps if he called again. If he came to the door and found her there in her stupidity. Perhaps if he weren't so drunk or said these things again tomorrow. It was not easy after all these years.

Lying in cold linen sheets in her bedroom directly above the morning room she realized that he had never said, "Don't go," before. It could be all right. It could work again. In the morning.

In the morning he had left. He probably never even went to bed. A check on his room proved it.

She waited for the letter that, if he followed habit, would arrive. He still wrote to her, the way he always had, regardless of blame, if there had been upset between them.

The blue envelope arrived three days later. It was the same blue as the very first one she had received from him. Instead of opening this one she found the initial letter and read that first. She wanted to be reminded of those fresh feelings and hopes, and she would try to find something in the latest one to build on. Remembering how she had walked to the lake with Gertie, who had long since died, she decided to do the same with her present two Labradors. She tucked the new envelope into her jacket pocket for later, after she had had the meeting with the builder to discuss the reinforcement of the slurry lagoon. He arrived and she replaced her jacket with a raincoat from the gunroom, where she shut in the dogs.

On her return Curtis told her they had set up such a racket that he had opened the gunroom door to see what was the matter, then they had escaped and were still loose about the house. He had spent the last hour rehanging coats and scarves they had pulled from the hooks, and mopping up water spilled from the bowl. Now he was trying to decide whether certain garments were worth mending. He held forth her jacket. It was ruined. The letter was gone.

She searched the gunroom, the dustbin Curtis had filled, and every corner of the house where the dogs had apparently been. She rang Muriel Fuller to help her hunt. Sixteen days later, when she was cleaning the inside section of the dog kennels—one of them had drunk milk from the churn left on the kitchen floor and had messed its sleeping quarters—she found the letter.

An hour of scrutiny only produced seven single words: "humiliated," "unforgiving," "privilege," "Kennedy," "Sleet," "existence," "Leon"; two words together: "with fate"; and three words at the end: "wait a week."

Delia telephoned Francis at his house in the Abacos to ask him when he would be coming to England again. He told her two months but that he wouldn't be visiting Sleet. He seemed to be expecting her to say something. She could not tell him about his letter, not on the telephone. She said, "Brown's Hotel, then," and set a date.

Two days before dinner in the brown of Brown's Hotel, there was a photograph in the newspaper of Francis, among others, at the opening of a nightclub in Paris. A girl who could not have been more than twenty was leaning with her back against him; his arms were wrapped around her. Her eyes were closed and he was smiling down on her head.

It's all the same, Delia thought. It'll never change and, if I'm honest, I do believe it hurts as much.

"You still make the nightclubs, then?" was her opening remark to him.

"I saw that too. Good picture, eh?" He looked ill.

"Pretty girl. Anyone special?"

"Let's order."

Through the first course she talked as she usually did, about Sleet. Francis was even less interested than he had been in the past. When he said, "So you still go on about it, then?" she did not understand but stopped. They were silent for some time.

"You took long enough to ring me. But that's it, isn't it? Your answer. You've always let me know how you feel by saying nothing. I'd just have thought that this time, this one time, you might have tried."

"I'm here now." Nerves made her abrupt.

"No you're not. You're at Sleet. Just like always."

"Thank you for your letter." She could not look at him to say it and, when she did, he was watching her so strangely she examined her wedding ring for distraction.

"You did read it, didn't you?" She dropped her head further hoping he would take the movement as affirmation. "Of course you did, you know exactly what I wrote there."

"I don't," she snapped. Now her frustration made her sound angry.

"That proves you do, honey." His voice was gentle. That sad, retrieved endearment that he had not used in years would take some wearing before it fitted again.

"I didn't. I didn't read it, Francis."

"You can't face it, can you, any of it?" His conviction that he understood made him kind, discreet, as though he were talking of a ghastly disease of hers that no one could do anything for. "But never mind, you mustn't worry. I'm not too old to die young but it's unlikely. We Sutherlands are long-lived."

"The dogs ate the letter. They got hysterical in the gunroom and they're usually so well behaved. I don't know what came over them. I didn't read it, Francis."

"Jesus, Delia." He pressed his palms to the edge of the table, tilting back on his chair. He was not kind anymore, he was cold. "Isn't it bad enough you ignored it? Isn't it enough for you to pretend not to have read it? But to say your fucking dogs ate it. Why do you do it to me?"

"You took away my trust and made me ugly." It rasped from her mouth. She was unaware of ever having had such a thought. It was as though some other woman had spoken for her. They stared at each other.

"Yes," he said at last. "Forgive me." Before she could think what to say next he was standing up. "I'll go now, if you don't mind." He left without giving her time to say she did.

There was no letter from him after that. She never saw him again.

PART TWO

Five

AUGUST, bloody August, the Sunday afternoon of the year; the suicide hour that lasts a month. There I was at my bedroom window giddy from David Rosen's "sad" rather than "bad" news. Francis, dead? Drowned in his own pool?

Outside my living day stretched on to poach the night while I cried. Dead after all this time? My love, no longer inhibited by his existence, presented itself with all the understanding required to bring us together again—the gentleness, the words, the small gestures that make it possible for one person to reveal himself to another and two people to share life. We would have come together when his hullabaloo was over. We were old enough to know what we wanted at last.

That night, the night before I went to David Rosen's office to hear Francis's will, I was woken by a dream. In this dream I was the invisible observer of the terrace outside Francis's house in the Abacos. A party was taking place inside. The feel of its sound decanted through glass doors into the humid Bahamian night. A white-coated servant placed candles on tables among the bougainvillae-covered arches. Two figures were seated in the shadows, unseeable but known, as things are in dreams.

The party emerged from the house on a silent swell of hilarity. Sleek people accustomed to dealing with idler's sunshine, some of them dancing only to explore a little vulgar love. Francis was one of those. He clutched a supple-bodied girl against him to soak her fragility into his aging frame, and licked her neck, palmed her short bright dress, his fingertips easing into the fold between buttock and thigh. He fumbled for her zip; a strap fell. The girl mouthed entreaty to the other guests who smiled and looked away. The dress slipped to her narrow hips where it remained supported by his hands, until he raised them and it fell to the floor and her body gleamed naked. She ran back to the glass doors but Francis barred her way; she ran across the terrace to the balustrade, climbed on to it, poised to dive. Now he was naked too beside her and making pantomime bows to his guests before launching himself into the night. The girl stepped back onto the terrace, laughing. They were all laughing and peering over and down, their heads black against sheet lightning.

Suddenly the terrace was empty and the two came, those from the shadows still unseeable, still known. Their tangible presence passing over glazed tiles to where Francis had made his dive and they looked over, as the others had done, only they weren't laughing. Far below, but impossibly detailed, was his crumpled body; his limbs in ghastly akimbo, head tipped back on itself, a stealth of blood staining the white marble of an empty pool.

Even the light of my bedside lamp didn't extinguish that last image so I turned it off, testing the validity of the dawn, and yes, there it was, tomorrow already. Too late for any more useful sleep, I'd be leaving for London at six to avoid the rush. Just how lonely had he been when it wasn't late and he wasn't drunk? How lonely? *Don't go, Delia. Don't leave me this time.* I never did. I was always there, waiting to be rediscovered. I'd have joined him in the Abacos if he'd asked me, little holidays from time to time.

He'd have come back, was beginning to; so many years bound us. He had from me that gift with subtle ties, freedom without complaint; subtle ties and guaranteed disillusion. He was going to come back. And now? Poor, poor Francis, dead.

David Rosen was short and in his mid-forties, a study in pale human colors with hair and lashes the shade of weak orange squash and fine skin dusted with light freckles which, in certain lights, appeared to oscillate.

When Delia Sutherland arrived punctually the morning after he had telephoned her, Rosen was standing by the door to his office talking to a junior partner. She was still a way from him when he stretched out his left hand to grasp hers from a distance. She would be seated in front of his desk before he allowed himself to be near her; then he would lean against the same side of the desk as she. All this was strategy he had developed to detract from their discrepancy in height. They would not exchange a word until they were settled this way. Over thirteen years, since he had taken over from the retiring senior partner to whom Francis Sutherland originally brought the affairs of Sleet, David Rosen and Delia Sutherland had come to know each other well enough to do without greetings; they liked it that way.

The daylight did not penetrate far into the room where only his desk lamp was lit.

He watched her place handbag and gloves on his desk, help herself to a cigarette. She had not done that for a long time. He held a marble lighter towards her and said as she lowered her head to the flame, "Filthy, isn't it?" nodding towards the rain at the window.

She let him scan her face for whatever it was he sought there and said, "Yes, but beautiful evenings at home, you know. The sun's brilliant from six on. Too late to dry the corn, of course, and get the combines out. A sort of meteorological 'up yours.'" She grinned at him with deadpan eyes. "Still, the last few days've been all right."

He expelled his laugh in a single breath and was serious again, wanting to study her more, like a doctor, she thought, looking for symptoms, and she allowed him, remembering that this was part of sorrow. You let people do this sort of thing for their sake.

There she was, hair swept up as usual, mannishness accentuated by a tailored suit, her presence haloed by the only perfume she ever wore, if she wore any at all. Rosen knew the name of it because it was the same one his mother had used, Arpège. Of course, Delia Sutherland had personalized it the way women do, in her case with a trace of dog. She looked powdery, worn out.

"I'm so sorry, Delia," Rosen said, and immediately thought: Blast, remembering her cold reception of his sympathy on the telephone the night before. He should not have to pretend with her.

"Well, one is," frowning away from him, to return with her expression adjusted. "Forecast is brightening up. With any luck we'll get into Pope's Bottom later on today."

"Good."

"Well, it *is* good."

Still leaning against her side of his desk he watched her, waiting for something. "Do you want any details?" he asked. "Some have filtered through."

"He drowned, you say?"

"Yes. There were others about. He dived from a terrace. Apparently the pool was situated . . ."

"I know where the pool was."

"Photographs?"

"No."

"You've been there?"

"Honeymoon."

"You never said."

When he spoke next he was monitoring his voice away from irritation. "So you'll know all about it, his dives, the party trick and all?"

"Yes." She did not, but she wanted to be the kind of wife who would have known all the things it would hurt to know, like the circumstances of his pleasure.

"Well, it seems he dived from the terrace and no one took much notice but he hit his head on the way down. Unconscious when he reached the water. It was too late by the time they wondered about him coming up again."

"Funny," she said.

"What did you say?"

"I don't want to know any more."

"But, Delia . . ."

"Does this have to take very long?"

He faced away from her. He had been frightened of her, when he first acted for Sleet. Gradually, during his visits there, he began to tell her how much he had been looking forward to it, and confided how he would remember their "walking the policies" (which is what Delia Sutherland called a businesslike hike across her property) and sitting up late at night drinking brandy, discussing plans. He was the one who had first asked her with rushed ineptitude, despite his having planned the question for months, "Are you ever lonely?"

"Lonely?" She had repeated it as though the word were a new one. It was the same question Francis would ask some years later.

"For a companion?" Rosen had said.

"I've got the dogs."

"I think I meant a man, Delia."

Her eyes had prized accuracy from him. "Sex, David? Are we talking stuffingtons?"

58

He had gulped his brandy.

Rosen went to the window of his office and stood with his back to her, twisting the ring on his little finger. "I last drafted Francis's will twelve years ago as per his instructions and he returned it signed, everything in order."

"I know." This time she did.

"Do you remember, the three of us discussed it once? That I felt you should know your position if just such an event as this occurred?"

"Yes, I do. And Francis and I have discussed it since then. We had our talks, David. We had our times. There were understandings between us that people didn't guess at." It was a childlike boast and made Rosen finally turn while she went on. "I was only thinking this morning in bed, that others never really knew what we shared. No, it wasn't a conventional marriage but we gave each other what a lot of married people don't: freedom. We were coming back together, you know. Well, you wouldn't, but we were. It was only a matter of time."

"Really?"

"Oh yes." She tapped and drew on her cigarette.

"Now then, Delia," brisk, all at once, "when dealing with wills the law provides a floor on what's left to a wife. It's judged in somewhat the same way as a divorce settlement, the same sort of amount. If the wife is left any amount lower than that floor she can contest and will almost certainly win."

Delia Sutherland was impatient; he was always this pedantic and it wasted time. She dropped her watch lower on her wrist, viewing it discretely, but he saw.

"Are you listening?"

"Yes, yes."

"Francis has left you well over double what would be regarded as the floor in this case."

"I know, David. I know the will." And now she spoke kindly, in an effort to stop him from trying so hard. It was just not necessary, all this.

"Not quite. Now, Delia, the fact is Francis has a natural son called Leon Kennedy."

Delia Sutherland stood up, walked to the other side of the room, wiping something from the palm of one hand. "I know."

"You do? I see. Only you've never mentioned him."

59

"No, I've not mentioned visiting the Abacos, I've not mentioned the boy. What's the matter with you today, David? What makes you think I should want, or need, to discuss these sorts of things? So I haven't mentioned him. Why should I? He doesn't exist as far as I'm concerned."

Rosen shut his eyes saying, "You take patience, Delia, you do take patience," and opened them again. "Francis has remembered him in a codicil to his will drawn up in Nassau. I've had it a while now, couple of years. There was an instruction not to open it unless he died. So I did, at eight-thirty this morning."

Delia Sutherland moved her scrutiny to the other palm. "So he's been remembered. His mother too, I should hope. What of it? I don't begrudge them anything." Rosen did not speak right away so Delia Sutherland added, "Well, has he? Has he remembered the mother too?"

"No. There's no mention of anything for her."

"That's too bad 'cause he should have. He should have."

At last Rosen sat down in his desk chair and scratched his forehead. "Delia, Francis has left Sleet to this young man."

With no pause, almost before he had finished, Delia Sutherland was saying, while glancing openly now at her watch as though determining whether or not she had enough time to put him straight, "No, no, no. Give it to me, the codicil." She shot out a hand.

He passed her the document and she read it, fast the first time, slowly the second. Pushing it back onto the desk without taking her eyes from it, she said, "I don't quite see. Clearly it's . . . what is it? What does it mean? Come on, David."

"It means Sleet, the house, the farms, the whole estate goes to Leon Kennedy."

Her gaze drifted past his shoulder to the window. She moved towards it and stood, staring out.

Pigeons. Pigeons there on the parapet opposite, squabbling, jostling for position. One is ousted. It lifts its wings, flies, circles, returns, and another goes. The rain had ceased.

"I think it's going to be a lovely day," she said. "Combines'll get into Pope's Bottom."

"Good old Pope's Bottom." The laugh he tried failed.

"Quite." She came back to her chair, sat down, leaned forward. "So how do we begin the fight?"

"We don't. You can make expensive legal waves, look for caveats, but in the end it'll be the same. You have shopping malls in Richmond and Clapham. A development site on the Isle of Dogs, the 1974 Offshore Trust, the 1983 Offshore Trust."

"It's not legal for him to inherit. He's illegitimate and he's not even British."

"It's perfectly legal. Francis acknowledged Leon Kennedy as his son, besides which he can leave his property to whom he likes. Young Mr. Kennedy is as British as his father, if he chooses to be, because Francis, as you know, always kept his British citizenship. There'd be no problem with immigration, particularly since there's little likelihood of him being a drain on the State."

"Stop it, I don't want to hear all of this," she said, and he rested his head in his hands, only too glad to stop. "The point is, Sleet's mine. It's my home. My family's home for a hundred and sixty years. I've never lived anywhere else. Now come on. What are we going to do?" He did not answer and she said, "David?" so softly she might have been waking him.

He pushed on quickly with words in order to forget that tone he had never heard from her before. "Francis has allowed for joint occupancy."

"What does that mean?"

"That you can stay on at Sleet as long as you like, but with the new owner, should he wish to take residence there. Of course it's absurd."

"Preposterous. What'll we do?"

His hands performed a meaningless mime masking his face. "I'm afraid it can't be a question of 'we' any longer."

"What do you mean? You're my lawyer."

His hands became purposeful, spreading possessively over two of the three thick files in front of him. "I'm Sleet's lawyer."

"And Sleet's mine."

"I'm Francis's trustee and executor."

"And Francis is dead."

"Precisely." From the dark hole of his sleeve he brought forth his cuff, fiddled with the plain gold links, moved the files to the left, the right. "There is a conflict here. I could relinquish my trustee and executorship on the grounds that I think the will is unfair to you . . . and I do, Delia, I think it's very unfair."

"Fine, do that."

"I can't. I've always believed one must respect the wishes of the dead. It's a principle. Francis bought Sleet from your father and now he wants his only child to have it. If he were alive I'd tell him I think it's unfair. I've spoken to him in the past about making the place over to you. I don't know whether he listened to me or not. I'd suggest to him that at least the place should be yours for life; let the young man have it on your death. But Francis can't speak for himself anymore . . ."

"Seems to be doing all right." Her voice came out of the dingy light in the far end of the room to where she had retreated again and Rosen had not dared look while delivering this speech.

"And I am obliged to defend his wishes." She did not say anything more so he added in a real voice and proper words, "Delia, I *have* to."

Faraway sounds revealed themselves, a vacuum cleaner somewhere, a typewriter, water pipes.

"Have you met him?" she whispered, close now and watching his face.

"Kennedy? No."

"He's black, you know." She rubbed at a chalk mark on her skirt, brushed her fingers, picked a thread from her sleeve, held it up.

Rosen laughed, too much because he was so relieved to have something to laugh at. "Oh, Delia, you are wonderful . . ."

"He's black, I tell you. His mother was an Exuma girl. They're the loveliest. She was a whore in Nassau when Francis found her. He liked them slender, dark and vulnerable. And she, well, she was the slenderest, the darkest, the most vulnerable."

Rosen took a deep breath and, forgetting the rhythm of breathing, held it. When it did finally rush out, the words "No odds, no odds" came too.

Delia Sutherland said vaguely, "Not mine?" Tears filled her eyes as the truth danced before her, but they ebbed without spilling as it danced away again. "I did try to be a little of what he wanted, you know, at the beginning." She addressed her fingers splayed on the desktop. "But it's not in my nature to allow myself to be altered by another. It's not a safe thing to let happen to you, David."

"No. No, it's not. You're right."

She squeezed her temples to dam the source of memory. "There were such a lot of women in his life. When he wasn't flirting with them they flirted with him in front of me. He didn't resist." She finished with surprise in her voice. "It hurt, actually."

David Rosen walked around the desk to where she sat. He drew her to him, so that her head was near his waist, in a stiff sort of way because she did not give in to the embrace. He had not expected she would. He had never seen her like this before and, despite himself, was glad of the moment.

"About the funeral, Delia. Would you like me to ask Francis's lawyer out there, Freeman Tucker, to see to it, or would you rather . . . ?"

"No. Him."

"That'll be all right, I'm sure. I believe Francis and he were rather good friends. Shall I tell them you'll be there for it?"

"Tell them I won't be."

Without warning she towered to her feet and he found himself facing into her breasts before stepping back to give her room to pick up gloves and handbag.

She moved so fast to the door he had no time for even one step. From the door she called, "Don't move, David," in her usual voice. He could not see her because the gray London light was all his end with a dab of amber from his desk lamp.

"I'm so sorry, Delia," and, Blast, blast, he thought.

"Well, of course you are, so sort something out, then, David. I'll call you later in the week."

Outside Rosen's office the rain had expired leaving a sheen on the streets. The sun dazzled in the tarmac, the windshields of cars, shop windows. It was hard to see and Delia Sutherland walked, sheltering her eyes with the large brown envelope Rosen had given her. Three times she stopped before reaching Charing Cross, abruptly breaking the current of pedestrians so people stepped around her, glancing, while she said, "No . . ." and turned back from where she had come, only to turn again, move on. At the end of a narrow lane leading to the Embankment was a tilting building with "Wines from the Wood" in flaking gold letters arced across its glass. She was prevented from entering by people surfacing from the cellar bar. Why so many coming this way when she wanted to go the other? Was this the end of the lunch hour or the beginning of rush hour? The day had lost its form. Not only could she not translate the hour, but the light, the leaves on the trees, the noise of trains and traffic were meaningless. There was nothing so simple anymore as a line of days leading to this one, or another leading away from it.

The attendant of a fuming barrow with a torn awning was snapping his fingers, jerking his head to music in his earphones. He raised his eyebrows at her and, assuming her stare was an order, flipped open the lid to plunge in tongs. She watched him draw out a hot dog, place it on a bun. She did not speak when he raised his eyebrows the second time, so in went onions, mustard and ketchup. He handed over the oozing affair, wiping his fingers on his sweatshirt with "Happiness is a warm pussy" printed across it, before holding out his palm and facing away, bored.

In the small park nearby was an open-air theater, closed, the deck chairs lined up, each bucketing its share of rain. Gulls stood one-legged on the umbrella-topped street lamps. Delia Sutherland sat on a bench, the river view blocked by a public lavatory. She placed her handbag on the ground between her feet, the hot dog on her lap.

David didn't believe me when I said he was black. He thought I was lashing about for excuses. But I saw him. He was playing around his mother's feet outside the gate of the house in the Abacos. I was driven through the gate when I first arrived and she was shut out; she and her baby. I turned round and watched her hoist him onto her hip and harangue with her fist in the air, until the sight of her was dissolved by the dust thrown up behind the car. She stood with the quality of a wanton twelve-year-old and must have been, what, seventeen, eighteen? Sometimes when I've been up early at home walking in the woods and come upon a roe deer close to, motionless, its alarm and scenting has reminded me of her. A creature all sense and intuition. Graceful; she was so graceful.

We went there, Francis and I, as part of our protracted honeymoon taken in fits and starts and which, Francis told me, in those days, would go on and on. We only used the road to the back of the house once, on arrival, otherwise we came and went by boat from the dock. The second time I saw her was the day after I arrived. I'd walked into the garden, over tough grass that wasn't grass at all but rough, close-growing weed. I'd skirted the beds of leathery things bright with bloom and walked the sandy, oleander-lined drive. We saw each other at the same moment, she on her side of the gate, me on mine. I probably said good morning. I would have said that. She didn't answer. I never heard her speak to me.

The following day I went again, not to see her but just the way one does in a house with a garden at a given point in the day when there's not much else to do. I went every day at the same time, in fact, over the period of my short stay. She was always there and each time I tried to speak to her. "Nice day," I'd say, ask the baby's name, that sort of thing. She always had the same reaction: she'd gather her baby close and back away, her hand firmly encircling the little head, pulling it against her breast so he couldn't face me. I hated the way it made me feel, someone the sight of whom could contaminate, endanger a baby.

When I asked Francis who the girl at the gate was he was easy about it. "It's only Jeanne Kennedy, she's all right."

"Is she mad?" I asked. He laughed and told me she lived in the cabana. I called her baby the Dust Baby and bought him clothes from a shop in Nassau before I left. It was early afternoon and she was asleep under a sea-grape tree. Her baby was wide-awake, watchful, sitting by the road with that insolently erect posture little ones have. He was playing with his fist inside a glass jar, banging it on the ground then licking it. Struck me as a dangerous thing for him to be doing. He stopped when I approached, stared at me implacably with his yellow eyes.

I could see his flesh was of that dense-celled compactness black people have, quite a different material from ours. Burrs of hair were scattered on his scalp; they were the same muted color as his skin, as though he were compounded of the dust he played in. Only his eyes were different, his brilliant tiger eyes.

His mother remained asleep, with one long arm across her Androsia print dress, a knee drawn up and fallen away, languid. The column of her neck was weighted to the left by the perfect sphere of her cropped head. And, coming closer, I could see her features properly. Her cat's nose was long, flat, progressing to form a finely molded triangle on her upper lip. Her cheekbones were like plums under the fabric of her face and her closed eyes had a crescent of natural shade where lid met lid. The cushion of her mouth stood proud from her face, an inspired afterthought. She was no muted color. Her skin, dry-glistening, was mulberry-black.

Her baby's motionless observance of me observing his mother must have woken her. She opened her eyes with a remarkable slowness, assimilated my presence. I put the packet of little clothes beside her like an offering and stood back. Did I stumble? Was I gauche? Need I wonder? How I must have looked, the bloody great English lady, agawk.

Her mouth pouted further, if that were possible. Her cheeks made minute undulations until, without so much as a quiver throughout the rest of her body, she fired a perfectly formed spitball which smacked my lip, swelled, slid down to my mouth. Before I realized what had hit me, my tongue was out, feeling and retrieving that warm, aerated slime.

I ran away. I only wanted to be kind to the Dust Baby. And now? Good God, and now?

Delia Sutherland blinked out of the heat and white light of the Bahamas into the face of a man with bad weather in his eyes. His massive head was framed by red hair that met beard spreading to his chest. He sat down beside her looking hard into her face then her lap. His fingers with corrugated nails pressed hard, moving north; she felt them separating her thighs through the tweed of her skirt, the rayon of the lining, the nylon of her slip.

"Can I?" he whispered. "Can I?" She frowned her confusion. "So I'll just go on, then," he said. "That's all right, is it?"

She saw the hot dog being borne tenderly from her. Holding it with both hands the man took a bite, slowly chewing, scrutinizing what was left, relishing the decision of where to bite next. Without raising his eyes from it, he wandered off, guiding with his belly a three-wheeled pram piled high with old newspapers and cardboard. Delia Sutherland looked down at her skirt stained yellow and red.

Your subconscious knows when it's encountered another who's impinging on your life, your love. It stands to attention, striking the air with a knowing finger. Ah, it says, let's see . . . and it waits while you go on living, telling yourself this peculiar state of suspension is the common sensation of being.

The memory of my encounter with Jeanne Kennedy and how I'd run away remained and I thought it stayed with me from shame. It was a friend of Francis's who told me the facts, one woman whom I do remember, though not her face. She was a Gaby Muir, just as Patricia had come to be a Patricia. It could have been any one of many faces opposite me in a fashionable Italian restaurant, a woman heavily scented, expensively ajingle. That's all I remember of her, the smell, the sound, the trace element of spite. It was the point in our marriage when Francis's absences from England were increasing.

Between zabaglione and coffee she said, "Did you ever know about Jeanne Kennedy?"

And I said, "Yes," because right away I knew what the question was telling me.

"Oh, so you do, then? Of course it was over some years back. I only mention it now because Francis is taking quite an interest in her little boy. It seems she let him run wild while she got on with her business—hate to think what that was—and he got nabbed by the police. Set light to a car with a gang of others. He's only seven. Francis pulled strings to get him out of trouble and into his old school, St. something's . . ."

"St. Andrew's."

"Oh. You knew?"

"That he went there."

"I see. So, well, his little boy's going there too. He'll be one of the first coloreds. Caused quite a stir, it has, the talk of the Lyford Cay Club. It won't be easy for him, poor little brute. I hope you don't mind my telling you, it's only that I thought you ought to know."

Conscious saluted subconscious. I asked Francis questions and I'm not sure my nonchalance was feigned. "That girl in the Abacos, the one I thought was mad. Whatever became of her?"

"She's fine. Set her up with her own bar in Nassau. Clever girl."

"Her baby, the Dust Baby, is he fine too?"

"You bet. He's a bright little person." The way he said it.

"So, he's yours, then?" But, you see, I asked that question, the final one, the only one that mattered, a long time after. Because we'd worked over that seam of conversation at infrequent intervals, in exactly the same order. It was nothing to add a question one year, and another two years later. "He's yours, then?"

"Oh yes," he said, not even bothering to look up from the menu. We were in Brown's Hotel. "The roast's always good here."

I wanted a baby. I'd wanted one, too. So, after all, Francis had been right in his assumption: the problem was mine.

Six

A GREEN PICKUP swerved across a field to follow a combine with a tractor and trailer traveling alongside. Without stopping, the combine disgorged a stream of grain into the trailer.

Delia Sutherland reached to the stack of cans on the seat beside her: it was Tom in the combine and Alec in the tractor; Tom was Heineken, Alec was Lilt or anything soft. She pulled up and ran after the still-moving combine, grasped the rail with one finger and sprang onto the vertical steps. The driver opened the door letting out a blast of Bob Marley, "No woman, no cry . . ." and a fume of the mothballs scattered to prevent mice from chewing the wiring. "Thanks," he shouted, taking the beer.

She rolled her shirtsleeves and crouched on the platform shouting back, above the noise of the engine and Marley, "I've just been checking the records. The yield's the highest for three years."

"Thought so. Long time since I've seen such a heavy crop."

"Another hour, you reckon, before you're through?"

"At least."

"The forecast said the weather should hold until Tuesday, then more rain. So when you're finished here take the combine on down to Pope's Bottom ready for the morning. Okay?"

"All right," he grudged, contemplating the hour it would take to drive it there.

She slapped him on the back. He nodded without taking his eyes from the spiked reel rolling below him. When she had gone he looked at his watch, and hissed. Reflected in his side mirror was Delia Sutherland waving two cans above her head; a hand appeared from the cabin of the tractor and she threw them.

Inside her pickup she was oblivious to the harvest dust caking the dashboard, sticking the panel windows open, masking the windscreen except for two fans of clear glass where the wipers reached. Moving into first gear the knob came off in her hand again. "Bloody, bloody foreign cars." She threw it aside, grabbed the shaft and forced it in gear. When a fox bolted towards the hedgerow, the dogs barked furiously. "Shut up, dogs," she yelled over her shoulder. It was a gun blast that silenced them. She stopped beside a man wearing T-shirt, plus fours, cartridge belt, and baseball cap back to front. He lowered his gun.

"Did you get it?"

"Naa. Got two before dinnertime, though." He pushed a can of beer into each pocket. "Thanks, I'll have those later."

"By the way, I found this on Piper's Drive yesterday evening," slamming open the back doors of the pickup. "Some maniac driver must have hit it." She stood back for him to see the roe deer.

"Looks like. Okay, Mrs. S. I'll get rid of it. Boil it up for the dogs. Too damaged for the dealer." He walked to a battered Land Rover with the carcass slung over his shoulder, its tongue lolling from the tenderly parted mouth.

Delia Sutherland curled her hands deep into her trouser pockets; her keeper loosely cradled his gun. They remained in convivial silence surveying the field, harsh-textured, sore, as far as the lapping wheat, from which, at any moment, a hare might rush, or another fox. Beyond the hedge untidy maize was bordered on two sides by plowed soil, speckled white with chalk. In a further field black-and-white cows grazed in unison. The terrain went on dipping and rising, a body breathing, spinneys, spires, housing estates and glossy-roofed industry trickling from its folds. In the distance detail was lost in a scrim of rain.

"Seen any broods?" she asked.

"Plenty of pheasant. No partridge. Though I seen partridge up on Cocky Down."

"Wonderful."

"The birds in Crendal Wood release pen are nice strong ones. Just have to keep the foxes off them now."

"I'll get over there later. Keep your eyes open, then. They'll be finished here in an hour."

He did not look at his watch. He did not have one. Frank Grimwood did not worry about time.

Ducking her head to left and right Delia Sutherland studied the woodland as she drove through Sleet: softwood plantations bordered by a line of beech. It was looking clean; the lower branches had been brashed. She left the pickup door hanging open to examine the first line of trees. The bark had been stripped away leaving a bright damp patch. She smacked the wound. Countless others had the same damage. Despite the coat of white lead paint at the base, despite the baited traps, still the squirrels ravaged the saplings, doing far more harm than the deer. She decided on a new campaign, Warfarin this time.

"Muriel, it's me."

"Delia, I didn't recognize your voice. How are you, my dear?"

"What are you doing?"

"I was in the garden. What else on an evening like this? It rewards my years of hard work a hundredfold. Do you remember the dump it was when we first moved in?"

"Yes."

"Would you like me to come over, or would you rather be alone a bit longer?"

"Do come over, would you?"

Muriel arrived with earth still clinging to her fingers. They sat in the last of the sun on the morning-room steps.

Since Delia said nothing Muriel began, "How was David? Did it go all right yesterday?" She was watching Delia's profile. Her mouth had contracted in a manner Muriel had not seen for years. Not since the days when Francis used to come to Sleet with his bright flock of friends.

"He's left Sleet to Leon Kennedy, Muriel. You know who I mean, don't you? Of course you do."

"Delia?" Muriel said on several notes, implying it was the wrong type of joke and the wrong time.

"It's true."

Muriel's incredulous gasp began with a "B" and went nowhere.

"It'll be all right, though." Delia was squinting across two fields to where a group of deer grazed.

"Well, it's got to be. It's your home, for heaven's sake."

Delia Sutherland smiled. It was reassuring to hear the protest she herself had made. "I know what I've got to do. What Francis meant me to do. I've got to buy it back from him, you see. God knows, he's made me rich enough. I'll make it all right, you'll see." The deer raised their heads, scented, and sped into the woods, the white flashes on their rumps bobbing against the green of the field. "He wasn't a straightforward man, Francis."

"That he wasn't."

David Rosen heard nothing from Delia Sutherland. Even when he failed to ring her later in the week, as she had commanded him to do, once he had sorted life to meet her expectations, she did not ring him.

He knew what she would be doing and why she had not called him. She would be at home continuing as before. After all, she was not a realist, not a worldly woman. She had not accepted it yet.

He contacted Freeman Tucker of Tucker, Higgs and Kelly, the Nassau lawyers. They confirmed Leon Kennedy had been informed of the will. Beyond that there was nothing to say. There was one hope which Rosen kept to himself and which would only come to light when Kennedy responded.

When Delia Sutherland did at last ring it was three weeks after their meeting and he was proved right. Her talk was all about the recent fine weather, the record yield, the completion of harvest—all but the linseed. She even said, "The worry is, how'll we better it next year?" and laughed.

Rosen did not laugh. He did not want to enter into that precarious optimism. So when it seemed the conversation was nearly over and, for the first time since he had known her, she appeared to have called for no reason, he was almost relieved to hear her ask, "Now then, David, have you heard from him?"

"Not yet, but he knows the will."

"Good. So it won't be long now."

Her airy finality bothered him. "What do you mean?"

"Well, of course it was frightful, the shock, at first. Driving home, though, I couldn't think why it wasn't worse. Do you see what I mean? Why I kept almost forgetting. Then I understood. You see, the boy won't want Sleet, David. It's quite obvious. I wouldn't in his place. He'll be a simple island boy. These, well, these natural children, for want of a better expression, are not at all uncommon over there. Francis once told me that his father, Scott, had two or three that he knew about. As for old Wallace Sutherland, well, dozens, by all accounts. What would a boy like that want with land in England? No, I assure you, he'll want me to buy him out, which I can easily do. Then he can be a big noise over there. Francis understood all of this, of course, or he'd never have done it. He only did it to, well, I don't really know. A joke, maybe. That's what it was. A little joke to give me a shock. That's why he made things so I could buy the boy out. And that's what I'll do. Simple."

"I'll confess to a similar hope, Delia. But I've made a few inquiries about him, discreetly, of course, from Mr. Tucker in Nassau. "Simple island boy" wouldn't seem to cover it. Did you know he's a graduate from Columbia University? Sociology? Well, you wouldn't, but he is. He finished last year. He's twenty-five now, Tucker told me, and he's been living with his mother in Nassau."

"That's all as may be. I just don't want it to take too long. It's an upsetting thing to have hanging about. I'm sure you understand. You'll put it to him as soon as possible, won't you? By the way, you must come down again soon, you know, for a little visit. I always enjoy your little visits."

You'll see then, she thought; you'll be reminded of the rightness of me, here. The unalterable nature of the place, and my presence in it, is obvious to anyone who lives, works or visits.

She had had visions too, during the three weeks since the news. Visions which confirmed that, of course, she was not only at Sleet, she was Sleet.

Checking the progress of harvest in Dog Trap—seventy-six acres of rich soil thrown among plantations of Norway spruce and Douglas fir—she strolled to the center of the field where there was a natural hollow ringed with arabesquing Scots pine. Down in the sun-filtered green of it were mossy, flat-surfaced rocks, bracken, and a dew pond. Three people were picnicking by the pond: a young man, a woman and a little girl. The girl had hair like a charred bush, and was wrestling with a tolerant Labrador, while the other two lounged laughing. The woman rolled over onto her stomach, reached for a bottle of wine, handed it to the man. He stroked her fair hair before taking it. Then he stood, lifted a bright golden saxophone against his body and started to play. The woman leaned her head, and her hair draped to one side. The little girl stopped her game with the dog to sit cross-legged, attentive. Delia Sutherland thought: An ugly little thing, that child, peripheral to those lovers, and: Damn, it's me.

The moaning combine in the field, the tractor and trailer with grain trickling from the back of it as it rumbled off to the corn drier, the waving haze of barley still to be cut, these things all fell into shade as the sun clouded over. But down in the hollow the sunshine remained and so did Delia Sutherland watching her father, her mother, herself.

In New Hope Copse she saw at a distance a man holding the hand of a small child, inclining to her the way adults do when walking with little ones, while his free arm swept the air to possess the oaks, the beeches, the ash. Delia Sutherland did not need to go nearer to know who they were—apparitions of herself, her father. No doubt other Caldwells, too, inhabited every shade, every trunk, rabbit hole and rut of Sleet.

She always visited the dairy during afternoon milking. When she saw Mike in the pit—Mike who had helped her dam the slurry lagoon four years before—attaching a cluster to one of a line of cows, when she slapped the flank of that cow, and shut her eyes to inhale the air loaded with the smell of blood-warm milk, udder wash and cow breath, she was utterly content in the conviction of her seamless permanence. That was something to have, she told herself, to know precisely where you belong, and to be as essential to that place as it is to you.

Nevertheless, having called Rosen, knowing that Kennedy was aware of the will and having had no word from him, was annoying. There were details to be arranged.

She rang again. "David, have you told the man yet, to tell the boy I'll make an offer?"

"To Mr. Kennedy?"

"Who else?"

"Yes, I have. We're still waiting. Tucker wants to know what's happening about Francis's personal effects. Do you want to see to those, or what?"

"I'll think about it."

Another week passed. It was purely silly that the whole business could not be arranged more quickly. "Well, David? Has he heard? Does he know?"

"Two weeks ago, Delia, I faxed Tucker right after we spoke and rang him again yesterday. He's passed it on. Mr. Kennedy knows what you'd like to do."

"And?"

"They're ringing me tomorrow afternoon. I'll call you."

At five the next day when Delia Sutherland telephoned she was informed that David Rosen was on the other line. She replaced the receiver but left her hand on it until Rosen rang back. "Yes? Well?"

There was amusement in Rosen's voice which faded immediately after he had said, "Good afternoon, Delia."

"Exactly. So?"

"Tucker's told me that Mr. Kennedy doesn't want you to make an offer. He's not interested in selling Sleet."

"That's ridiculous. He doesn't even know how much yet. I can pay for it. Does he know that?"

"He's adamant. No offers."

"Oh, David, really, that's only because he knows perfectly well he'll sell when we say how much. We're talking about a great deal of money, after all."

"That's not how Tucker made it sound."

"That's how it is. Really. I know. I'll speak to the boy myself, then."

"He's not a boy, Delia. He's twenty-five and Tucker said that he's specifically declined any offers at all, and that he doesn't want contact with you."

Chuckling as one familiar with her own unalterable flaws she said, "No, I don't expect he does."

After that she sat on the morning-room steps watching the day slide off the face of Old Carrots Field. For the first time that year she sniffed autumn.

Alone in the dining room, having eaten the half grapefruit set in her place by Curtis, she helped herself from the sideboard to fish pie cooked by Mrs. Files. Later, she watched the *Nine O'clock News*, shut the dogs in the kennels. She wound the bracket clock on the letter table in the hall, the marble mantel clock in the serious chill of the ballroom, catching the pendulum, releasing it, listening for the rhythm of ticks stuttering into the vastness. In the morning room she wound the French clock, the one with lovebirds entwined on the top of it. She tried and failed, as always, to synchronize its chimes with the hour. In the upstairs passage she opened the long case clock, knowing very well it was broken, that the weights had not descended for years and the hands remained at twenty to one. But this was Thursday evening and that's what she did on Thursday evenings, wound the clocks. She sat on the edge of her bed for a few minutes, digging dirt from under her nails. Shortly after ten-thirty she switched off her light.

Nine and a half hours later she rang David Rosen at his home. "I'm going over there, David. I'll sort out Francis's stuff in the Abacos. And after that I'm going to see the boy myself, make him understand. We can't go on waiting about like this."

I must leave all of this awhile. I must postpone reliving the stages of failure because it's too much, too much for me at once. You never failed. Let me tell you now, you didn't. You had perfect pitch, my love.

Instead I'll describe my hotel room here in Marseille which, although large, is really quite featureless. The impersonal style suits me. It'll be easy to leave when the time comes. When you come.

They call it a suite, that's because there's room for a sofa, I expect, not a very nice one. No effort has been made to enhance the room, unless you count three small prints randomly hung on separate walls, *Une Baigneuse* by Seurat, a Degas of a woman drying her hair and a Bonnard of another woman in a bath. Someone has specific taste, haven't they? But this is my dwelling place and has been for nearly four months now. My goodness, how long it takes to write all this, this life of mine. Is it all right, I wonder; am I clear? Will you understand?

I make a point each day of leaving the New York before lunch to walk along the Rue de la République where, fifth on the right, is a fine flower shop. I always bring something back from there—today it was iris together with something white and richly scented; I asked the girl twice what it was called but couldn't catch what she said—I arrange the flowers in the vase I bought soon after I arrived.

My hotel is a first-floor one on the Vieux Port with narrow stairs leading up to its reception. There are two windows in my room, three-quarter-length casements with elaborate iron balustrades. I lean there. My eyes skip the busy road that sweeps around the head of the port and is divided by a great oval flower bed, garishly planted. What I'm watching is the fish market on the far side. I watch it from my seat in the New York as well, which is down below to the right; I can see the top of its maroon awning. The fishwives pack up at lunchtime. The trestles supporting shallow wooden trays painted blue, red or yellow, and which have the vendor's name and telephone number roughly inscribed on the front, these are all folded away at about twelve-thirty, until the next day. By two o'clock there's no sign the market was ever there, except for a residual odor on stiller days. So, you see, I've entered, as completely as I can, the scene on my postcard; I'm part of it.

I'm here. I'm not going.

Seven

DELIA SUTHERLAND stood in the immigration queue at Nassau Airport. She wore a safari suit and khaki hat perched on her slipping load of hair.

The unkind brilliance of the tropics depressed her. She had not liked it before, did not like it now, and the throng of tourists who had also disembarked, wearing baggy floral shorts, trussed with the straps of cameras and rucksacks, was irritating. So was the welcoming goombay beat pounded out by two drummers and a guitarist at the back of the hall.

Seeing her name on none of the placards paraded outside the customs hall, she retreated to the shade of a wall opposite the terminal. At last a car drew up. A fat man alighted and, with the unexpected delicacy of the very fat, nimbled across the road, his belt buckle riding high on his belly. He entered the terminal building, then returned to stand with one hand on his haunch, the other sheltering his eyes to the right, then the left, where Delia Sutherland was sitting on her suitcase, unaccountably invisible to him.

"Mr. Tucker? Are you?" she called, and he swung round, his hand hovering over his oiled, blond hair.

"Mrs. Sutherland. Mrs. Sutherland." He spread short arms in greeting, relief then wonder as she rose to her feet. "My, my," he murmured to himself and, bowing, he announced, "Freeman Tucker. Tucker, Higgs and Kelly. Welcome to the Islands."

Twenty minutes later the Tucker, Higgs and Kelly Cessna glided off the runway at Grant Bahama Island and tip-tilted one hundred and six miles north to the Abacos, cays where Sutherlands had dwelled since 1789. After years of persecution as loyalists in independent America, they had fled their lush Carolina plantation with their slaves, believing the Bahamas to be British, rich and fertile. All it was was British. Within years their cotton plants were decimated by a tiny bug and the Sutherlands resigned themselves to a meager living from farming. They acquired the skill of boat-building; first dinghies and smacks, then sloops, eventually large cargo schooners.

During the Civil War, when the Yankees surrounded the Southern ports, the Sutherlands made a fortune running the blockades with war supplies from the British and French, as well as helping the cotton export to flow from the ports of Wilmington, Charleston and Savannah. They invested their money abroad, avoiding the poverty suffered by most Bahamians when the Civil War ended.

"So, no more Sutherlands in the Abacos now," Tucker shouted above the noise of the plane he was piloting himself. "Not now Francis is gone. Seems a pity, don't you think?" He was not looking at her, did not see how unaffected she was.

"It happens with families. They die out, you know," she said without raising her voice or removing her attention from the crowding clouds.

"You say something, Mrs. Sutherland?" Tucker shoved his earphone aside, creasing up his face to hear better. She did not turn and he shook his head, presumably on her behalf.

The thirty-minute flight was followed by twenty minutes in a truck to a dilapidated harbor where a black-skinned man hauled himself from a motorboat onto the patched wooden dock.

Tucker called, "Hey there. How are you today?"

"Hah, Mr. Tucker. I's fine."

"Good, good. Now, this is Mrs. Sutherland."

Shy-eyed, smiling, the boatman passed a hand before his face to remove a veil of sleep. "Hah, Mrs. Sutherland. I's Fwinky," tossing up a grin, sharing a joke about his identity with the sky.

"How do you do, Fwinky?" His handshake rippled to her shoulder.

Tucker said, "You've worked for Mr. Sutherland some years now, haven't you? Must be five, could be seven, even more." The hum of agreement was no confirmation of time. Tucker confided, "Good man, that. Haitian, you know. Hardworking, reliable."

Later, in the boat and shouting again because of the whoosh of water behind them as well as the noise of the engine, Tucker told her, "We could've gone round by road but this way you get a better feel. I've got a small place nearby on another cay. Beautiful, eh?"

leveling stubby fingers with pride at oyster-pink sand and casuarina pines shimmying at the sea chambered turquoise and petrol-blue.

She shut her eyes against it all; shut her eyes to open them again onto the harmless horizon. Tucker saw her do that and decided what kind of a woman he was dealing with.

The coastline crept low, green with intermittent houses, each a different interpretation of the same dream: sea life in the sun. They all had their own finger of dock with a greater or lesser craft. Francis Sutherland's dock stretched farther and was better kept than the rest. Tied to it were two speedboats, a smack and a powerboat equipped for deep-sea fishing.

Having handed her suitcase up to Tucker, she clambered ashore and retrieved it from him. She hurried forward with her head down so as not to see the diesel-and-hemp-smelling boathouse where she and Francis had once kissed and kissed; or the two canvas shoes pushed on dock posts to dry and which she was certain had belonged to Francis. How long had they been drying there now? He had been dead five weeks. Still she had not reached the end of the dock. There was the holding tank to pass yet. Inside were grouper, dolphin fish, conch, and lobster on the bottom. From Francis's last trip, were they? His prey surviving when he hadn't? A white plastic bag containing two loaves of bread was huddled against one of the last dock posts and she was relieved to see it, something belonging to today, to the living. Must be Fwinky's, she thought. Now there was no choice but to raise her eyes and let herself see the house.

The whole building was made of the island pine. The steep, shingled roof shone in varying shades of gray, and there was the terrace in front. The pool below was hidden behind imported rocks. Before she climbed the wide wooden steps, where a frenzy of bougainvillea covered the handrails, she looked back down the jetty. Tucker had remained beside the boat, staring after her, while Fwinky padded barefoot with a petrol can towards the boathouse.

"Well?" she shouted. "You are coming in, aren't you?"

"Right there." He saluted and advanced.

The house was entered from the left into a sheltered deck area running its length and surrounded on three sides by louvered shutters. There were tawny wicker chairs heaped with cushions. Three gold-bladed fans in the ceiling stirred limp currents into the air.

When Tucker caught up, Delia Sutherland was standing with her hands up and her back to him, saying, "George? Can it really be?

79

All this time?" She stepped forward, brought her hands to her knees, solicitously bending. "Speak to me, darling."

She was addressing a massive and gaudy macaw perched in the corner, side-facing her suspiciously. He held out a black claw which she stroked. "That's right, baby. So it is you, then. Well, fancy that. After all this time. 'Fat white,' remember? 'Fat white,' go on."

The bird cranked out, "Fat white lady nobody loves. Whydu whydu whydu."

"That's amazing. Mr. Tucker, this is George; we're old friends. One forgets how they live on, poor things."

"Yes, that's right, we've met often." Tucker trilled his fingers self-consciously, embarrassed at having not previously registered that the bird was human.

"It was Francis's father, apparently, who taught him a lot of tum-te-tum poetry. He knows another one about Heraclitus being dead, you know."

At last this difficult woman was animated, and to sustain her Tucker pointed enthusiastically to a cage in the opposite corner.

"Parrots too, Mrs. Sutherland. Come over here."

She barely glanced at the bright creatures. "Yes, I know, Mr. Tucker. But they're not really people, are they? Not like George here."

When Tucker caught himself shrugging apologetically at the parrots he knew he was out of his depth. He slung his jacket over his shoulder and, anointing his fingertips in the breast pocket of his shirt, ascended the two shallow steps leading into the main part of the house.

It was one great, shadowed room with bedroom suites flung, at first-floor level, to left and right. Guests would stay in a cottage in the garden. All the cooking, eating, living went on under this vaulted ceiling with its skylights, around this central fireplace, on this limestone floor knuckled with the imprints of fossils. Still caressing George, Delia Sutherland heard Tucker cry, "Luney."

"What?" She stepped up into the deep cool of the room.

"Mrs. Sutherland, come and meet Luney. Luney, Mrs. Sutherland." Tucker was holding his hand towards a still presence and a flare of white at the back of the room near the kitchen area.

Delia Sutherland offered her hand to a young girl in an overall. She was short, and as dark-skinned as the boatman, which was darker than most of the Bahamians. The front of her hair was flattened by a battery of pearl clips and left to rise at the back in Styrofoam peaks. She allowed her hand to rest in Delia Sutherland's, whispering to one side, "Luney," following with a palm stroke to her lips, brushing off the word.

"How charming. Now, 'Luney.' How do you spell that?"

Swayed by the drawing of her breath, the girl took a moment to dream, then said with a far-off resonance, "You don't spell dat, ma'am, you sez it."

"And so I shall. Thank you, Luney," using the removing of her hat to hide her amusement. The girl vanished, apparently without movement, to be heard clanking saucepans and chopping. Delia Sutherland fell onto the cream leather sofa with her arms stretched across the back of it, her legs stiff in front of her, laughing uncontrollably. "Oh dear, oh dear, I'm so sorry, Mr. Tucker." She curled up to tourniquet her laughter. "I always did that with them, said the most ludicrous things."

"With whom?"

"With them. The blacks. 'You don't spell it, you sez it.' Perfect. She's so right."

She laughed more and Tucker was smiling, intoxicated by the sound escaping from her, which shook the sofa, reverberated in the rafters and made the parrots screech. She had steadied herself when Tucker, who was chuckling too, nodded at her. She heard him say, "And you have joy, Mrs. Sutherland."

Her hand went so quickly to cover her profile and her mouth became so taut, he thought she was going to weep with the same energy. "Oh no, Mr. Tucker," she choked. "You're quite wrong there. It's been very hard for years, and now, to be back here, you don't know what it is for me. Here, where I could've done better, if only I'd understood, if only he'd helped me; if only this, if only that. God, what am I saying? I must be very tired."

He touched her arm. "Mrs. Sutherland? I only meant that you have Joy, the gardener. He works the plot over the road, the Yamacraw. He's Haitian too, like the rest. Immigrants, you know. Life's better for them here when they're lucky enough to get in. And they don't mind work. May I take your bag upstairs?"

"I'm quite all right, thank you. I know the way."

He called to her when she was halfway up the open stairway to the bedroom she had shared with Francis; Francis's bedroom. "May I say, Mrs. Sutherland, that I understand it can't be easy for you? But that I'm so glad you've come here to see to his personal effects this way? You see, he was my client, sure, but he was my friend too and it seems right, to me, his wife should be the one to tidy away after him."

A great bed with a dark carved headboard like an ecclesiastical panel reaching halfway up the wall, a chest of drawers supporting a mirror between brass pillars, a desk dropped open exposing drawers and pigeonholes stuffed with papers: these high-polished, somber items, out of keeping with the rest of the house, subsided within the airtight hush of the room curtained and shuttered against the light. Delia Sutherland put down her suitcase and closed herself in there.

It wasn't like entering a room at all. It was like entering Francis himself, the undead essence of him. Not the young Francis either, in whom I stood a better hope of experiencing the odd happy memory, but Francis as I'd last experienced him with the tang of his Lucky Strikes, last night's whisky and dejection all togged up as *joie de vivre*. The spirit of his meticulousness was in the pile of freshly laundered shirts and handkerchiefs at the foot of the bed. It would have been no one's job to put them away. Everything in his life had its place; long-sleeved shirts to the left, short-sleeved to the right, belts hung this way, not that, this painting, this woman, this sock, each just so, and only he knew how.

Escaping from under the pillow on the bed was the hem of a caftan, the soft kind he'd slept in all the time I'd known him. The mirror on the chest was tilted down, reflecting a dish of cuff links, a pencil stub, crushed boarding pass, loose change, the ivory brushes he never used, and the plastic hairbrush he did because it was more effective. How could I have known that detail? It's the sort of thing a lover would observe. Or a loving wife. I pulled his hair from between its spikes, not so gray as mine. It smelled dry, of his skin, of his life. I was rubbing the dusty ball of his hair against my cheek as I turned over papers on the desk.

In his handwriting one of them began:

Darling, darling, Here I am, with you again. Writing to you is being with you. The nearest I can at the moment. That'll change. We'll have more, much more . . .

I didn't read on. That was the way it had always been, my love daring the slightest signal only to find his love was elsewhere. And who was she these days? Who had he been making beautiful? He was reaching out from death to hurt me in the same old way, only this time I didn't have to know. Later when Tucker was gone I'd be alone to burn every paper there without another glance.

There was a photograph of me—it could not have been taken more than five years before. In it I was crossing Old Carrots, coming towards the house, a stick in one hand, the other pushed into my hair. I was clearly alone. My face had that closed concentration of the solitary walker but I looked happy. No. I looked tranquil, contained. But isn't that the sum of it, happiness? To think he'd stolen that secret image of me, taken, no doubt, from an upstairs window with a fancy lens. In recent years he had often carried cameras with any number of attachments. Never saw the pictures he took. Now this one. As I held it, I knew if I looked over to the bed he'd be there, hands behind his head, stealing, this time, an image of his widow. "Hello, Francis," I said, to have the sound of my voice ground me. It made his presence more complete.

I felt the cuffs of the cotton jackets hanging in the cupboard, smoothed the scrupulously scruffy trousers. I opened his razor in the bathroom to rub the powered residue of his beard in my fingers, and wondered if it was still growing on his dead face. I held his toothbrush, left-handed the way he'd have done, opened a container of cotton buds, pulled off a length of dental floss, examined a bottle of eardrops.

"So soon, Mrs. Sutherland?" and, "Oh dear. Here, here, have a drink."

They lunched in the lilac light of the deck shuttered against the day, slips of sun crossing their faces, the table, the floor. Delia Sutherland watched the coming and going of Luney's bare feet as she brought the food she had prepared.

Tucker would have liked to say something to amuse Mrs. Sutherland. He was sorry her laughter was gone. But then why should she laugh, it was a sad business. "Sad business."

"What?"

"Too bad. Man like Francis. Silly accident."

"So he was your friend? I've often wondered lately who his men friends were. Are there others?"

"Not many. He'd become reclusive. He'd do the parties now and then as he used to. He'd get very wild those times, like he was making up for something. Mainly he was happy to fish. In fact the night he died, the Saturday, we'd been fishing all day, just the two of us. It was his birthday and I'd planned this surprise party for him. The same old crowd, but he'd been seeing much less of them. I took him off so the house could be got ready and everyone arrive. We came back to this great reception and the party began. I think he was pleased. I like to think he was pleased."

Was she at the party, the "Darling, darling" of his letter? Was she someone's wife? Was writing to her the nearest he could be? I wouldn't look. I wouldn't read. I didn't have to know. And Tucker was saying, "He spent more time in the Islands these past years than ever before. More like his pa did. Now Scott Sutherland was a big man here, very involved in politics. But I don't blame Francis not going that road. It's not so easy anymore. Things are different here since Pindling and all." Tucker crossed his short arms, tenderly rocking himself, his own baby. "We got fond of each other, Francis and I. He was a generous man, a rare thing these days. And, like I say, I'm glad it's you sorting the stuff. As you know, his sister inherits this place. She lives down in Atlanta and she's way older than Francis, isn't she? Some fifteen years? She didn't make the funeral either. There weren't too many there, to tell the truth. All those that took his hospitality, where were they, I'd like to ask? I've seen pictures with him duck-shooting on Andros surrounded by girls in bikinis and all sorts. But, excuse me, you won't want to know such things."

That's true, I don't want to know; don't have to know anything I don't want to. A small fire in the garden will settle the contents of his desk.

"Is the cemetery near by?"

"At the top of the hill beyond the town. He's there with all the Sutherlands. I've had a fine tomb made, Mrs. Sutherland. You'd be pleased. I had to pay to have them work as fast as they did, only I didn't want my friend's grave marked with just a cross in the sand for any longer than it had to be. We could go over if you'd care to."

"I'm not ready, Mr. Tucker, but thank you for all you've done. I didn't come to the funeral because I was too angry. I didn't understand at that point."

"Of course, of course." Organizing a meeting of his fingertips, he peered round them to inquire, "Didn't understand what, exactly, Mrs. Sutherland?"

"That Francis expected me to buy Sleet from Leon."

"Oh no, that would be a misconception. That's not how it is."

"Forgive me, Mr. Tucker, but despite everything I think I understand my husband better than you."

"Yes, of course. However, I'd hoped you'd come over understanding that Leon doesn't wish to sell his property called Sleet. He's most adamant, Mrs. Sutherland."

"He won't be when he hears my offer."

"It's not the money. He's a tenacious young man."

"Do you know him well?"

"Got to, over the years. Francis had me watch over him since he was a kid and his mother couldn't cope. He got into some trouble down in Jumby Village."

"I heard about it."

"Did you know his ma asked Francis to take him off her hands when he was seven 'cause she was too busy with the bar?"

"No."

"Well, that's what happened. I was the one that took him from her and it wasn't a good scene. I'd never want to have to do that again. Even though I'd found a fine lady to take care of him. Aldina Simmonds. She still lives in Fox Hill. It's all Nassau. She was then in her sixties and a fine black church-going lady with a number of boys and girls from similar circumstances. But you see, Mrs. Sutherland, he handled that and being one of the first nonwhites at St. Andrew's School. Not easy. Not easy. All this makes a boy something. In Leon's case, tenacious, I'd say. Vacation time Francis arranged for him to caddy at the Lyford Cay Club to keep him out of trouble. You know it?"

"Slightly."

"Leon's bright, like his ma. He learned from those guys he caddied for, sophisticated stuff too. Why, why you know, I've even heard him speak a little French?" Tucker smiled to himself. "He was always a cute kid. Sad."

"Why sad?"

"Well, excuse me, Mrs. Sutherland, but a kid with no ma, no pa but they're both alive, living nearby and rich to boot, while some matron, fine though she may be, is paid to take care of him and he works vacations? I'm not saying it's unusual but it's sad and tough too."

"His mother's rich, now?"

"Big success. Smart businesswoman. Got a club called the Big Bamboo on Wulff Road. Gambling, dancing. Named after a famous place that burned down."

Was it Jeanne? Was she still the "Darling, darling?" A bonfire. A bonfire on the beach tonight when it'll be too dark for my eye to catch a few stray words of love.

"Are you married, Mr. Tucker?"

"Nope. I'm a solo act. Broke up with my wife years back. My daughter visits with her kids, summers. Kids like it here."

Delia Sutherland pushed a shutter wide. The sun hit her face, her throat where her shirt was unbuttoned. "I saw her once—Jeanne."

"Jeanne?" He frowned. "Oh, Turpie. He always called her Jeanne, didn't he? I'd forgotten that. I asked him why he did once and he said it was a more beautiful name. But Euturpia's nice too, that's her real name. Doesn't use Jeanne anymore. You don't get too many Exuma girls with a name like Jeanne." Tucker broke off some bread, wiped his plate with it, chewing with dainty relish before dabbing his napkin to pursed lips and fluting his fingers.

"Is she still very lovely?"

Tucker massaged his knees, contemplating the conch salad left in the bowl. He would have liked some more but it did not seem appropriate. Not now. "She is."

"I want to talk to her, Mr. Tucker."

"It's not a good time, Mrs. Sutherland."

She examined the palm of her hand. "Couldn't—"

"Something the matter there?" he interrupted. "You got some irritation? Rash, maybe? It's the heat. I've a spray that's good."

"No. No, thank you. Couldn't Jeanne, Euturpia, have seen to his stuff? Why didn't you ask her?" coloring from her effort at detachment.

"Why? Propriety, Mrs. Sutherland. You're the wife. Besides, she wouldn't Not Turpie, not now."

"It was you who prepared the codicil to his will?"

Tucker's fingers traveled in search of a resting place and settled for their usual breast pocket. He made a noise of agreement. "It was."

The wine was half-finished, there were mangoes, sapodillas. He rose from the table forlornly, addressing his attention to the crease on his trouser leg.

"Mr. Tucker, I have to persuade the boy—"

"Leon, Mrs. Sutherland. He's called Leon."

"—Leon—to let me buy back Sleet. Do you know the circumstances?"

"I am familiar, yes. Even if he'd change his mind, and he wouldn't, his mother wouldn't like it. I've talked to her. She wants it for him."

"So she influences him? They're close?"

"I don't know about close. They've found each other. After I took him over to Aldina Simmonds when he was just a tot, Turpie and Leon never met. That's how she wanted it. Only last year, when he came back from college, did he go to live with her. Seventeen years apart, they'd had. Now she has this fancy residence in Delaporte, big Spanish-style house, built with all her own money, and he's the college graduate. Like I say, they've found each other."

Delia Sutherland closed her fingers around the inside of his elbow with a pressure that could have been the overture to an embrace but he knew it was not.

"Mr. Tucker, I must see Leon. I have to talk to him. I want to make him an excellent offer for Sleet, one impossible to refuse. Where do I find him?"

"He's not in the Islands right now."

"He's avoiding me."

"Not necessarily, but he won't sell, Mrs. Sutherland, and like I say, he's not here."

"Then I'll see her. She's a businesswoman. I insist you arrange a meeting."

His eyes trailed from her hand, the penetrating warmth of it, up to where her expression conscripted his obedience. "You're some piece of work, Mrs. Sutherland, you know that?"

"Is that 'yes'?"

He pushed plates aside to lay his briefcase down, clicked it open, clicked it shut again, before descending the wooden stairs to the dock.

"Mr. Tucker, is that 'yes'?" she shouted after him.

"That's 'yes,' Mrs. Sutherland," stepping away lightly, a balloon in ballet shoes.

At the last minute a sense of something unsaid made her hurry after him. He was already in the boat. "Mr. Tucker? Well, I wanted to say thank you. I mean, thank you for everything." The boatman was untying the guest line. "Fwinky? Now you will look after Mr. Tucker, won't you, Fwinky?"

"Yes, ma'am."

That was better. Yes. She felt all right now and when Tucker came as close as he could to her, confidentially crooking his finger, she was only too pleased to lean precariously forward over the dock, ear to his lips. He whispered, "The name's Franky, only he has trouble with his r's. The Haitians do, you see?"

In the kitchen Delia Sutherland found matches and Luney, without a word, watched her take them. She closed the bedroom door, drew open the curtains, folded back the shutters. The noise of the boat departing with Tucker in it grazed the afternoon silence. A door slammed downstairs. She seated herself at the desk. From the window was the sight of Luney ambling across the garden below, away from the house. Still watching the retreating figure, she let her fingers drag papers from the six pigeonholes, pull open the small drawers to find more. Collected under her hands they made a thick pile. Perhaps they were not all love letters? Perhaps she was making a mistake? Her eyes slipped across and down to glimpse any words not covered by her fingers spread over the top page: "hours," "be with you," "your name," "love," "last night."

Before sleep
Darling, darling, Here I am, with you again. Writing to you is being with you. The nearest I can at the moment. That'll change. We'll have more. Much more. I was in Nassau on business today but couldn't keep my mind on it because I'd already decided to come up here tonight and be with you. When I decide to talk to you this way, my hours are spiked as if we really have a date planned. I was counting these pages last night and gave up at forty-two. I say your name and pretend you're here with me. I'll ring you tomorrow. I really will. Good night, my love.

Sun up, Tuesday
Been looking at your picture again. The worn lions of your beauty, fiercer, finer than ever. I'd like to hold you. Touch you.

I've done it with other women. Still do, just sometimes. It's not a thing with me anymore. I want it to be you. That's all.

After lunch
I go to buy the bread from Ulrich most days. Like I did when I was a boy. I'd take a smack along there and he'd give me a cinnamon cake. He still does, like there's no change. Like I'm still a boy. He was old even then. I tell him about you. Why can't I pick up the phone and say, Come on, darling? I guess because if you said no there'd be no more dreams. I didn't used to be one to leave dreams be. Had to make them real. What happened to me?

Late
I'm weak. I have to sit down now and then. Just in the middle of doing something I have to sit down with my mind blank and filling, like a pitcher, with sadness. I'm frightened of the dark. I see things that aren't there. And I'm scared of the light when it comes because I see things that are, like my face getting old.

Sunday
Went to Jeanne last night. She gave me stuff. It passes the time. Makes me feel good for a while, then bad. It's worth it. Saw my boy. He's sometimes in the hall when I pass on the way out. I say hey, kid, he says hey. I'd like to know him. It's like seeing myself in the shadows there, all choked up. I guess I'll do it. Get him over. We'll go fishing. I have a son. I have a son.

First thing
I was awake last night and suddenly remembered the time you made me rise early to flight the duck. And what did we do? We screwed in the bushes till breakfast. When I remembered that I panicked. If I could have forgotten that, even for a while, what else is gone and I don't know? I pretend you're here. When I came back from fishing yesterday you were beside me in the lean-to gutting the catch with me. It's the kind of thing you liked doing when you were here. The light from the hurricane lamp fell on your hair. How long since I've seen it loose? The first time I saw it loose. The honor of that intimacy. Few women have anything so remarkable in their armory. I remember waking with my face in it the first whole night we spent together. I opened my eyes into a black web. I thought: no man has ever

slept in her hair before. I have that and the privilege of her laughter all my life. Then I fucked up.

Last thing, Friday
The privilege of your laughter. I wrote that to you once before, in the letter you pretended not to read. Was it because of my "game with fate," Leon inheriting Sleet if I should die? Was that what you couldn't face? I don't think so. Besides, why should I die, honey? People don't, especially when they've had enough and wouldn't mind. He's more likely to die than I am because he loves life, his mother tells me so. Or did you pretend not to read it because of my invitation to make a real life together? That's what I believe. That there may be no hope. I guess that's what stops me ringing. But I will one day. I will be the man I was. I can still hear your laughter when I said, "Who's Patricia?" and still don't know why it was so funny but, God, you looked fine.

Evening
Today I had four baths to fill in time and I invented you. We sat with George looking at the sea. We didn't turn on the lights. Those stars. Jesus, the nights here. All my life and they still amaze me. I look up at all those stars and I think: He's one strong sucker, God is, but he sure doesn't give a shit about me. I want you to know you're not a fantasy for me. I know you and the value of what we could have shared. I'm the impotent one. What does a man do with a woman like you? I'd send every letter I've written you since we last met if I thought you wouldn't do it to me again, humiliate me again. Sleet's not good for you, my darling. You don't know that and you might never know it.

I don't know the day.
I don't know what the day is anymore
I rang you just now and you did what you do, not speak. I listened to you listening till you cut me off. You're right. The wound I made in you has healed in an ugly way. If I opened it up could we take care of the healing together? Make a better scar? I'll call again tomorrow. I'll just pick up the phone and, how'll I begin? It'll have to be me. I'll say, Delia? You'll say, Francis, what is it? But you'll say it like an accusation. I'll have to

remember that and not be put off. I'll say, How're things? Like a signal to let you know I want just to talk. Fine, you'll say. You'll be thinking I haven't just rung to talk, that there's a motive. There will be. To tell you I want you to come back to me. That I love you. I'll wait to say all that till we've talked some more. You'll say, So how's life? I'll say, Wonderful, why wouldn't it be? And then I'll have told a lie, the first, but soon after, because of it, I guess, we'd say good-bye.

Night before my birthday
Fishing with Freeman tomorrow. That sweet guy. Plan to go way up by Double Breasted Cay. I know it's 'cause there's a party planned for my birthday we're going so far. We'll come back and they'll all be here, all those ones I don't want to see anymore. But Freeman's done it all in friendship, so what would I say? Luney told me about the party. She knows it's not a good idea to surprise me. Not like the old days. What if someone made you come? Only no one knows what that would mean to me so they won't. But it could happen anyway. You might be there. And if you were I'd be so good to you you'd stay. And the next day I'd say, Let's go see Joy awhile, see what's growing. You'd like that. Every day I go to him, pretending you're with me. And you will be. Good night, darling.

Eight

I READ throughout the night, glancing at the bed from where, earlier the same day, I had been certain Francis was watching me. Not anymore. The room was emptied of his essence. To reconjure it, so palpable when I first entered, I pressed my face into his clothes again and couldn't, couldn't retrieve his scent. His hairbrush, razor, everything I'd previously touched, had relinquished his identity. All that remained of him were the words of his confused hopes, swimming on the pages.

The qualities I had cultivated to help me through, such as diligence, such as dignity, such as keeping my peace, had been, after all, weapons which isolated me and made me loathsome. I had wasted my life and Francis's. Content with humiliation, satisfied with disappointment, I had been too selfish to reach out.

I heard Luney arrive, heard her talking to Franky and then the boat going away. The hours expanded in deeper and deeper heat, until the air split and the rain was all but blinding.

I lay down with Francis's caftan in my hands. Luney didn't disturb me. Perhaps, accustomed to Francis, she'd become unquestioning about others' ways of life.

There were over a hundred letters covering the two years since our meeting in Brown's. Some pages were long, illegible, others no more than a line. Although he'd written that I was not a fantasy for him, he had dreamed me, written me, into a woman far less flawed than I am, or ever could be. But I would have tried to be anything to have him back and be able to say, Look, I've come. Late for the party, but I've come.

During the second night a headache forced me to stop reading. I found a canvas bag in his wardrobe in which I laid the pages, handling them as though they were living and in pain. As though they were Francis. And they were.

Opening the door I found the house in darkness. It was hard to walk, my legs were so cold, although the night was very hot. At the top of the stairs I thought I was going to be sick and returned stiffly to the bathroom. Kneeling, with my head bent over the lavatory, it was some time before I realized this sickness was not a thing I could throw up. I shuffled away and at the bottom of the stairs the back of my hand accidentally knocked the rail, hard. It was a shock. I raised my hand to my eyes wondering how I could have hit it so hard. I banged it again, purposely this time, and again, and again. I stood there trying to destroy my right hand. Using the walls for support I made a slow tour of every inch of the building, stopping frequently to squeeze the dizziness from my skull.

No Francis. No Francis, anywhere. I knew I was alone now. That the dead are dead. When I slumped onto the sofa George acrobated his way to me and I stroked my face against the armor of his feathers, nosed into the softness beneath. His scent of desiccated sweetness was peculiarly consoling.

Outside on the terrace, at the point from where Francis used to dive, and made the dive that killed him, I looked down into the moon-flecked pool. I had become a tenant of my own dream. There was no wind, no movement, but for the dark shapes of the boats breasting the dock. The vibration of my heavy steps along the jetty shuddered down the poles, swelled in the water. Through the grimy window of the boathouse a night light old-mastered Franky's sleeping face.

Back at the house I found a note had been folded into the handle of the screen door. My derangement had me believing that this, too, could be from Francis. The letters were lopsided and inaccurately formed:

PLEASE MY BOSS LADY. AM RONT YOU LUL ME $14,000 GO TO HAITI. PLEASE MY BOSS LADY ON MONTE OCTOBRE. AM RONT YOU LUL ME. PLEASE TAKE $BY WIKS. AM RONT SEE MY BEBE.

L.

I had planned to stay only a few days in the Bahamas. Dealing with Francis's belongings had been a useful excuse, when all I had really wanted was to meet with Leon Kennedy, arrange a conclusive deal. One which would have left him rich and me in possession of Sleet. Now I understood Francis's will not to be so simple a matter, also that he had believed I knew about it. Everything he had done had been in the light of a life he believed we would, one day, share. I could no longer leave right away. I wanted to live awhile among those who had been part of his childhood and his last few years. I would stay to invent him, the way he had invented me.

Late on the afternoon of her third day Delia Sutherland left the house for the first time. Slowly she walked the oleander-and-silk-cotton-lined drive, out to the road where the sea-grape tree, twenty-four years on, had spread its branches low to the dust. No place there anymore for a Jeanne Kennedy, Euturpia, Turpie, to sleep with her baby playing nearby. She crossed over the road in search of Joy in the Yamacraw—fifty acres of fruit trees conjured from blowaway soil.

A track led her through haphazard planting into a clearing where three shacks listed companionably on limestone supports. Their planking was patched with corrugated iron, their roofs shingled with flattened tin cans. The window spaces were covered with greasy cheesecloth. A fence made of tree limbs, a Pogo stick, three golf clubs and some broken implements was draped with barbed wire low enough to step over. Creeper grew out of a wheelless Cadillac raised on blocks. A toaster, a pram and a hostess trolley, all lay wreathed in weed. Inside the chicken run—mesh bed bases tied with baling twine—the hens nested in a fridge. Their soft quibbling, a television muttering from one of the shacks, the buzz of a distant light aircraft, these sounds were subdued, deferring to the dusk.

A man with skin like an old passion fruit lay asleep under a butterwood tree, a machete in his loosed grip. He jumped to his feet, screeching, when Delia Sutherland's shadow fell across him. His bare, bony chest heaved. His lower half was engulfed in army-issue shorts held up by one of Francis's old school ties. He retrieved a cap with "Bahamas" in blue letters on the front, smacked it, dropped it on his head and squinted up.

"Would you be Joy?"

"Yeah. Ah's Joy. Ah been sleepin'." He looked behind, confirming that his body had joined him from the ground. "When I see you I finks you zombi."

94

"No, I'm Mrs. Sutherland. How do you do." He took her hand while his toothless mouth gaped. "Would you show me round, please? I'd like to see what you're growing here."

"Sho, Joy show you." He strutted ahead lashing his machete about. "Mr. Fwancis, he do this with me. He always like to do it, even when he was little boy. Look, dem's sapodillas, dem's mammy supporters, limes, mangoes. Lots a diffwent fwuits. Ah stays round stop 'em teef de fwuits."

"Animals eat them?"

"No. Teefs teef 'em if dey don' see Joy. But Joy always here. Joy come here for Mr. Scott when Fwancis just a little boy."

"Over forty years, then?"

"Mmm." Another noncommittal song, as Franky's had been, and she thought: Quite, what can it matter, forty, fifty, who cares?

"I came here years ago," she said. "But not for long and I never came over to the Yamacraw. I didn't know you were here."

"But you eats my fwuits. Lotsa people don't know they eatin' Joy's fwuits. For a long time Mr. Fwancis didn't come but he did lots before he die like that."

Joy pulled down avocados and sugar apples, offering them in his tortoise-belly palm. He showed how he planted the young trees in potholes where the soil was richer and she saw that after all there was nothing haphazard about the planting; it had the symmetry of necessity. She bent with him to examine troubled roots, spotted leaves, patchy bark. When they arrived back at the butterwood where he had been sleeping he showed her a white fungus around its base. She shook her head. "I don't see it coming on, Joy. Do you, really? I think you'll have to expect the worst."

He shook his head too, and they stood together without speaking. He touched her arm, beckoning her down to his glittering eyes, and asked in a rattled whisper, "Miz Boss Lady, you like see Joy's cock?" and was nearly knocked over by her abrupt straightening.

"I don't think so, thank you, Joy. The fruit'll do nicely."

"Joy got fine cock. Mr. Fwancis lul me de money. I buy 'im."

"Fighting cock, you mean?"

His strip of mouth opened but his eyes did the laughing. "Dem's good."

The stench of chicken droppings choked her as soon as he opened the door to one of the shacks. Inside were two cockerels in opposite corners, sore, bald things with a vestige of feathers. When Delia Sutherland entered, they took off, squawking, thrashing the air on a collision course, but crashed in a cloud of dust and straw on reaching the end of their short tethers.

Beneath a haze of cobwebs the walls were painted with clouds, hefty angels and Disney characters. "Was this a nursery, Joy?"

"One time. Mr. Scott give shack to Joy when Fwancis come big boy." He picked up a cockerel by its feet, stuffing it under his arm. Outside he allowed her to examine the bird.

"Cruel business, this cockfighting."

"I jes breeds 'em," he told his innocent feet.

"Oh well, that's all right, then, isn't it?" she told hers. "You've children?"

Joy swiped the air in the same manner as Luney and Franky. This time she understood it was the drawing not the lifting of a veil. "All gone 'way. Got dish now. Lotsa channels."

"Well, thank you for the fruit."

"You come on find Joy 'nother time?"

"I'll come tomorrow, if I may."

The following morning she walked towards town along a road tumored by tree roots. In half an hour only one small truck passed, a satellite dish rocking in the back.

The town began all at once, with no outskirts; neat lines of pastel-colored clapboard bungalows, their garden paths painted to match, each dwelling with its own dish in the yard. The rows were separated by concrete lanes, toy-town tidy. The only traffic-bearing road ran between the houses and the waterfront.

Figures rocked on porches, hunched on stoops. No black faces, only white ones watching her without greeting. Even between themselves there was no calling, no chat. These were descendants of humble loyalists, and of the sailors who had accompanied them from America. The two or three families who had come without money or slaves, and who had kept themselves rigorously segregated from the few black people they found already on the island, were still shunning newcomers. Their energy and physique had been sapped by interbreeding. Their pale skins were raddled with melanosis. There was little boat-building anymore. Money was made from fishing and selling tourist junk made in Taiwan.

Delia Sutherland stopped calling her unreturned greetings, tried to ignore the many pairs of sun-tired eyes, slow-moving behind glaucous panes, as they measured her progress past the wooden church, the school, the town hall, the firehouse, the inn.

She was stalked by one small girl who was joined by a boy, until, keeping a distance, a group of silent lint-haired children followed. When she glanced behind they vanished around corners in a bouquet of arms and legs, to peep out at her with drained blue eyes. The end of town offered nothing but the turn-around, so she struggled over the dunes, through razor-edged grasses. There was the sea again. It was restless here on the windward side of this spit of island.

She took off her shoes and paddled. There were voices in the wind, as there often are—no words, just voices. When she sat in the dunes brushing the sand from her legs, the voices persisted although now she was sheltered: *Go home, go home. Francis is dead.*

No. Too early. Too early in the day for this. She stumbled down the beach. The voices followed: *Go home, go home . . .* They were not imagined. The dunes were stippled with the white heads and sore-burnt faces of the children. *Go home, go home, Francis is dead.* Delia Sutherland ran towards town.

Teenagers were gathered on the steps of the one-roomed town hall—big-boned, inactive boys and blond girls in a twilight between ethereal beauty and overheavy womanhood. Save for the tinnitus of a Walkman no noise came from the group, no foot-tapping or nudging, no jokes, flirts or smiles.

Standing in front of them with her hair awry Delia Sutherland panted, "Did any of you know my husband? My husband, Francis Sutherland? I'm sure you did. Perhaps you ran errands for him, or went fishing with him?" Lids were lowered, gazes shifted. Down left was a boy with cotton-wool hair and eyes too small for his face. "Did you know him?" He slow-motioned his head away. She had turned and was a few steps off when she stopped. "What? Did someone say something to me?"

"Past the 'otel hover there." The boy with cotton-wool hair lazily lifted his long arm towards the sea.

Francis used to imitate the Abaconian speech, dropping aitches from where they belonged, slipping them in where they did not. "Thank you," she said, although what he had said made no sense. She walked to the harbor. The heat was intense.

"Hah, Miz Sutherland. You ront go back in boat now? You don' look too good, Miz Sutherland."

"I'm not, Franky. Not really. How did you know where I was?"

"Luney sez you's gone so ah comes and ah waits. Couldn't be nowhere else."

"I couldn't really, could I? Let's go home, Franky."

When the boat was under way she looked back and there were the children running in the dunes, waving to her like children anywhere. She waved back and thought: They're right, of course. He is dead. No harm in saying so. And she waved harder still.

When she returned she found Luney crouched, chin in hands, her back against the cooker.

"What are you doing there, Luney?"

"Waitin'."

"Is there something cooking inside?"

"No, ma'am."

"Then what are you waiting for?"

"You, ma'am."

"I see. Come and sit next to me."

The girl uncurled and slow-stepped towards Delia Sutherland. She trailed a hand along an imaginary banister, sweeping the other behind where the skirts of a ball gown would have trailed and was so tangibly created that when she sat down on the sofa Delia Sutherland moved to make room for the folds of that gown.

"Is it about this, you're waiting?" holding out the note from the screen door.

"Mmm."

"How old is your baby?"

"She's three."

"How old are you?"

"Eighteen."

"Luney, now you must answer me truthfully, you've nothing to be afraid of. Nothing will make me angry. Who is her father, Luney?"

Luney rolled her eyes away, covering them first with lids, then a hand and another hand. "Come along, I think I should know. Don't you?" Delia Sutherland spoke softly. "Is Mr. Francis the father of your baby?"

Luney screwed up her face and her laughter squeaked like a party whistle. "No, no. Not Mr. Francis, ma'am. Ma bebe's papa's a minister."

"Thank God," she said.

"No, it ain't thank God 'cause he took 'vantage o' me, my aunt says."

"A politician? From here or Haiti?"

"From Kansas. He were a minister of the church. My aunt, she run a house for them visitin' ministers to Port au Prince. I'd fix rooms, make 'em nice. Turn the sheets an' such. My aunt show me how to fix things nice. He were a minister along of his delegation to Haiti. He were real nice to me till he ront go back an' I had ma bebe. My aunt keep ma bebe while I go make money some other place. So I works for Mr. Francis. He give me money see ma bebe. He always do that."

"How often?"

"Each time he go way en monte Octobre."

"Do you want to stay here, now Mr. Francis isn't here?"

"Yes, ma'am. Mr. Tucker says I can. He says ah's needed here."

"So you are. Did you like working for my husband; was he kind?"

"Sure was, but times he was mighty crazy. He get so wild, shoutin' an' screamin' at fings which ain't there. Luney hide when he like that. Then I come along and finds him sleepin' on the floor here like a big bebe an' I cover him up." She twirled a knob of hair and crooned as though having described a trifling scene.

"That was kind of you. I'll make sure you have the money to see your baby."

"Yes, ma'am."

"Luney, he talked about my coming here, didn't he?"

"Lots."

"What did he say?"

"That you's beautiful. You's fine. And you's comin'."

This was said with such an earnest effort for accuracy that Delia Sutherland smiled. "I see. Anything else?"

"He said Luney, when Ma'am Sutherland get here she ront take dat talkin' from you. Ah laughs and he do too. He say I have to learn behave myself if you come. You ain't so bad. You look sick, ma'am."

"I'm sad, Luney, that's what it is," and she wished Luney could cover her the way she had Francis, as though she too were like a baby. Luney crossed the garden to the hut where she slept, nodding and gesturing to inhabitants of her air-drawn world, which was no longer a ball. Now she was apparently surrounded by children and was patting their make-believe heads. And why not? What else should she do while the day expired in this fearful heat? Then what, when evening came? She could be with Franky but there was nowhere they could go to eat, drink or dance. It must have been like that for Euturpia, when she was turned out to the cabana. And for Francis too, the lonely, empty afternoon followed by similar evenings. Wasn't Sleet the same if, for once, she was honest? "No, my love," she said aloud, "my love, my love," and was flooded by the days she had called him that. "You were never committed here the way I am at Sleet."

Every afternoon for twelve days Delia Sutherland visited Joy. Her visit became a ritual, as did her daily walk to town. There the children never failed to stalk her, calling different messages, some days more friendly, some days less. Once she heard the chant "Lonely lady's husband's dead, Lonely lady's husband's dead . . ." On listening harder she became certain the chant was "Bony lady's husband's dead." That's good, she thought, bony lady, that's me.

She spent hours sorting Francis's quantities of clothing into piles for Franky, Joy and the boys on the town hall stoop. When she set the boxes in front of the teenagers, drawing out the bright shirts and linen trousers, the girls were the first to come forward. Only then did the boys stir themselves, to stop the girls from grabbing everything. They thanked her in quiet voices, told her the clothes were "cool," but no one said they knew Francis. The city suits and ivory silk dinner jackets she gave to Franky.

In the afternoons she lay on the bed with the canvas bag beside her. Unable to sleep, night or day, she withdrew the letters at random. Some she knew by heart.

On the morning of the day before her departure Delia Sutherland was sitting in front of the fruit and toast Luney set daily on the terrace, and which not once had she been able to eat.

Franky was leaning against the boathouse whistling while Luney, a basket in one hand, primping her stiff hair with the other, meandered towards him, chattering in an unfamiliar language. They would be going off in the boat together because that is what they always did in the mornings, to return in half an hour. Having accepted this as routine Delia Sutherland was suddenly curious.

Gripping the banister of the wooden steps with both hands, she called to Luney who did not hear. Her voice was hoarse. Luney was already stepping into the boat when Franky saw Delia Sutherland halfway down the steps.

"Hah, Miz Sutherland. Fine day." He waited while, hand over hand on the jetty rail, she made her way towards them. Such a different walk from the day she arrived and had carried her own bag into the house. Nor had she pinned her hair securely; it was beginning to break loose.

When she was very close and could finally be heard, she said, "Where are you both going?"

"Ah's takin' Luney to the bread man. You wanna come along, Miz Sutherland?"

"Is he called Ulrich?"

"Yeah, that's him."

During the trip the wind finished the business of her hair. She knew what had happened but could not be bothered to deal with it. Franky struggled to keep his attention on the way ahead, preferring to nod at her in admiration.

Ulrich Barker's house was along a still band of water broken at the edges by crowding mangroves. His dock was strewn with beer cans, oil drums, fishing nets. A sign slipped from its nail read: ATTALUS BARKER: BOATS FOR RENT. GAS. BREAD. WATER. Stretching up to a paint-peeling house was a patch of watermelons and tomatoes. The soil around the plants was dark from recent watering. Two dogs rushed at Delia Sutherland, growling and scattering dust. She knew she did not have the strength to throw her voice through the stillness so she knelt on one knee. "Good boys, steady now. There's fellows."

They stopped to feign distraction from another direction, jaws hanging.

A bow-legged fellow in a straw hat watched her approach with his dogs at her side. His eyes and mouth were diminished by his nose, an overripe fruit in the middle of a face littered with sore patches.

He allowed her "Good morning to you" to blister and drop. "Are you Ulrich Barker, by any chance?"

" 'S me."

"How do you do, I'm Mrs. Sutherland."

His eyes remained set on a point beyond her shoulder. "You the missus of Francis done kill hisself?"

"Absolutely. But he didn't."

"Die?"

"Kill himself. It was an accident."

"That so? You gonna live here now?"

"I leave tomorrow, I'm afraid." At last he pulled his eyes towards her and she rewarded his effort. "I would have done, you know. I would really have tried," she insisted to someone he could not see.

" 'E'd been saying 'ow's you's coming hover. Coming hover to live. Guess you couldn't make it before." He thought awhile before concluding, "Too late now, I guess," with the dispassionate perspective of the very old.

He beckoned her into the house. The room was divided by waist-high partitions into kitchen and two sitting areas, one for himself, one for customers. A counter was stacked with plastic bags containing loaves.

"It's bread you want, right?"

"Yes, please."

"Cinnamon cakes too, they're good. Try one." He dropped a heavy thing glistening with syrup into her hand.

She bit into it. "Certainly is good. Can I have some? You knew Francis well, didn't you?"

"Baked his bread."

"Well, there you are, then. Did he come to you every day?"

"Most days, poor man, an' talk about the time he was a boy. Long time ago now. Talked about his missus too."

"That's me," she reminded him.

"Yes," he responded vaguely and she felt less real.

"Why do you say 'poor man'?"

"I say that 'cause he weren't a 'appy man. Some his some haint. He weren't. Such a sweet, 'appy kid he was too."

"And Jeanne, did you see much of her?"

"Dunno no Jan."

"Euturpia?"

"Turpie? Sure thing. She'd come get the bread back when Willa Mae baked. Made you laugh, Turpie did. 'Ad names for hall of us. She'd watch then baptize 'cordin' to what she saw. Names fit so well some still 'ave 'em, though she haint been round for years. Willa Mae was 'Sunny Face.' Heveryone called 'er that 'fore she died. Mind you, Turpie weren't halways that polite.

"I'd give her little one a cinnamon cake. He loved 'em. Hall the kids do. Gone now, hall of them. Francis, Turpie. And she haint got no little boy no more."

"Why not?"

"He growed up. My boy Hattalus done that too. He growed."

"Is that your son's boat business on the dock?"

"Was. He's gone. Married a Chicago girl. She couldn't settle. Kept going off 'ome, comin' on back. She'd leave the little one along of Willa Mae and me. When she was here they'd go out late and leave him then too. He's sleep hover of us."

"Your grandson?"

He checked her face for sincerity before going to the other room, returning with a photograph in a fancy tin frame. Holding it close to his face between two big hands, speaking to the picture, he said, "Sweet child. We'd give him cakes. Put him to bed. I'd collect up the photos and put 'em hon the bed. He'd look an' look. Laugh till he slept. I'll tell him who they hall was. They hall look different now, see. Them as haint dead. When Willa Mae died Sally went on to Chicago for good, took the boy. Hattalus went hafter them. Never came back. I heard from them once these five years. They sent me this picture." He stroked the glass, reaching through to the living face. His breath rattled. "Miss 'im, sure do miss 'im." An amen silence. "Still, it's hall sent to try us."

"You're alone now?"

"Guess so."

"How old are you?"

"Ninety-four."

Was she to be sentenced that long?

Later, after she had visited Joy for the last time and he had filled her arms with fruit, as he had on every visit, she made her way to the cemetery. It was an isolated place exposed to every sand-carrying wind. Elaborate memorials were sunk in it, urns and angels' faces worn away by it. Simple graves were almost obliterated, but for the tin cans blown over, stiffly retaining plastic flowers, and the curling photographs in cellophane tacked to wooden crosses. Even the newest graves, their flowers still fresh, were misshapen by icing-sugar waves of sand.

Delia Sutherland did not see the children among the headstones. She was unaware, this time, that they had followed to pick noses and scratch, contemplating her from a dozen hidden places. The audacious ones stood in full view when she mounted the surrounding steps to a white marble sarcophagus. She shouted things they could not understand before lying face down covering up the words:

Francis Sutherland
Who Fell Asleep in Jesus
8 August 1936—8 August 1989
"Frail Children of Dust"

The children played hide-and-seek and catch until dark, when they filed past her. Two grubby quick-bitten fingers reached out to tickle her leg. She raised herself and saw pale-headed shadows hop-scotching the graves, disappearing through the wrought-iron gate wedged open in sand.

She arranged Joy's fruit where Francis's feet would be inside all that stone and left.

I stayed in the Abacos just over two weeks, waiting for the return of his spirit, to reassure me, give me some indication of the future.

Night after night I sat on the sofa looking out to sea, the way Francis had. I moved, as I've described, among the people of his childhood, and those, like Luney and Franky, who had cared for him lately. I didn't sleep at all until, one daybreak, I sank into unconsciousness for several hours. On waking I found myself unexpectedly, profoundly, homesick. All I could think of was Sleet without me in the autumn. The fields would be plowed and drilled; the cows calving, dropping their loads in secluded corners. Francis was gone and I remained the woman I always had been. Like a persistent current, my sorry nature would resume its course.

Franky looked fine in Francis's clothes. To escort Delia Sutherland to the main harbor he selected a navy pin-striped suit with matching waistcoat. The trouser hems flapped way above his ankles and bare feet. From the helm he waved to the world skimming past, to a fisherman in a rowboat with a long-legged dog sniffing the air from the prow; to a capsized windsurfer, and three children running on a strip of sand. All the time he threw away laughter, at one with the day and his life.

"Fine place, eh, Miz Sutherland?" he shouted over his shoulder.

She sat on the toolbox, pressing her hat to her head, and looking not this time out to sea but at all that was passing and being left behind. "What?"

"Pity you gotta go so soon. Next time longer and Fwinky take you fishin'. Some beautiful place, huh?"

"Yes, Franky, it's a lovely place."

He did not hear but saw her smile and was pleased.

When he shut the door of her taxi twenty minutes later he leaned in through the window. "Next time Fwinky and Boss Lady catch some big fish," he whooped, sweeping his arms wide.

"Thank you, Franky, I'd like that. Take care of George, won't you, while Luney visits Haiti."

"You bet. Ol' George okay with Fwinky."

The taxi jerked away before either could speak again. From the back window she saw him swaggering along the dock, a hand on his hip, throwing keys in the air with insouciant authority. A perfect imitation of Francis.

Tucker sent the company plane to fly Delia Sutherland to Nassau. He did not come in person. There was an evening to pass before the midnight flight to London and, despite Tucker's adamancy that Miss Kennedy wouldn't see her, she taxied to the Big Bamboo on Wulff Road.

"Are you a member?" A huge ebony man crossed the worn glitz of the lobby.

"No."

"I'm sorry, members only."

"May I become one?"

"Recommendation only, I'm afraid. There's a nice place down the road. I'll point you the way." He held open the door.

"Is Miss Kennedy here?"

"Your name, please?"

"Mrs. Sutherland."

He bowed, not to her but reviewing their exchange. "I'll show you to a table, Mrs. Sutherland."

The thin, conditioned air inside carried smoke, sweat disguised in a hundred bought perfumes and an electronic beat through spangled darkness. A bar glowed in petrol-blue neon. Candles bloomed on faces, talking, drinking, kissing. Dancers, waiters, wandering shapes were countlessly reflected in smoked mirror walls. The clientele was elegant and mostly black, men in beautifully tailored white suits, well-dressed women.

Delia Sutherland ordered a whisky and waited, uncertain of recognizing Miss Kennedy when she came. An hour passed. Could she be the one with the little skirt and thigh boots? The one naked beneath a white chiffon blouse? Or the languid treble clef at the bar, clasping and reclasping long fingers, who, feeling herself stared at, removed dark glasses to fire hatred? She was none of these women. Nor was she in the gaming room with its low lights on green baize tables, circles of hands restless with chips, cards, cigarettes, while the tension adjusted itself with each soft call of the croupiers.

Eventually Delia Sutherland returned to the lobby. The big man was not there so she opened the only door marked "Private." Kidskin sofa, a satinwood desk strewn with papers, overturned plastic cups, the surrounding chairs askew. A trolley was heaped with beer cans and plates of half-eaten burgers. Lace underwear and a slipper trimmed with marabou lay among the sheets on an open divan.

"You're wasting your time, Mrs. Sutherland."

The source of the packing-paper voice was hidden by the door. She closed it and saw, through glass in the far wall, the interior of the club again. There was a clear view of the table where she had sat for so long.

A woman was leaning, forehead on arm, against the glass, observing the noiseless throng. A red silk kimono clung around her skeletal ankles. When the woman turned her head to smoke the cigarette held near her viciously straightened hair, Delia Sutherland said, "So you are here. You were watching me all the time."

Euturpia Kennedy turned untenanted eyes in a face laid waste; even her lips, emptied of succulence, were hardly there but for the outlined ridge. "I watch everyone. You have to in a place like this, every move they make." She crossed the room unsteadily, reached over the desk for a bottle of pills. "What do you want, Mrs. Sutherland?"

"You know very well that I want to make an offer to your son.

That I want to buy back Sleet. Will you please listen to my suggestions, or at least have him meet me?"

"Forget it."

"What about him? How does he feel? It would mean a great deal of money."

"He's his own man. He does what he wants."

"I don't know if I believe you. I've been in the Abacos, you know, at the house."

"So?"

"You were still friends with Francis, weren't you?"

"Yes," very quickly, to have the confirmation over with. "Yes."

"What happened to Francis by the end? I found letters to me. Some read as though he were losing his mind."

"Your husband was lonely, bored, disappointed. He came to me for stuff to forget all that. He wasn't a serious user, but maybe sometimes he got a little crazy. I wouldn't know."

A refrigerator buzzed in the corner of the room. Curious how you couldn't hear the music at all. Her silk kimono rasped; bright lacquered seedpods and gold chains around her neck chuckled with every movement. Was she a serious user?

"Francis didn't dream he'd die so soon, Miss Kennedy. He thought he'd grow to be an old man. Did he tell you he wanted us, him and me, to be together again?" Their attention locked on each other. "Why would your son want Sleet when, if he sold it to me, he could have anything he wanted? Why leave these islands for somewhere like England?"

"Because he must get away from this." Euturpia Kennedy held up two pills, tossed them into her mouth. Her hand shook as she filled a paper cup with vodka, drank it, refilled then pointed into the club. "And that. Right? He doesn't need money. I made plenty of that. He needs distance. A place far off with responsibilities to hold him down. Somewhere safe. This isn't safe. Francis gave that place to Leon and he's going to take it."

"But it's not just 'that place.' It's my home."

Euturpia Kennedy's eyes pursued something in Delia Sutherland's expression until, finally, she said, "I remember the last time I saw you. Never will forget. I was shut out . . ."

"Yes, I remember too."

"I was shut out my home. Francis told me to stay in the cabana while you were there 'cause you were his wife. Never knew he had a wife till then. I'd been with Francis three years, living in his house, sleeping in his bed, caring for our child. Even when he wasn't there he'd let me stay on. Then he shut me out for you. You who never came but once. One day I uncovered myself in front of him, stroked my body, my breasts, my ass. I had some body then. I said to him, 'You want that bag of bones more than this, and this and this.' I called you the Bony Lady. 'You want that bony lady more than me?' " She bared her shoulder, traced her breasts with her fingertips. "Not so good anymore, is it, Mrs. Sutherland?" She cradled herself in crossed arms. "Francis taught me all kinds of stuff from books and talked to me. He'd changed my name and changed my head before he tired of me. But I'd had the taste. After that nothing's good enough anymore. I wasn't going to be no whore in Nassau. Yes, he bought me the bar so I'd be quiet and leave him alone like a good girl." She beckoned with her finger, dropped her voice. "Want to know what I really wanted? I wanted to be you. I wanted to be the Bony Lady, and have him love me like he loved you. Right up to the end I wanted that. And where were you, lady? Where were you all the time he wanted you? And me? Me? He gave me nothing."

Delia Sutherland searched her lap for the offers, the arguments, the good sense. All she found there were her hands, big blue veins on the backs of them, not pretty at all. She understood now that any deal would be no more adequate than baby clothes thrown into the shade of a sea-grape tree. "You have his son, Miss Kennedy. It's more than I have."

Euturpia Kennedy closed her eyes, allowed her head to fall far back. "Yes, yes. I have Leon."

"But he's away at the moment, so Mr. Tucker says."

"I think he said that so you'd leave us alone, don't you? Leon's with me. Not for much longer but he's with me now. So would you go, please, and do like Mr. Tucker wanted, like we all wanted, leave us alone?"

PART THREE

Nine

"WELL, THAT'S IT, then, Mrs. Sutherland, I'm retiring. No more to be said." Mrs. Files brushed the whole matter from the front of her apron, chasing it down, across and off her lap. "My family won't be sorry. I'm sixty-one as it is and, truth told, I couldn't work for one of *them*." Her vowels turned in the syrup of her West Country accent. She was seated, with Curtis, before the desk in the morning room.

Before Delia Sutherland could make up her mind about how much to say, and to whom, she was forced into an explanation less than an hour after her return. Curtis had dropped the *Echo* onto the dining-room table, where she was drinking her morning coffee, and he remained beside her. She twisted her head around, up to his face, followed the line of his arm down again, to his hand, to his finger pressed against the newspaper. She read the headline, "ALL CHANGE AT SLEET PARK," and in smaller letters, "Sutherland Son to Inherit." Underneath were outline facts about Francis Sutherland, his childless marriage to Delia, and Leon Kennedy's inheriting the estate.

"How on earth did they get hold of this?" she exploded.

"They do, Miss, these paper people. They telephoned three times while you were away."

So she asked Curtis and Mrs. Files—who had been watching Delia Sutherland's reaction from the service door—to come with her into the morning room where she explained the situation as frankly as possible.

"It's nothing personal," Mrs. Files said. "I'm sure they're as good as we are but, they're them and we're us. And that's that. Don't expect they'd give a thank you to work for me neither."

111

"I quite understand, Mrs. Files. And as you say, you're past retirement anyway."

"All right, then. It's settled. But I'd like to say now, it's a shame. What Mr. Sutherland can've been thinking of, I don't know. There was me thinking the place was yours too. Then he puts you out like this. Fancy. Don't seem right."

"No. Well." It was satisfactory that Mrs. Files should come to that conclusion. Curtis had said nothing.

"Here." Mrs. Files leaned conspiratorially forward, her arm across her knee, glancing round the room before continuing. "Is he very, like, though, you know?"

"The only time I saw him was years ago; he was just a baby with his mother."

"And was she, like, very?" Concluding with a nod intended to provoke disapproving confirmation, wanting Mrs. Sutherland to draw on the fund of resentment that must surely be there.

"I went to see her, actually." Delia Sutherland mused at the pen she was threading in and out of her fingers. "She's terribly ill—her looks are decimated. It was appalling."

Dismissing that, Mrs. Files pressed on. "Yes, but, you know?"

"What? Black, Mrs. Files? Dear me. Yes. She's black. Good heavens, I think your plan to retire is for the best; let me know if I can help in any way. Curtis? How do you feel?"

His face, paled almost to blue, was crackled with thread veins. The tremor of his head, which had begun only lately, had grown more distinct during this conversation; starting low and shuttling up as though following a fly on a windowpane.

"Curtis?"

"I don't know what to say, Miss. There are no words." Speaking appeared to calm the agitation. "I'd thought I wouldn't have to move again, that we'd be all right, you and me, Miss, a few more years yet. I'm too old to change. Seventy-one. It's a bolt."

"I'm sure Mr. Kennedy'll let you have your old cottage back. I'll ask Mr. Rosen, if you like."

"No, Miss. Too much for me now with the garden and all. And the memories of Maurice. I wouldn't want that."

"We'll apply for a council flat, then. Somewhere central. How would that be?" She knew he would be friendless, that, beyond the house, the few people who worked in it and herself, there was no one.

"You'll be all right, Mr. Curtis." Mrs. Files nudged him. "I'll come visit, bring along our Auntie Megan."

"Not Auntie Megan, thank you, Mrs. Files. See enough of her in the kitchen, as it is," nostrils flaring, mouth dipping. "I'd be grateful, Miss, if you didn't mention my age to Mr. Kennedy. I'll retire, of course, but I'd like more time to lay my plans. Besides, I might be of some help settling the young gentleman."

"Quite." Fair enough, she thought, why shouldn't he work on and "settle the young gentleman?" Nevertheless. "All right, then. I promise I won't mention your age or retirement. Leave it all to you, as it were."

"I'm sorry, Miss Delia. And Mrs. Files has it, it doesn't seem right, the place being taken from you. Nothing'll be the same."

"That's for sure. There's not much else to tell you except that he could be arriving anytime. I intend to be gone when he does. I'm looking for a smallholding in the north of Scotland. Room for a flock of fifty sheep. That'll keep me quiet. I've missed having sheep here these last few years." She gazed accusingly at the sheepless landscape.

When she turned back again her expression made Mrs. Files stand to reach her arm around Delia Sutherland's shoulders. It was their first embrace in thirty-five years. "There, there, my dear, there, there. It's not right. Just not right. Come along, Mr. Curtis, I think Mrs. Sutherland'd like to be alone for a bit."

Delia Sutherland gave a short blast on her nose and stuffed the handkerchief back up her sleeve. "Thank you, Mrs. Files. I'll be telling the others in the morning. No need for secrets."

No need for secrets, so Mrs. Files telephoned her daughter straightaway, then told Frank Grimwood who came by with four brace of partridge from yesterday's let shoot; who stopped Alec on the tractor with a load of silage behind; who met Tom in the grain store; who found Mary in the estate office when he went in to fill out his time sheet; who confided in the postman when he came with the afternoon mail; who amazed Mrs. May in Forester's Cottage when he delivered her *Freeman's Catalogue* and a postcard from her son holidaying in Pouket; who stunned her husband when he came in from the sawmill. "Holland, duck, you'll never guess what."

Less than two hours after her meeting with Mrs. Files and Curtis, Delia Sutherland received a call from Muriel Fuller.

"Delia, what on earth happened out there? Is it true? Is it really happening?"

"You saw the paper, then?"

"No. I only arrived from London a minute ago. I stopped at the garage to fill up a can for the mower. Steve, you know, Mrs. Files's son-in-law, who works there, he told me. What he actually said, just between you and me, was, 'A black man's inheriting Sleet.' I didn't say anything. What did happen, then? Surely he's agreed to let you buy it back?"

"It wasn't exactly . . . You see, when I was there I found . . ." Her stomach contracted and she retched.

"Stay there. I'm coming over."

She arrived within fifteen minutes and found Delia Sutherland in the morning room, with her face pressed into the wing of an armchair. Muriel held the broad shoulders and was surprised at the strangeness of the proximity, just as she had been surprised at the sight of Delia's loosened hair some weeks before. "Come on, tell me."

"I've been wrong all the time, Muriel. I've wasted years and it's too late. I mattered, you see? Look." She pulled some of the letters from the thigh pocket of her combat trousers.

Muriel read slowly, tapping her mouth with her fingertips. Twice she removed her eyes from the letter, matching what was written there with the woman in front of her. When she had finished she stroked the letters back into their creases, muttering to herself, "Of course, of course." She closed her friend's hand around them and, without letting go, pressed her dry lips very hard against Delia's forehead. Muriel did not know precisely what she was trying to convey—more than consolation; nothing she could have explained. Later, to her husband, she said, "It's pathetic, Tom, she's no idea how to love and considers herself unlovable."

"Did you speak to him at all, Delia?"

"No. There wouldn't have been any point anyway. He won't sell. The lawyer described him as 'tenacious' and I believe it. I went to see his mother. She's very sick, Muriel. It was horrible to see. She used to be so lovely."

"I know, we met her, Tom and I. We went out to stay with Francis, years ago. It was after you two were, well, less together. Tom and Francis remained quite friendly until—" She changed her mind about continuing, which made Delia Sutherland more interested than she had been.

"Until what?"

"Something happened. So what'll you do?"

"Go."

"Good. I hoped you'd say that. Things are never so bad when you just let go. I promise you that, and you'll go before he comes, I hope?"

"Long before."

"I can't see it, you know, him here at Sleet. I just can't see it working. However, let's be practical. What'll you take with you?"

The next morning, when she returned from her early visit to the estate office, Delia Sutherland found Frank Grimwood waiting to speak to her.

"I haven't had breakfast yet, Frank. Will you join me?"

"No, thanks. I'll come straight out with it: rumor has it a black's taking over here."

She eased into her seat behind the desk in the morning room. So early, so early in the day. "Please sit down."

He would not. "Mrs. Files gave me some of her talk yesterday. Then I was down at the Chough last night and everyone was on about it. Dawn was dishing out the details with the beer."

"Dawn?"

"She's behind the bar there. Steve, who works at the garage, his girl. Mrs. Files's granddaughter."

"I see."

"Well?"

Having explained once more she added, "I'd intended to tell you all together this afternoon."

"It's no good, Mrs. S. I'm not working for no black. One or two of the others feel the same but they can speak for themselves. I'm giving my notice."

"It'll have to be to Mr. Rosen, Frank. Strictly speaking, I've no role here anymore. Are you sure you're wise? Have you another job?"

"I'll have to see about that, won't I? Young Martin's been out of work for a year now, ever since he left school. He's made sixty-three job applications and had fifteen interviews. Nothing. If those blacks weren't here things would be different."

115

"I don't want to get into that, Frank."

"But you are, Mrs. S." He jabbed a finger at her.

She was startled, confused by his anger and weary too. With an effort she said, "Listen, Frank, and you can pass this on if you want to: I've not given Sleet to Mr. Kennedy, nor sold it to him. It's been taken out of my hands. There's nothing I can do. If you feel you can't stay, then so be it. Just think before you make a move, that's all. I'll do all I can to help. Now if you'll excuse me."

Frank Grimwood sat down, watched her making big business of cleaning her spectacles. "I'm sorry, Mrs. S. Don't suppose you're none too pleased either."

The spectacles fell from her fingers. "So if that's all, Frank." She collected papers, set them down, opened a drawer, shut it. She would not allow him to see her face. She had wanted to be strong to the end, give no evidence of what this overthrow was doing to her. And here she was, with Frank Grimwood of all people, shaking so much she could not fix her spectacles on her nose.

His chump hand came down on the desk, giving her a point of focus. "Here," he said gently. "You know that old badger up by Crendal Wood?"

"Yes?" Shadow cleared from her features. "Yes?"

"Well, he's pushed his set right on up through Ragge Down. Come up in the middle of it, he has. I swear it's the same old boy. Twenty yards, it must be."

"No? Really?" She reached for her keys. "How wonderful. Let's go and see."

The next morning, when Delia Sutherland met the men before work, she was treated to opinion and advice. "Don't you settle for it, Mrs. S." "You should see someone. Take it to court." "No, but you can see his point, Mr. Sutherland's, that is. After all, it is his son." "What about our jobs? Will we be all right, d'you think?" "What's he like? Sort of Michael Jackson, is he?" "Is he called Sutherland, then, like his dad?" "Will his mum come too? Night-club owner, fancy. Can't picture them here, somehow." "What can he know about farming, anyway?" "Well, so long as he does know about it that's all that matters. No offense, Mrs. S. Oh, sorry."

She backed away, appalled such details should have been passed around so soon, and that people were confronting her with them. The imminent change had already stolen her distance; she did not feel safe anymore. There was nothing familiar in this intimacy. But it wouldn't be long. Not long and she'd go.

"Work on," was all she could advise them, "as though there were no change. I've no information as to the future. Nothing's discussed with me anymore. No doubt you'll be receiving letters. Meanwhile, farming won't wait, will it? So, Alec, I expect you'll finish moving that dung today. Warren, you and Tom can dehorn the calves."

The weeks passed into November, December, January. Everyone worked on "as though there were no change," including Delia Sutherland. Several times during that period Muriel implored, "Aren't you ready to go yet? Just don't leave it too late, will you?"

At last Delia Sutherland said to Curtis, as he stooped into the dining room with her breakfast coffee, "So then, Curtis. Here it is. It's happening. That was Mr. Rosen on the telephone. He's arriving with Mr. Kennedy on Sunday evening."

"Sunday, Miss? Sunday?" His tremor had worsened in the past weeks. A mild oscillation had become a violent jerk of the head. "Surely not a Sunday?"

"I know, I know. I tried to explain that no one's really in. And there's no need to come in, Curtis. They can go out for a meal. So long as their beds are made, don't you think? Will you get the trunks out? I'll start packing today. Off Saturday."

"Oh, Miss Delia," he said, patting around his head and the back of his neck the oven glove he had used to hold the coffeepot. "Oh, Miss Delia."

"Sit down, Curtis, here." She pushed a chair behind him and he dropped onto it, sitting forward, gripping the sideboard.

"Oh, Miss Delia."

"I won't be taking much. There's not much I'm allowed to, actually, by the terms of the Trust, but even so . . ." She did not go on to explain that to remove anything would be wrong as far as she was concerned. The least ornament was integral to the whole; anything she took would create a space in the picture of her history, the only thing in her life left intact. "We have three days. More than enough."

Sunday night and there I was stalking the hall. My shadow lapped the outside steps because the doors were open letting out the heat, wide open because I hadn't bothered to bolt them, and the side door was open too, creating a through-draft that made the fire smoke and the dogs restless. They knew something was up even before my car was loaded. They'd known for weeks and stayed by me, anxious when I was out of sight, whining in the daytime when they never used to. Curtis had closed that side door twice but I'd found reasons to go back through, the dogs' bowls, checking the padlock on the cellar and, somehow, I didn't bother to shut it. It didn't seem to matter. My three trunks were upended in the corner ready for Curtis to send on the train.

"I'll stay over, give you both dinner," I'd told David. "It's only civil, after all." He wasn't happy about it and extracted my promise not to try, on any account, to negotiate.

Sunday night and there I was.

Headlamps swung into the top of the drive, caught me midway across the hall.

Not here, I thought. Not here, after all. I want to be in the morning room. He'll see me by the fire, leaning against the mantelpiece, and know how things really are; how they ought to be. But had I ever done that? Leaned by the mantelpiece?

I called the dogs and they crowded behind me into the morning room, clip-clipping to their place with the chewed blanket and the bones. I went to mine, the fireplace, the place of possession. Right away I had to leave it to answer the telephone. It was the elderly widow of the village-school caretaker, whom the council had tried to evict from the flat that went with her husband's job. When that failed they attempted an exorbitant rent so I intervened. She was ringing to say she was settled in a new council bungalow and it was thanks to me. This was the best of it, I thought; such actions and such responses had justified my life. I forgot my circumstances talking to her, that I no longer had power to help, that in a few hours I'd be gone, and I said, "Of course I'd love to visit you, I'd be honored. Good-bye." After replacing the receiver I must have said aloud, "Bloody bureaucratic bullies," because I heard, over the racket the dogs were making, David's voice. "Another victory over red tape, Delia?"

Just for one moment I hope they saw, David and the young man next to him, a radiant woman, generous, strong, sure of her place in the world. I hope they saw that because it wasn't going to last.

"Delia, may I introduce Leon Kennedy? Leon, this is Mrs. Sutherland."

How did I see him then? My impression is overlaid by so many later images. He was taller than I was. His wiry hair, so sparse, nondescript when he was an infant, had become thick and dark-brown, russet where the light struck. His eyes, those tiger eyes, retaining mine from the moment I turned, were the ones I remembered; steady, with no fear, without bravado. He was not black, nor could he be mistaken for white. His hairless skin, with a bloom of well-being, was in a territory of its own. When he moved his head I caught sight of minute areas along his hairline where there was apparently no color at all, as though the bistre shade of his face were a mask. Tear it away and he'd be insupportably white. He had his mother's beauty and strength of feature: straight-bridged nose broadening at the base, below which the line of his upper lip was a flip of Matisse's brush. His mouth was wide, beige, blunt-cornered. What had really locked me over there, kept me rigid, foolish by the telephone, was the way he moved; like an athlete, a dancer, with the ease of one glad to be in the world. I knew him.

"How do you do, Mrs. Sutherland." He held his hand out to me.

The point is, Francis was back. His spirit had come with his son. Not one feature was the same, or even similar, but the slide of his identity came and went, coalescing with the presence of this young man. Behind the movement, within the breath, Francis was there.

"How do you do . . . Leon."

Then he did a terrible thing. He touched his eye with the back of his hand.

David Rosen centered himself between the two tall people with his arms raised, a referee weighing his introduction. Delia Sutherland, having given Kennedy's hand a cursory grip, backed to the fireplace, heels on the fender, gaining two inches. Her fingers buttoned something at her neck where there was nothing to button. She dropped her hands, rubbed her bottom, twisted palms out to the fire, delivered him the room with her eyes and chin.

Here it is, our room, a Caldwell room and, very slightly, a Sutherland room. Everything here has been chosen by us, cared for by us. She watched him seeing it all, feeling it all, assimilating his surroundings with no fidget or fluster. He was genially detached, as though brought along to Sleet for no better reason than to admire and be pleasant. She wanted to say, Now do you understand that it's all mine and always will be?

She smelled the newness of his clothes, his tweed jacket, the soft shirt, the corduroys. He had tried hard to dress the part, succeeding only in appearing too English. When she noted this minor failure a peculiar sensation slid inside her, like pity, like an ache resting at a way station to fear.

"I suppose you'd like a drink, both of you?"

"Don't move, Delia. We'll help ourselves. Leon? Anything?" Rosen crossed towards the drinks trolley but she was there before him.

"I'll do it, thank you, David. I'll do it," and "Shut up, dogs," over her shoulder.

The dogs, who had sustained monotonous barking at Leon Kennedy since he entered, now submitted to aloof ecstasy as he kneeled to massage their ears. "All right, my friends, that's enough, now." His voice, though deep, trailed a feminine note. There was no show in his words to the dogs, he was speaking privately to them in a way she approved of.

Bottle in one hand, glass in the other, she said, "So you do like dogs?" as though the world had told her otherwise.

"Yeah, I like them. I have one back home, I mean there, Nassau."

And she thought: So you're not decided yet, are you?

When he stood up, brushing his hands, the dogs came at him, barking with greater confidence than before, as if they had learned his secret and wanted to tell. They would not let him pass.

Delia Sutherland continued preparing a drink. "Funny things, aren't they?" holding it to the light, checking the measure before giving it to Rosen. "Place, boys," she said without conviction, but they scuttled away, relieved to be let off. She considered the trolley again. "Well, Leon?" He was still standing. "Sit down, for goodness sake. What do you want, then? To drink, I mean?"

"Bourbon would be fine."

"Well, I don't have that. One doesn't much in England, you know."

"Scotch and water?"

"Splendid." She watched Rosen feeling for a cuff in his sleeve. "Perhaps it would be a good idea to take our drinks upstairs? Have

120

a bath or change or whatever before dinner?" Leon Kennedy had just seated himself. "You're in North One, Leon. David, you're East, as usual."

Leon Kennedy's lips restrained more than a smile. "I'll go fetch my bags." Near the door he groped in his inside pocket, brought forth a package, held it towards Delia Sutherland. "By the way, this is for you."

"Me? Gosh. What is it? I say . . . Arpège. The very one I wear. How did you know?" He gestured to Rosen. "Oh, I see. Well, thank you, Leon, how nice."

He was on his way out again when she called after him, "You'll find Curtis lurking about out there. He'll show you to North One," and crossed her arms, saying to Rosen or herself, "North One is where Francis slept, so that's all right, isn't it?"

"He gave me a lighter. Rather charming."

"You don't smoke."

"No, but I can light other people's now. It is nice of you to have stayed to greet him, really. Sorry if I didn't sound too keen at first. I just thought it'd be hard for you. But it'll be okay, won't it? I imagine you'll be leaving early in the morning?" While she stared at the floor Rosen continued, "I do hope we have time to talk alone before you go."

There was activity in the hall and Curtis's quavering voice.

"David?" she said.

He put his hand on her arm. "I mean, Delia, we've had such a long association and a successful one, I'd like to think, well, I don't want to just lose touch."

"David?" She had not removed his hand from her arm, or let her arm fall to make his hand fall too; so he moved his hand to cover hers. She was still looking at the door. "David?"

"What, Delia?"

"He doesn't say much, does he?"

An unfamiliar sound came from the hall. Curtis was laughing.

The dining table, long enough for twenty, was laid with makeshift formality on a damask cloth bulkily folded to cover three places. There were silver-covered dishes on the sideboard. Portraits of ancestors covered the walls; their faces advanced and retreated with a pulse in the electric current; a shuffling audience straining to see the play. Leon Kennedy surveyed them, his attention returning to

121

the one in front of where he sat, a dark, curly-haired man, wearing a red velvet coat and an arrogant smirk.

"Ah. There you are, Curtis," Delia Sutherland said as he backed through the door with a tray. "I take it you've met Mr. Kennedy. No need for introductions?"

"No, Miss. And Mr. Kennedy was chilled in North One so I've taken—"

"Seriously, Leon? Chilled in North One? There's a bar fire, isn't there?"

"Curtis kindly brought me another." The darkness of his jacket made his eyes even yellower. Sitting straight, self-contained, his wrists resting on the table, he dipped his head to emphasize certain words. "And, say, he was telling me how in your mother's day there were coal fires in every bedroom and how . . ."

Francis was lingering; he was there, even in Leon's voice.

Delia Sutherland stopped listening. Her fists mounted on each other, she stared beyond the picnic patch down the molasses shine of the table.

So here he is, then, walking about, asking for heaters, getting them; hearing the stories. It's begun. Please, God, I want it to be over but I don't want the ending.

The candlelight drained her life, stressing dark hollows in her cheeks and eyes; tendrils of hair strayed around her face with shadows of their own.

"I guess it takes time to adjust." Leon Kennedy said it gently, almost an apology.

"What? Adjust? What do you mean, adjust? I'll never adjust."

He was leaning imperceptibly towards her. "To the cold, Mrs. Sutherland. I'm talking about me and the cold. Nothing important." A smile glided to his mouth. "And, say, Curtis was telling me about these things, these weird things. What are they called, Curtis?"

"Thermals, sir."

Leon Kennedy slumped in his chair, laughing, and it came to him with the same elegance as movement. His laughter bred laughter in Rosen, and even Curtis was unusually breathy going about his business with the plates.

"We'll help ourselves, thank you, Curtis."

"Very well, Miss," sharing the pretense that there had actually been an intention to serve them.

While speaking Delia Sutherland had noticed that Rosen was staring at Curtis's feet. He was wearing bedroom slippers, tartan with pom-poms on the front, the same as Delia's own, only his had the sides cut out to ventilate bunions. "It's Sunday, you see," she said when Curtis had closed the door behind him. "Help yourself, Leon," indicating the sideboard.

"Sorry?" Rosen said.

"You were looking at his slippers, weren't you? They're because it's Sunday. It's his little statement. He doesn't normally work on Sunday evenings but if anyone does come"—she paused—"as you have"—another pause—"he'll come in to cook because Mrs. Files is off and she won't come in. But he wears his slippers to remind one that he doesn't really have to."

"Gosh. I see."

"All right over there?" she called to Leon Kennedy who was peering into a dish, tilting it towards the light of a portrait above. "It'll be kidneys."

"Are you sure?"

"Yes. They go with the slippers on Sundays. Don't have them if you don't want. I'll give them to the dogs. I usually do." He returned to his seat and she went on, "Anyway, I don't see what's so funny about thermals. Very useful, they are. Wear them myself."

Leon Kennedy passed a hand across his face, drawing off expression and swallowing. "You do? Well, you're going to have to tell me all about that because . . . because . . ." His voice was spiraling up to laughter. "Thermals, thermals. I'm sorry, but I just can't get over it. It just sounds so silly. Say, Curtis is great, David. Just as you said. He's cool."

"So you've been describing us, have you, David? That's nice," adding before Rosen could answer, "More new clothes, Leon?" She touched the fold of hair at the back of her head.

"Who, me?" Leon Kennedy turned his fork on himself.

"Yes. You," she answered to the ceiling.

"Hey. That's right. It's cashmere. Really soft. Do you like it? How did you know it was new?"

"The smell."

He dropped his arm, shook his head incompletely, taking it to one side, half decision, half dismissal.

"By the way, David"—she turned from Kennedy's eyes—"my keeper, sorry, *the* keeper is leaving. I did tell him to write to you.

Didn't he? Oh well, people don't, you know. They won't. And there's Mike too, at Home Dairy. Now he's not happy," mustering the bad news.

"Delia, let's not bother with all that now, shall we? Let's just, you know . . ." Blanched by the candlelight, Rosen stirred in his seat.

"Well, you'll have to find out for yourselves, then."

"That'll be fine."

"Will it? And naturally Curtis is retiring."

She had not planned to say it. But did they know, did Rosen and Kennedy have any idea how much all this was hurting her?

"Do you mean *that* Curtis?" Leon Kennedy pointed to the door leading to the kitchen. "He's not going to be here anymore? He's leaving?"

His confidence was subsiding, along with his smile. Now Delia Sutherland gave him proper attention. "No, Leon. He won't be here. He's well past retirement. He only stayed on for me. More wine?"

"Leon's been touring England for the past ten days, Delia. Wasn't that a good idea? To see around the country a bit?"

Rosen eked out a conversation with her and without Leon Kennedy, who was sewn into an isolation that made him more powerfully present. His laughter had been natural to him, but this, this removed tranquillity, was more so.

She wanted to watch him and then say something to find out how hard it would be to retrieve him from such self-preservation.

"Not hungry, Leon?"

"Not really."

"She's retiring too, Mrs. Files. My cook."

"Oh, Delia, please." Rosen threw down his napkin.

Leon Kennedy did not react. He returned his attention to the picture opposite. "Who is he?"

"Not family. He's the man who built this house then gambled it away. All the rest are ancestors, every one of them."

"Ah."

"Mine."

"Yes."

"Look here, Leon—"

"No, Delia, you promised," Rosen broke in but he did not know it was an evening of broken promises.

This she had to say. She who had been refused any kind of hearing, now she would be heard. And Leon Kennedy would understand. She knew finally why she had stayed to suffer in this way, so she could explain to him and he would see. Then he'd go. Nothing to it.

"You know very well how many times I've asked to see you, speak to you. The proposals I've made. Francis made his will in a moment of madness. That's all. He loved me." With a short triumphant nod to Rosen she insisted, "Yes." Then back to Kennedy, "This is my home, Leon. There are so many reasons why it won't work, you taking over here, but—"

"Delia, for pity's sake."

"Pity, David? Pity? Look I'm entitled . . ."

Leon Kennedy stood up. At the sideboard he crashed two covers onto silver dishes. Delia Sutherland, Rosen and the ancestors blinked. He punched the sideboard with both hands then opened a fist, leveling his hand on the air in a private calming gesture. With his back to them he jabbed a finger to the floor. "You told me, David, you told me she understood. You said we wouldn't have to do this thing. Talk this way."

"I know, Leon, and I did. Christ, Delia, help me out here, can't you? Have I not explained that?"

"So." The sideboard knocked the wall as he swung round and the noise groaned in the room that had not known such life since the night Francis Sutherland, drunk in front of weekend guests, told his wife, self-assured and aloof on the distant coast of the table, that she was a frigid bitch who needed seeing to and he didn't care who did it. He had clawed the cloth from the length of the table and a slow-motion avalanche of plates, food, cutlery, decanters of wine in silver coasters, candles and engraved Bohemian glass, creatures carved in silver, a bowl of roses and two Paul de Lamerie dishes all shunted beneath sixteen pairs of bewildered eyes, and no one thought to hold the cloth, prevent the steady crash of destruction at Francis Sutherland's end of the table. It seemed to take a long time. When it was all over and the table was bare and no one could think what to say, then they noticed that Delia Sutherland was gone. It was past her bedtime anyway.

Leon Kennedy was next to her now, one fist gripping the back of her chair, about to pull it from under her, his other hand clenched on the table near her own which she snatched to her lap.

"No, Mrs. Sutherland, you look at me because I want to see you understanding what I'm going to say 'cause I'm never discussing this again with anyone."

His face was very close. Her shoulders attempted a shrug of indifference but remained defensively hunched.

"Sleet's mine now, Mrs. Sutherland. Everything else is history. I'm not saying that nothing belongs anymore—like those pictures, this." He picked up a silver owl, holding it at her face. "Or anything else that's here. Even you. All of it, everything, has its place that began somewhere in the past. Now I'm here and I have a place too and nothing's going to change that. No suggestions. No deals. You can stay or go, it's the same to me. But I stay. Do you hear me, Mrs. Sutherland?"

He did not move away from her so she slid from beneath the arc of his body, her napkin fell to the floor. She passed around the table but slowly, and touched the back of one of the seventeen vacant chairs to steady herself. She had reached the door, was almost through it, when she called wearily, "Come on, boys."

Leon Kennedy pointed a questioning finger between himself and Rosen, who was paralyzed in a protective lunge between his and Delia Sutherland's chair. Rosen shook his head, indicating the dogs under the sideboard who were staring after their mistress, equally uncertain. They shifted their gaze to Rosen who grimaced sympathy at them, nodding. Still they did not move until, on hearing a more familiar tone, loud, irritable, from the hall, "I said, 'come on, boys,'" they scrambled.

I went out with the dogs into the volume of the night. It felt cold and good and free. Real night, country night, is a very complete thing with a limitless density, unlike the sham night of cities; a density that allows no belief in dawn. And that is what I wanted then, to feel I could remain safe from a future and past, safe from time.

There was a new swath of light among the stars. It hadn't been there before and no doubt wouldn't be tomorrow; resting, I expect, on its journey from one universe to another. I tried to believe there were things beyond possession, greater belonging, greater satisfaction, but I was tied by resentment, self-pity and a mad belief that the past could be resuscitated. I could only think of that oh-so-English phrase "It's not fair." I've been told there's no real translation in any language for the English conception of fair, which is oblique justice redefined for every circumstance.

I leaned against a chestnut, one of a bib of trees leading down to the Wild Garden. Through its low branches I had a latticed view of the buildings that made up my home. To the right was the outline of the dovecote where, as a child, standing in the doorway with my back to the sunlight, I fought my shadow with a wooden sword. When I was bored and ready to win, I kicked shut the door. Inside I would sit on the dirt floor smoking cigarettes stolen from the drawing room. My throat would itch with the dust of doves who inquired and conversed on the same few notes, while the heavy ticking of the estate clock at the top of a rotting ladder reverberated around the eight chalk walls where game used to be hung. After the dovecote came the wall connecting the stableyard to the house, the yard I'd crossed every night I could remember to collect the dogs' bowls and return them full. After the yard was the house that was built for, and due, so much more life than I'd ever been able to give it. Perhaps that was why it was being taken away from me; I couldn't do it justice.

If I could have departed then, never reentered the house, it would have been with some strength of mind.

I told myself I was waiting out there for the signals to let me know David and Leon had gone to bed, lights switched off at their bedroom windows, at least some movement of the curtains.

There was no need to see him again; I was leaving very early. Only I had to feel, to see one more time that elusive spirit of Francis; despite repeating to myself, "It's not you, is it, Francis? It's not really you?"

David Rosen came to the steps and peered into the darkness as though into a room where he had no right to be. "Delia? I say, Delia, are you out there?"

She was not going to answer but he remained, so she said, "It's all right, David. I'm coming in now." Although she made no effort to be heard, the night carried her voice just the same.

"No kennels tonight?" Rosen followed her to the gunroom where she pressed her head against both dogs, murmuring inaudibly to each. She sighed, picked yellow hairs from her black dress.

"No. They won't like it in here, too hot; but it's quicker for the morning, otherwise I'd only have to cross the yard to get them.

And that's how I always start my day, isn't it? Crossing the yard to get the dogs. Mustn't do that tomorrow. No routine tomorrow. Nothing familiar tomorrow."

"I'll be down to say good-bye."

She was at the bottom of the stairs, he was two steps up. "Do you mind not, actually, David?"

"I understand."

"So. Good night, then," facing away.

"Yes. Well. Quite."

She frowned. "That's what I say, isn't it?" And her laugh was halting and light and willing for more fun. It was the laugh of a girl, how she might have laughed on the night of the dance where she met Francis. It seemed to her there was something more to say. While she was thinking what that might be David Rosen bent from the height of his two steps and kissed her cheek. She covered the place with her fingers, preventing one of the many drafts of Sleet from carrying it away.

"Thank you," she said.

"Good night."

She bolted the front door, checked her car keys were on the hall table, turned off the lights, all this briskly. There had to be an end. All ready now. Nothing to do but go upstairs and sleep; only the lights in the morning room and she could turn those off without entering, just reach around the door. No need to see again the possessions she was leaving. She felt inside to the glass plate on the right and swept three switches upwards, blacking out one more cuddy of the past.

The door was nearly shut when she heard, "Please don't do that, Mrs. Sutherland."

She flicked the bottom switch. One table lamp by the window shone onto the Chinese figures.

Leon Kennedy was standing in front of the fire where she had chosen to stand all that time ago at the beginning of the evening.

"Oh, I see," she said. "I'm sorry. I thought you'd have gone to bed."

"No. Because I thought you'd have said good-bye."

"Of course. So, well, good-bye, then."

"Okay. Yes. Good-bye."

She remained by the door with her arms crossed. The tangled fringe of a rug was suddenly very interesting, the back of an armchair, its cover taut from washing, the wide oak floorboards. Anything but to raise her eyes and see him there where she ought to be. She wanted to say in her other voice, the one she had mislaid outside, So here you are at last, on my estate, in my house, at my place in front of the fire. She decided she would say it, noticed how her body rearranged itself for the tone that would come. She was surprised that to be herself and speak her mind required such physical effort. Had this always been the case? Never mind.

Fingers tapping her upper arms, she focused on him, "So here you are, then . . ." and stopped. She refocused and saw a man, very young, a stranger in a room made, lived in, loved by others; a room he would possibly never make his own. She saw a young man afraid and pretending not to be. "Do people say how like your father you are?"

"Well . . ." Hands in pockets, he lowered his head, taking the question as a compliment. "You think?"

Her fingers rested. "What's it like? Not belonging?"

He tensed. "You mean here? Sleet?"

Her gaze roamed, she half-raised a shoulder, fingertips, an eyebrow.

"Ah. That. I understand," he said and pointed to the drinks trolley. "Would you like a . . ." but he repocketed his hand. "No. Of course, you do that yourself."

"A drink, you mean? Brandy, then. Perhaps I'm not so keen to have this day end after all."

She let him pour it for her while she threw another log onto the fire, smashing a cathedral of embers. There would be nothing but heatless yellow flame for a while. Her armchair already felt unfamiliar because her spectacles were not in their place beside it; there were no files waiting for attention, no newspapers, even the armchair itself felt different. She reached to the gap between back and seat where years ago she had stuffed a cushion that made all the difference to that small problem with her spine. It was gone. Gone already. When had they done that? Like they could not wait to abolish her conveniences and idiosyncrasies. She scanned the room for other changes. Yes, the chrysanthemums had been moved from there to there. Or had they? And there was the desk, something about that too. But of course there was. She had cleared it herself.

She clutched her forehead, drew up her legs. After all these years, at bay in her own armchair. Through the spinney of her fingers she saw Leon Kennedy standing again by the fire watching her.

"It's a place to be," he said, "like any other."

"What? What are you talking about?" She organized her limbs, pretending ease.

"Not belonging. You asked."

"Did I?" It was a trick and she knew it, to ask a personal question then appear to forget it so any answer would seem to be volunteered with all the humiliation of confession. But Leon Kennedy's eyes did not hold humiliation, only the assembling of a special hatred. The kind she had encountered from the languid woman in the Big Bamboo. She hauled herself upright. "I'm sorry. Of course I remember. You could've told me to mind my own business."

"I know that." He came to sit on the floor near her chair with his elbows on his knees, hands linked.

He's very relaxed, she thought. How quickly he becomes relaxed if I allow him. My hand could touch his hair from here, he wouldn't even know. "So not belonging's a place to be, is it?"

"That's right."

"Will I like it?"

"You'll never be there. You belong. You always will."

"Is there anything you want to ask me before I go? There must be things you need to know about Sleet."

"There must be."

"Well, then?"

"I guess I'll catch on."

She pictured herself getting up, going from the room. In a minute. "Did you see much of your . . . of my . . . of Francis?"

"Some. He'd come to our house in Delaporte from time to time. Are you familiar with Delaporte? It's a nice part and my ma built this really beautiful place there."

"A highly successful woman, your mother."

"I guess," he said, viewing something in memory unhappier than success. "So anyway Francis would come to our house late, after Mamma was home from the club." He realized what he was saying and glanced at Delia Sutherland.

She stroked any possible offense from the air in a good imitation of worldliness. "She gave him drugs too, didn't she?"

"Nothing serious. He was low. He liked a little help from time to time. You asked if people say we looked alike. Well, I don't know his people, the ones that knew him. He never had anything to do with me until I graduated from college nearly two years back now. The very first time I saw him he stopped on his way to the front door, three, maybe four in the morning. I'd been waiting. He kind of smiled at me and he said, 'Hey, kid,' then he said, but more to himself, you understand, he said, 'Jesus, it's like looking at myself.' So that's who said we look alike, Mrs. Sutherland. Good authority, eh? Or maybe you don't think so?"

"After that?"

"I'd make sure he saw me every time before he went out the door. He turned round often enough to let me know he was look-ing for me. He'd say, 'Hey, kid,' and I'd say, 'Hey.' " Leon hit his breast. "I mean, I was twenty-four. 'Hey, kid.' But that was okay."

"That's all?"

"That's all."

You're here, Francis, aren't you, seeing all this happen to me? You're very close. Am I doing all right? Will you stay near this time?

"So here you are, then, Leon." Disbelief swirled inside her.

"You keep saying that and, yes, here I am."

"Because your mother insisted."

"Absolutely not."

"If it hadn't been for Sleet, then what?"

"Social work. Family therapy, difficult kids and such. Makes me laugh when I think how things turned out."

"Makes you laugh, does it, like a lot of things?"

"I guess. Take you, for instance, only don't take it wrong. You're a cut-out English lady. I met thousands of them back there and they're all like anybody else except for the voice, French, Germans, Americans. Give or take. But you, Jesus, you're the one God made."

"Thank you so much. But I'll have you know this cut-out lady is a woman in terrible pain; a woman who's leaving here because of a whim of her husband. So this figure of fun is going to bed now. And when you've finished laughing perhaps you'll turn off the lights." She was already crossing the room when she smacked her forehead. "What am I saying, what do I care about the lights?"

He reached a hand in her direction. "I'm sorry. You misunder-stood. Not funny, Mrs. Sutherland, really. Talk to me. Tell me about the house in the Abacos? I've never been there, talk to me about that."

Her eyes linked them until she went to pull together the curtains she knew very well had never met properly. "Well, of course you've been there. I've seen you there."

"Seen?" From within the arena of armchairs and sofa he had been mirroring her progress about the room, two steps forward to the drinks trolley where she placed her glass, four steps to her eight over to the window, three back on her way to the door again. "What do you mean, 'seen'?"

She could not bring herself to say, You were shut outside the gate. "You were a little boy. Playing. Your mother was there too."

"Oh, she would've been." His voice was suddenly loud, strained. "Mamma was always there by me. She, why she, throughout my life, has always stood by me to help me make big decisions . . ." Delia Sutherland had stopped to face him while his voice rose still higher. "And when she came to school for me . . ."

"St. Andrew's?"

"Sure, St. Andrew's. Why not St. Andrew's? Columbia too. She'd visit and the guys'd say how beautiful she was. Because she was beautiful and couldn't do enough for me, that's for sure. I guess you could say she spoiled me and—"

"All right, Leon. I heard you. You needn't go on." She quickened her pace towards the door. From the other side, leaving only her fingers around its edge, she said, "Good night. Good-bye."

"Mrs. Sutherland?"

"What?" Her voice doubling about the hall. One of the dogs barked from the gunroom.

"Don't go."

The wind cartwheeled, slamming up against the windows, resting awhile before starting again. Chimes from the clocktower trailed in the clefts of movement. A log split, resettled; another cathedral in the making.

Delia Sutherland reentered, keeping the door as a shield. "What did you say?"

"I said, 'Don't go.' "

Her eyes searched among the possessions and in the folds of the curtains for familiarity but there was nothing to reassure. In the moments she had left, the room had changed its allegiance and there was nothing safe here anymore. She felt her voice collecting inside her. Her body flexed. "I'm very sorry, Leon. It's late and I have an early start."

"I don't mean that, Mrs. Sutherland. I mean don't go. I can't do it on my own."

Ten

THEY'VE DONE IT, they've taken the outside tables away. You can understand; the weather's too cold now for any normal person to want to sit out. And they look so dank, all those unoccupied chairs, not good for business. Besides, there's a lot of rain, even I can't sit out in that. I haven't been in yet because when I do I want to have bought the silk flowers for the old lady. I'm not quite ready for that, for acquaintances. I'll remain in the open where I'm easily seen, easy to find. What I do now in the mornings is walk, the way I do at night. I go to the quarter behind the Quai du Port, it's old there and very poor. So I walk, I think, and return to my room where, sitting beside the window, I pin down butterflies from inside my head.

How many times had I prayed for the impossible? To have that evening with Francis once more, not all of it, just the moment when I was through the door and heard him say, "Don't go, don't go," and I wouldn't have gone, and my story would have had a different end?

Funny how turning points can visit in plain clothing and only on looking back is the impression found, an impression made by the weight of a moment so apparently modest it's hard to recall.

I fell asleep that night saying: Thank you, God, Thank you, God, and with images of myself explaining to Leon the rhythm of the forestry and fields, teaching him love for what I loved. That was all I'd ever wanted, I thought. This time I'd make it right.

———

At seven the next morning Delia Sutherland let the dogs outside, yelling after them so her voice might slip through the window and heavy curtains of North One.

Leon Kennedy did not come down. At seven-thirty she had started the engine of the Subaru when he came running out of the house.

"Get in. We're late." She pretended not to see David Rosen who appeared on the step as they drove off to talk to the men at the place where they gathered before work.

She was prepared for hostility towards Leon. Very well, she'd tell them, leave if you must, but I want no abuse, is that clear? Frank Grimwood would not be there, they would see him later. The men were going to be surprised, of course, because she had said her last good-bye on Friday. She wanted to study Leon beside her in the pickup without him knowing. Did he have any idea what he was in for? He was only half-awake.

As they approached the workshop at the Piggeries—there had been no pigs there since her grandfather's day—she saw the clump of men, half-turned away, appearing uninterested.

"Yes. Well. Here I am," she said to them, suddenly shy. "Staying on a bit, you see, to help Mr. Kennedy here."

Their cheer did not go far in the brittle morning air but it pleased her. She would never have expected a cheer. She patted her pockets in the way she used to when she smoked and was in search of her lighter. "So, Tom Sutcliffe, Stuart Macdonald. Alec here's on his year out from college, Donald's our mechanic, Warren . . ."

"Hi there, Tom," Leon Kennedy said. "Stuart, great to meet you. Alec, hello. Say, Donald. Warren, hi."

Each man looked at anything other than Kennedy so long as his eyes were on him. The minute his attention was removed to the next, Kennedy was appraised from head to foot. Every gesture was judged and measured, while they concealed their interest behind beard-scratching, nose-stroking, brow-rubbing hands. Delia Sutherland was thinking: Who'll be the first, which of you will speak up?

"Now, then." She was just inside the workshop doors with the fertilizer shed behind her, stacked to the roof with one-tonne sacks. "We're in a quiet time at the moment, Leon. January always is on a farm. The best thing is for everybody to get on as usual and Mr. Kennedy here can ask anything he wants to. There's nothing to it, really."

He was standing between Delia Sutherland and the others, facing her. Although his features were almost hidden by the collar of his goosedown parka he nodded and did something with his eyebrows that made the company smile.

"Right, then?" She was disconcerted.

"Yes, Mrs. Sutherland. That's okay by me," Leon Kennedy said. "I'll ask what I don't know. Like what's that you're standing on?"

"This? This is a Cambridge roller used after the fields've been sown. Gives a sort of tidy look to it all. That there's a seed drill, there's a fertilizer spreader, plow," indicating the line of machinery outside.

"And the white sacks in there?"

"Ah. Urea, Leon. Urea."

"Oh, really. Nice."

Now they were laughing and Delia Sutherland did not understand. "Right. Let's get on. Tom, where are you today?"

"Plowing Top Field. Spring barley."

"Oh, that's right. Well, you can't. They rang on Saturday morning to say the repair to the tractor'll be three thousand and that's the only one that'll take the big plow. But three thousand is too much for now. So you'll just have to hang on a bit. There's the fencing to get back to." Tom made a noise like a horse blowing. "I know, I know," she said. "We won't have to wait long, though. Martin, Warren, you're still on fencing, aren't you? Well, Tom can lend a hand there. Any questions, Leon? Happy with that?"

"Terrific."

The men stamped their feet, restoring their circulation, as they walked away. "See you later, guys," Leon called after them. "And, say, we'll get that tractor fixed right away, Tom, no problem."

They stopped to look back at him. Tom raised his arm, mirroring Leon Kennedy. "Thanks."

Someone else said, "See you later."

"That's right," said another, "see you later." The men went away chuckling.

"Funny mood they're in," Delia Sutherland said as they drove towards Home Dairy. "They're curious about you, of course."

"Course." He let his head roll against the window and she could have believed he was doing something with his eyes to the countryside, the way he had done with his eyebrows to the men. Something to enlist the support, the complicity, of the fields, the planta-

136

tions of spruce. She had wanted to see him wake to the possession of all this beauty but he watched its passing impassively, stirring only to ask practical questions.

"That's fifteen of those big ones down. Why leave them lying about like that? It's a shame. An eyesore," he said of the oaks fallen in the park.

"Since the hurricane. There's no money in them and it takes the right machinery to cut them up. That's expensive, so they stay. We have five hundred acres of forestry here. But you know that already, don't you?"

"Yes." He refolded his arms, closer this time, pulled his chin into his collar and withdrew.

He's returning to somewhere safe when he does that, she thought.

Mike was in the pit between two lines of cows. He showed no surprise on seeing Mrs. Sutherland and called out angrily, before she could speak, "Mrs. S, we've had the MMB cell count. It's far too high. Our price'll drop even lower. We've got to replace the tank washers."

"I know, Mike. As soon as we get this month's check."

"But you said that last month."

"This is Mr. Kennedy."

"Oh yes." Mike rubbed his hands into a cloth pulled from his green overalls. "That's right, I forgot for a moment. It's your problem now, isn't it? Well, we won't sell the milk at all if the washers aren't replaced and that's that."

"Jesus, money, money, money," Leon Kennedy said, walking away from the dairy. "You're really strapped for it."

"No, actually, Leon, you are." And just for a few minutes she savored the circuitous routes of pleasure.

Frank Grimwood was having breakfast when Delia Sutherland knocked and entered his warm kitchen. "Morning, Frank. Don't move and don't be surprised to see me. I've stayed on to settle Mr. Kennedy here." She pocketed her gloves and gripped her cold fingers around the rail on the stove.

Frank Grimwood showed no sign of moving, or even of lifting his eyes from his plate, except to flick them at Kennedy who was standing by the door.

"So I've come to introduce him. Leon, this is Frank Grimwood, our head keeper."

"Thought you were leaving," Grimwood said before Kennedy could speak. "Scotland, wasn't it?"

"Like I said, I'm staying on a bit. Mr. Kennedy arrived last night. He's met some of the others already."

Shoving crockery aside with his forearm Grimwood linked his fingers in mute concentration on the table.

"How do you do, Mr. Grimwood?" Leon Kennedy held up his hand, more of a proclamation than a greeting. There was no response.

Delia Sutherland regloved, giving herself time to consider her unexpected anger towards Grimwood. But wasn't he the one she knew? The one she trusted? Wasn't he the one with whom she'd grown up at Sleet when his father was head keeper before him? "Do you have anything to say to Mr. Kennedy, Frank? Even, for instance, what you told me a few weeks back? How do you feel about that now. You've not mentioned it again."

"I might have something to say when I'm ready. Not before."

"Okay, Mr. Grimwood," Leon Kennedy said. "When you want to talk about anything you'll know where to find me." The door rasped on the red-tile floor as he dragged it shut behind him.

"Really, Frank, I don't know. That was too bad of you." She had intended this to be no more than a comradely rebuke.

"I'll thank you to mind your own business, Mrs. S."

The inside of her mouth was suddenly bitter. She wanted to swallow, only the muscles in her throat were stiff.

Driving back she scanned the fields, the forestry, the ditches at the sides of the road, anything but Leon Kennedy. It wasn't her fault, she was thinking, he'd have to get used to this sort of thing. He'd got off lightly with the men earlier. There were bound to be some who felt as Frank did. That's life. She would have to think of something to say in a minute to break the silence.

When they reached the house, five minutes later, she had to nudge him awake.

"No breakfast?" she called when she saw him striding up the stairs two at a time.

"God, no. It's too early. I have to sleep, Mrs. Sutherland."

"What do you mean, sleep?"

138

"I mean, seven-thirty's too early for me. I need more sleep than that."

"Good heavens. So, sawmill at eleven, then. We'll meet Holland May there."

David Rosen was watching Mrs. Files's scrambled egg on his plate. "Still here, then, Delia?"

"Slight change in plan." She leaned through the service door. "Curtis? Morning. Have trunk "1" unpacked in my room, will you?" She joined Rosen with a cup of coffee and an apple. "Don't you like your scrambled egg?"

"I've reached an understanding with it. What about Scotland? The smallholding you've just signed for? The sheep?"

"It's a little house with vacant land. There are no sheep yet. It can wait."

"He doesn't need you, Delia. You're making a mistake."

"Last night he said he couldn't do it alone. And of course he can't. And, David, with the best will in the world, you can't teach him. It's something only I can do."

He dropped one word into the shelter of his newspaper.

"What?" she asked over the top of hers.

"Nothing."

"No, well"—looking at her watch—"I must be getting on. You here for lunch?"

"No, but I'll wait for a word with Leon."

By mid-morning Leon Kennedy had not arrived down so Rosen left a letter for him on the hall table and returned to London.

At eleven Delia Sutherland found Curtis teetering upstairs with a tray. Both ignored the fact that yesterday they had said farewell to each other and a way of life.

"Are you safe with that? What is it, anyway?"

"Mr. Kennedy's breakfast, Miss." He moved on when he saw her expression.

At lunchtime she found Leon Kennedy in the morning room, dressed in a tweed jacket, soft shirt, tie, different ones from the day before. "Oh, there you are, Mrs. Sutherland." The pleasure in his voice disarmed her.

He did not look so much like Francis today. He was reduced in some intangible way: maybe it was his youth; perhaps his essence had not yet unfurled to fill the room the way Francis's used to.

"What's the matter, Mrs. Sutherland? Are you all right?"

"Yes. Yes. Of course. Why wouldn't I be? Where were you at eleven?"

"I overslept. Isn't that terrible?" as though speaking of another's transgression.

"So you didn't meet Holland May, my forester. The head forester."

"I'll catch up with him."

"Jet lag, is it? Makes you sleep like that?"

"Not any longer."

"Idleness."

"Boy," he breathed quietly, distancing himself without movement.

He ate little at lunch and she thought: Well, he wouldn't would he? He's only just had breakfast. She told him about the new high-tensile fencing they were putting up, and the ten acres of daffodil bulbs they were planting as an experiment rather than consigning the field to set-aside.

"Set-aside? Is that some kind of fertilizer?"

"No, it's when the government pays you not to grow crops in the fields."

"They pay you not to?"

It was more interesting to him than high-tensile or daffodils so she tried to explain the principle until his interest faded. "May I borrow your car to go downtown?"

"Leon, we don't go 'downtown.' "

"We don't?" He pushed away from the table as he had the previous night when he had lost his temper. He hunched his shoulders, drawing in his elbows, clenching and reclenching his fists, buffeted by invisible punches. "Not go downtown? But, Jesus, that's . . . I don't understand you. How can you not get out?"

"No. I mean we don't say 'downtown,' we say 'to town,' or name the town."

He dropped his head, hoarding the laughter she would hear coming from the hall a minute later. "Well, good for you, Mrs. Sutherland."

"You can borrow the car and I'll see you in the office later to go over the VAT files."

"Sounds cool."

140

"Hey," she shouted after him. "You don't know the way to town."

"That's okay, Curtis said he'll come too."

The front door slammed. Delia Sutherland remained where she was, examining something unfamiliar in her spirit, something that under X-ray might show like a patch on a lung.

The hall clock struck the half hour, the three-quarter, two o'clock, and still she sat. Vanity? Was that David's word? It wouldn't be like him. Weightless with introspection she observed her hands as she had in the Big Bamboo, with their veins like injured worms—big, workaday hands—and hid them between her army-surplus thighs.

Mrs. Files hesitated with a tray under her arm when she saw Delia Sutherland still there at two-fifteen. For years lunch had been a twenty-minute affair.

At first Delia Sutherland could not place this slim woman with thick red hair lapping her head in curls. "Mrs. Files? What have you done to your hair?"

"Done? Done? Done that two months ago." She sounded light-hearted.

"It makes you look so young."

"So I just been told. Feel young too."

That glory of hair gone and she had never noticed, not even on Saturday when they had said good-bye. What had her eyes been seeing all this time? And Mrs. Files had a family to look young for, people who loved her, wanted to see more of her, who would be glad if she retired.

"Two months? Really? Fancy. Dinner for two, then."

"I know that."

"How?"

"Mr. Kennedy came to the kitchen and we had chats."

"Chats?"

"About food and such. He's interested. So that's all right. Only he says eight-thirty, not seven-thirty."

"Ridiculous."

"So what'll it be?"

"Seven-thirty, of course."

Mrs. Files let her shoulders answer while she stacked at the sideboard. Delia Sutherland thought of asking, So when are you actually retiring, Mrs. Files? But that would only bring, When are you leaving, Mrs. Sutherland? So she went on watching and noticed for the first time that Mrs. Files had lovely hands, long-fingered, fine-textured, graceful in their mundane task. Thirty-five years and she had never noticed her hands. Family to be young for and lovely hands. "I said seven-thirty."

"I heard."

Later Delia Sutherland was sitting at her desk under a fluorescent tube in the estate office. The yolk-yellow walls were layered with seed merchants' calendars, charts and various photographs of herself in a white coat holding a haltered bull, his forehead dabbed with rosettes, from the days when she bred Herefords. The filing cabinets and chairs were a union of postwar utility and the cheapest modern plywood.

It was after five and Leon Kennedy had not tried to find her. She knew he was back from town, had seen him earlier through the window.

Muriel telephoned. "What's happening, Delia? I rang the house to find out if you left all right this morning and Curtis said you were still there. That I'd find you in the office as usual at this time. What's going on?"

"Well, I've decided to stay on a bit to settle him."

There was a long pause. "I see." Another long pause and, "So you'll call me soon, will you? Let me know what your movements are?"

"Course. Bye."

Walking the dogs kept Delia Sutherland out of the house until six-thirty. She stayed in her room until seven-thirty. On her way into dinner she heard music from the morning room. The kind of music she had not heard for a long time.

The food was not in and when she pressed the bell underfoot there was no response. Dinner had never been late before. She circled the table while her progress was marked from the darkness under the sideboard by four white crescents of dog eye. "Stay, boys." She left the room.

"There you are, Mrs. Sutherland. I've been waiting for you. It's nice to see you. Look." Leon Kennedy spread his arms. "They're for you."

White roses filled the room, one still in his hand.

"Dinner's at seven-thirty."

"I said eight-thirty, Mrs. Sutherland. I'd get sick eating so early and anyway it's no fun then. C'mon. Do you like them? Roses."

"Fun? No fun? And of course you'd want some fun this evening, having done nothing all day. Where were you this afternoon? Have you no sense of responsibility?"

"I was buying a car. And I got you the roses."

"Well, there used to be flowers in our own greenhouses."

"Yeah. But not now. Not anymore, yet. And this is a flower, Mrs. Sutherland. This is a beautiful living flower." He approached her, holding out the rose.

"Keep back." She had not meant it so loud; so harsh.

He threw the flower down. Before he could speak Curtis appeared. "Dinner is served."

"What?" She flew round. Seeing Curtis at the door in that way she did not need him to repeat his announcement.

How long since the formality of "Dinner is served?" For how many years had she entered the dining room at eight-thirty in the morning, at twelve-thirty, at seven-thirty, eaten the food she found there and gone? If she had a guest it was never more than one and the hour was always the same.

They began with a cheese soufflé. Delia Sutherland had no idea Mrs. Files could cook a soufflé. The pink lamb cutlets were flavored with rosemary and brandy; the raspberry sorbet was served with a melba sauce, ground hazelnuts and crumbling biscuits. She ate without comment but there was nothing left for the dogs.

"I'm going up. Good night."

"Mrs. Sutherland? It's not yet nine." Leon Kennedy followed her into the hall.

"Some of us have been up since six-thirty and I like to read. That's what I do, you see. I go up at nine and I read."

"Why are you angry with me?"

"It's not working, Leon. This. My staying."

"Don't say that. It will. It's only the first day."

"Twice today I've waited and you've not turned up. Twice I've wanted to explain things about your responsibilities here."

"So there's tomorrow. It's evening now. It's time to relax and talk. You come down here and tell me about the time you went to the Abacos."

"I don't want to. There's nothing to say. It's Sleet that should be interesting you but apparently it doesn't. Good night."

"You come on back here, Mrs. Sutherland," he shouted. "You come on back here and talk to me."

"Don't you shout at me in my house." The vibration in the banister under her hands traveled down to him; "house," "house," "house," all about the walls.

"It's not your house."

"Your house, then. What do I care? It's your responsibility now." The dogs whined in a cringing advance towards her. "And put the bloody dogs in the kennels."

So the first day finished with me lying sleepless, listening to that familiar music coming from below as it had years before, the jazz records my mother used to play.

I slept and woke to find the house quiet, settled from the anger that had shaken it. I thought I heard birds, despite the sky showing no signs of thinning. I've heard them before like that, distanced but there, singing beyond the night in a daytime of their own. Perhaps it's the pipistrelle bats and that's why, if I looked, I wouldn't see anything outside but a disturbance of shadow. Then I heard a new sound: a thin wail more certain than the birds, coming from inside the house, balancing between the shuffling drafts.

Tightening the cord of my pajamas, blinkered by my loosened hair, I listened outside the door of North One, where the sound had led me, a musical instrument playing a familiar tune, I couldn't recall the name; playing it so far, stumbling on a phrase and returning to the beginning. Suddenly the whole melody came through. Not only could I still not think of the name, I couldn't determine the instrument. This troubled me so much that when, in the morning, I found Curtis running the polisher over the hall floor, I asked him, "Did you hear that in the night, Curtis? What was it?"

"Music, Miss." He didn't even look up.

"I know it was music, Curtis, I know that. And don't tell me I have no ear." I headed out of the house.

Back in those hours I had remained a long time outside the door of North One, being filled by a sorrow so complete it overflowed, and I covered my ears not to hear any more. I had run to my room, my bed, pulled a pillow over my head.

"Curtis? Curtis? Where are the dogs? I told Mr. Kennedy to put them in the kennels last night. They're not there."

144

I searched the house, the gardens; and drove over to Frank Grimwood, interrupted his breakfast. Had he seen the dogs wandering? No, he hadn't.

"Get him," I said to Curtis and pointed to the stairs. "Wake him. I want to know what he's done with my dogs." And when he returned, "Well? Did you wake him?"

"No, Miss."

"Good God, Curtis, what's come over you? I want to know where the hell my dogs are."

"They're asleep on the bed with him, Miss."

I would have left had I not seen he was wearing something I hadn't seen on him before, and had to ask him about it, certain I knew what the answer would be. "Incidentally, what's that copper on your wrist? Do you have rheumatism?"

"No, Miss. I haven't got rheumatism. Mr. Kennedy gave me this. Isn't it attractive? See how it's engraved? Perhaps he thought it might make me nip up a bit quicker with his morning tray." He twinkled with his joke.

He played that music every night, that other music in his room. I'd listen outside, still not knowing the instrument or the name of the tune he practiced.

Once he came into the passage and looked around. My chest ached with a child's fear while I cringed in the deeply recessed doorway of North Three. When he went back to play again he left his door ajar and I could see him in there naked to the waist, head bent. A clarinet was in his hands. Of course, of course, a clarinet. A terrific heat eased from his room, welding with the air outside making it into a different zone from the rest of the house, like the Gulf Stream off Scotland. Curtis had taken advantage of it and put an azalea on the table in the passage, a yellow one with a pungent scent. Leon always opened his door after that and, standing in the same spot where I could see him, he would play.

I never discovered for certain if he knew I was watching him. Perhaps, like his mother, he was aware of his beauty, wished to have it admired, although nothing in his daytime demeanor was vain. But I was admiring him and remembering Francis; how he had been, once; what it felt like to touch and be touched by him. My thoughts hadn't run in this way for years. Now, nightly, when Leon

145

had finished playing and had closed his door again, I would be left sleepless, confused by the force of my neglected senses.

After a week of that I decided one night to leave in the morning. I wrote a note to Leon, left it on the hall table for him to find when he came down at God knows what time, and went in to breakfast.

From the dining-room door I saw him. He was standing by the window tilting a folded newspaper to the light, which left his other hand free to knead his hip with an unconscious sensuality so familiar. Apparently he hadn't heard the door and I stood there until slowly, still reading, he set his head in my direction and smiled. Gradually he removed his concentration and gave it to me. "There you are, Mrs. Sutherland."

I forgot the note on the hall table and he found it later, came to me distressed. "You're going?"

I took it from him. "No. I changed my mind."

"You could do that, Mrs. Sutherland? Go with only a note? That easy?"

"Please, Leon, just forget it. Put it out of your mind."

"You could. You have that capacity, don't you? Promise you won't do it that way. Promise." He watched me with an anxiety and a pity so powerful I walked away.

No, I didn't leave. Not that day or on any of the countless occasions I resolved to, because I was sharing my house with Francis again. It was Francis with his head back laughing, inhaling all the joy of the world; Francis delighting in the flowers he threw together with branches and invited me to enjoy. It was Francis—it hurts, this, to remember—it was Francis who, bewildered, touched the back of his hand to his eye. One time, after he had done that, I found somewhere dark, and the Bony Lady cried; cried as she should have done years back.

To the world, of course, I was busy, self-assured Mrs. Sutherland; the world did not see my breakwaters sinking lower every day.

In gratitude for what I thought God had given me, a second chance, I ignored Leon's boredom as I talked him through the files —just as I was ignoring Muriel's messages to call her—and I ignored his rarely appearing at meetings with agricultural reps and men from the Milk Marketing Board; ignored his non-involvement with any of the humdrum things essential to the running of a place like Sleet. Instead I closed him out, continued without him and became absorbed in my old routine. Only that is a lie.

Nothing was as before because he was there and if I did not persevere with my patronizing offers of involvement it was because my confusion was worsening, the patch on my spirit growing. The only cure would have been to leave. I couldn't.

I avoided him instead, sometimes even for a day and most of an evening, until I was in the mood, strong enough, weak enough, who-knows-what-enough to take a sip of Francis. Then I'd find my fantasy broker—he was never very far—and use his company to restore my past and make it right.

There is a particular incident I remember when he came to me. I'm not certain why I should remember this unless it was perhaps my first, unacknowledged, awareness that he was himself and not another; and that that self was, in a dignified, quiet way, reaching out to me.

The outer door to the estate office slammed and the inner one opened with its uneasy stick and snuffle past the strips of draft-excluders worn down and added to over the years.

"Ah. There you are, Mrs. Sutherland." Leon Kennedy leaned against the door to shut it and watched her.

"That's right, Leon. Here I am. Good timing, actually. Sign this, would you?" She adjusted her half-moon glasses, reached for a document to her left, held it out to him; all without looking up.

"What is it?" He turned the paper in his hand.

"It's the improvement-grant application for the slurry lagoon at Home Dairy. I know I mentioned it. Just sign there, at the bottom."

He placed the paper directly beneath her face, leaning across with his pen, forcing her to tilt back in her chair. Having signed he lifted his head which brought their faces close. He did not move away. His skin smelled of soap and newly turned soil.

"There is another desk, Leon."

He capped his pen. "So there is."

"I've also been sorting out the dates for the let shoots. The first'll be in September, partridge, on to pheasant in November. It's profitable let on a single-day basis. I don't participate anymore but . . . Are you listening to me?"

147

"You been drawing cows, Mrs. Sutherland?" He pointed to cards in front of her.

"They're pedigree forms. Look, left side, right side and front. I draw in the markings of each Friesian heifer—they're all unique, you see—and send them off to the breed society, then they're registered."

"You know each one that well? That's something, that's really something."

"One does, you know." She watched him sifting the batch of cards, momentarily intrigued.

"Want a walk?" he asked.

"Don't be silly, it's dark."

"Would Bung or Ho like a walk?"

"Not in the dark, Leon. They don't like it."

"I looked for you earlier when it was still light."

"I had a school governors' meeting. Otherwise I've been here. What have you done since lunch?"

"Took a nap. Read some. Went downtown on a few errands."

I thought nothing of that incident until, maybe a year later, there it was installed and detailed in my mind.

He was living in the real world beyond my contorting imagination. It was always by accident I'd come upon him with others and watch him converse with people I'd known nearly all my life, lighting them with his interest, vignettes in which I played no part.

Late one afternoon on my way to the kennels with the dogs' bowls I passed the lighted kitchen window and stopped because I heard his voice. My view was mostly of the aluminum saucepans dangling from a rail above the range. Shut behind glass doors on one wall were copper pots and jelly molds which I'd never seen used. Three lightbulbs with white glass shades coated with grease on their upper sides hung in a line over the table where Mrs. Files sat, a chopping block in front of her. She was shredding something by holding the tip of the blade and moving the handle of the knife around in an arc, her head on one side. I could hear singing and moaning from a far corner. Megan must have been there, Mrs. Files's senile aunt whom she brought to work when there was no one else to look after her.

Suddenly a hand shot up in the foreground of my view, something glistened purple in its fingers. I moved backwards and by standing on the low wall that bordered the towering yew hedge, I gained a level view of the kitchen.

Leon lay on his back on the table, with one leg crossed over the other, the preparations for dinner all around him. He was holding an aubergine at arm's length above him, twisting it about, judging it.

"I swear to you," he was saying, "it was this big, Margaret, I'm not kidding. And it kinda looked like this too."

Mrs. Files picked up a tea cloth, buried her face in it, laughing, then shook it at him with delighted outrage.

Margaret. He called her Margaret.

I went inside. I think I thought I wanted to be part of that companionship too but knew it would conclude with my entry. But that didn't have to happen because he was closing the kitchen door behind him as I arrived in the passage.

His face was devoid of any warmth or humor; there was no residue of the merry encounter with Mrs. Files only seconds before (I would never be able to think of her as Margaret).

This was my first understanding of him. What had happened in the kitchen was a calculated wooing, tease, flirtation, safely outrageous. He charmed, teased, involved then abandoned, his mind already on the next thing. He knew just when, and how, to tap, in order to receive at a deeper level than he gave. That was his sadness. He required everyone to love him. Hence his small tokens, unexpected gifts, to me the Arpège, to David the lighter—when David didn't even smoke—to Curtis, the copper bangle. No doubt he had just given something to Mrs. Files.

Dreaming, Leon almost crashed against me, there in the kitchen passage. "Mrs. Sutherland, where are you going?"

I pushed past him into the kitchen. There she was, still radiant from his company, smiling with that freshness that had come over her since his arrival, reflecting on her exchange with him. The imbalance of feeling between them shocked me. "Mrs. Files?"

She glanced up. There was no doubt I intruded even now she was alone. She bustled to the dresser and tucked—I saw it—a small package deep inside the drawer.

After spying him through the kitchen window with Mrs. Files, so much himself, so much not Francis, I thought I didn't want to see him at all. I was even beginning to consider myself freed, until dinnertime that evening.

Every evening he would come down wearing the black cashmere jacket he had worn on the first night, and in a mood that was somehow expectant. "There you are, Mrs. Sutherland," he'd say, as if the sun had risen on seeing me or, indeed, I was the sun. He said it so often I was beginning to expect it, listen for it.

What he imagined those evenings would hold, what possible excitement, was beyond me. I think I just assumed he was that sort of person and nighttime did that to him. Francis was the same.

What happened was an apparently significant incident, like all the rest. Simply that he pushed his plate away, turned sideways in his chair to face me, then stretched, crossed his legs. "What this place needs is proper heating. Only lunatics live in this temperature. An Eskimo wouldn't," he said.

We stared at each other. I was thinking: Why did you do it? Die like that? See how happy we could've been. Look at us now.

I reached over, lifted his hand from where it was resting on the table, toying with a piece of orange peel, and he leaned forward with it, allowing me to take it as near to myself as I wanted. I held it between my own, uncovered it to see the fingers lying on mine: a square hand, fine-boned, fine-textured, not large. I turned it over, turned it back, recovered it. "There are so many things we disagree about," I said. "I wish it wasn't like that, it wastes so much time and that does run out in the end. We know that now, don't we?"

"All right, then," he softly prompted, as though I were speaking lines, "go on."

"Go on what?"

"Go on about the heating. About why not."

I relinquished his hand, heard my voice alter. "I've told you a thousand times we can't afford it, or rather, I'm not going to afford it. It's not in the character of Sleet and besides—"

"Mrs. Sutherland?"

"What?"

"I pay now, remember? And I've never mentioned the heating before." He wasn't looking at me when he said that but into the air at his side as though reading a sad text written there.

I knew it was Leon's hand I'd taken into my own. I may have been speaking to Francis but I'm not certain of that. I believe, perhaps, even then, I was speaking to him, to Leon.

In the usual way we'd have gone to the morning room after dinner and sat awhile. I might have read, checked papers before going up to bed. I had to explain more than once that that was what I did—go to bed early—until he stopped asking. What I was really doing, up there in my private darkness, while below he played my mother's old jazz records and new ones he'd bought, why I really went so early was to have longer imagining him into his father. He was his own father down there and it was that night again when Francis said to me, "Don't go," and this time I hadn't. I was still there, you see, rearranging my jigsaw heart.

That evening Leon didn't follow me into the morning room to sit in the armchair opposite mine, slipped deep into it, his elbows on the arms, fingers linked in front of his face. That evening he didn't come into the room at all.

After waiting some time, instead of going to my bedroom and packing again, as before dinner I'd been so certain, at last, of being able to do, I went in search of him. I called his name in the hall with the dogs standing beside me. His car was still outside; it was the open-top Volkswagen Beetle he'd bought himself on that first day straight from the showroom window. His bedroom door wasn't shut and I listened to the stillness inside. He was obviously not there but I called his name again just the same.

Dinner had been cleared from the dining room, which looked self-conscious and redundant, as dining rooms do when not in use. All that space, all that pomp, for just a bit of food. The kitchen lights were off, Mrs. Files had gone home. There was no one in the staff sitting room, but then, there hadn't been for years.

The dogs followed me along the back passage. I stopped calling Leon's name and felt unreasonably furtive, wished the dogs weren't with me, they made such a noise. At the top of the back stairs I made them wait. On the far side of the landing was the door to Curtis's flat. The knocker was the odious face of a gnome.

I don't know why my search drew me to that part of the house, except that Curtis was the only soul in it other than myself and Leon. I could hardly ask him, Where's Mr. Kennedy? I was hoping, on seeing his face, an excuse for disturbing him would occur to me.

I had gripped the gnome's face when I heard the weaving, low registers of Leon's clarinet. I strained to hear if it was a record but it was that tune, broken in his usual stumbling places. Then a piano joined in. The playing stopped and I could hear their voices, Leon's and Curtis's, just the two of them in there. I didn't knock.

151

I didn't think about Francis anymore that night. I didn't leave either.

Leon gave up wearing the new clothes he'd bought in London, curiously dated, formal stuff, even then, even to my eye. Instead he wore jeans, old ones that had been molded into his own shape. The first time I saw him wearing them was an isolated spring day trying its feet in winter. He was on the lawn outside the morning room throwing a ball for Ho who'd obeyed his commands of "Sit," "Wait," "Go," until I arrived. Even before he saw me Ho lost interest, began scenting about. Leon threw the ball high, running for it himself and falling to catch it just for the pleasure of movement in sunshine. I ambled towards him.

He lay on his back at my feet. I said, "You should wear a sweater, it's not as warm as you think."

"No, but it's sun, Mrs. Sutherland. It's sun." He breathed deeply with his eyes shut and I smelled a baked saltiness coming from his jeans and was reminded of Franky. It was even possible to scent resin oozing from the hot wood of a dock, the air of warmth and freedom. He must have worn those jeans on countless beaches and fishing trips. Looking down at him there on my English grass, under my English sun, I knew he was pretending a tie-dyed sky, glass sea, breeze in a fast boat.

Do you miss it? I wanted to say. Is it terrible, your homesickness? I've known it too. "Lunch is in."

"Mrs. Sutherland?"

He came after me with his arms wide, still dazzled and dazzling in his private powerful light; those pale jeans already crumbling for want of their accustomed humidity. "Mrs. Sutherland, please." He was going to hold me. Intoxicated by a short measure of dilute sun, he was going to hold me.

I waited there on the grass too long. He came very near. His arms nearly enclosed me. "No, stop it. Get away."

But it was I who got away to the steps up to the morning room, Francis's sorry steps.

I did see him, though, standing, looking after me as if he'd been struck, very quiet, very separate. And yes, yes, his hand moved up towards his eye. The sun went in.

We had lunch as usual. He was polite.

Eleven

"M ORE RAIN."
    "It'll pass. My christening . . ." Delia Sutherland's finger
pressed a black-and-white photograph of a woman lifting her hair
away from the grabbing hand of the baby in her arms. "And me on
Mushroom, a Shetland we had once. Not for long, the Caldwells
aren't horsey people."

She had found Leon Kennedy in the ballroom in a wing chair
near the window, a leather-bound photograph album open on his
knee, more on the floor beside him. A sweep of light remained
between frayed brocade curtains, without a gleam on the parquet
floor. He was tipping the album towards the ungiving light, scrutinizing the wide pages. When she entered he said, "Hi there,"
quietly, without removing his attention, his voice resounding along
with her footsteps.

"Albums?"

"Yeah. What a lot of people once. Shooting parties, picnics, fancy
dress. Then the same bunch of faces pop up, standing in exactly the
same positions, doing exactly the same things in front of different
houses. They sure got around."

"People did."

She was drawn closer and ended up sitting on the arm of his
chair, craning past him. "Me at the seaside." She touched the
image of a gawky-limbed child in a knitted swimsuit.

"You always wear that ring, don't you?"

She pulled her hand away, curled it in her pocket. "It was my
mother's. Not good, though. All the good stuff went. Speaking of
which . . ."

"Oh, don't," he said because her voice had changed. He had brought her close by stillness. Now she was gone again.

"No, it's important, Leon. A bill's come in. Seventy-five thousand."

"That's a lot." He reached for another album.

"Seriously."

"Yeah, seriously, that's a lot," utterly impassive.

"Good God, you really have no grasp, Leon, do you? It's my fault, this bill. I changed the fertilizer order to once a year instead of quarterly. It was just after Francis died. I didn't think it through. But it's due and the farm accounts won't take it. You're going to have to sell something and there's hardly anything left to sell. I have to say this is the first time I've been in this position since I took over."

Standing beside one of the fireplaces she touched a dark oil painting. "It's a pity, but this'll have to go."

"No. I like that picture with the little girl passing the corn. It's just so, I don't know, right, somehow."

She made a noise like a laugh. "Leon, you're not even looking at it."

"Not this minute, but I have. It's a favorite of mine."

She angled herself onto a stool. He turned another page. "Who's this baby and you, like, tiny, next to it? Looks like another christening. Same robe."

"My brother. Cot death. Do you know who painted this? He's very famous."

"Sure. I wonder what it is, Mrs. Sutherland, that makes you believe I'm an uneducated man? Hey, the Coronation. Your mom and dad sure had a fine view."

"You've no choice but to sell it. I've run Sleet for twenty-five years. I know what's what."

"It's not business, Mrs. Sutherland, to throw good money after bad."

"You don't know what you're talking about. Buying fertilizer isn't bad money. It's essential."

"Fertilizer's shit."

"Ah." She hurried to the door. "Now I see: you want a row. Well, you're not getting it. I'm going out, but before I go I'll tell you one thing. In all the years Francis and I were married I never asked him for a cent. I ran Sleet myself; under my care it's broken even . . ."

"You mean broken."

He did not say it loudly and she was not sure she had heard right so she continued. "I brought it back from the brink, made the farm, forestry, the shoot self-supporting. And if you think I'm going to bail Sleet out with the money Francis left me when you can't even be bothered to learn the most basic elements of running an estate then you're mistaken."

"Sure. Was there a call for me this morning?"

She was not going to answer but, yes, there had been a call when she was in the estate office waiting to direct a consignment of creosote to the sawmill, otherwise, being a Saturday, the office would have been shut. A man had rung asking for Mr. Kennedy.

"He's not here. Mrs. Sutherland speaking. Can I help?"

"You the secretary, or what?"

"I told you I'm . . ." She rested the receiver. If her name did not explain her then she was no one; not anymore.

The man said, "That is Sleet Park?"

"Yes."

"Only, see, I want the proprietor, Mr. Kennedy. Look, love, never mind. Just give him a message, would you? Say Happyhol Cabins confirm they'll be over Monday to erect. He knows all about it. There's a dear. Bye for now."

"Actually, there was a call. Some nonsense about cabins."

"What did they say?"

"Erecting Monday. So you know about it?"

"Yes."

"What's it all about?"

"A surprise."

"And the bill, Leon?"

"The cabins'll take care of that, Mrs. Sutherland. It's so brilliant I can't wait to tell you." His enthusiasm carried him to her. "I was in the estate office waiting for you a couple of weeks ago and this firm rang. It's such a good idea. Genuine prefab log cabins hitched up to the mains. They're fixing one on Monday so I can see it but I've already talked to other people who've done it and they're so popular. Course the groupings wouldn't be anywhere near the house . . ."

"Groupings?"

155

"Well, you know how people like to be together, even if they're pretending to be in the wild, so I was thinking of groupings of four to six cabins per lot."

"Lot?"

"Yeah, maybe five to six lots to start. Each cabin'll take a family of four."

"I don't understand." But she did; only could not believe.

"Hey, hey, hey." Palms towards her, he sidled past, backing from the room. "I know that face. See you later."

"Come here."

"No, Mrs. Sutherland. Not when you speak to me that way."

"You can cancel that ridiculous little man this minute. How dare you not consult me?"

She followed him to the gunroom, shouting, while he picked up a tweed coat. "I've tried to introduce you here. I've stayed on to help but not once have you met me so much as halfway. If you think I'm going to play manager while you carry on in your feckless manner with lunatic ideas, ignorant of what really . . ."

He passed her, holding his face away from every shouted word, interspersing them with his own but not loud enough to be heard: "Stop it," "This is destructive," "Don't say these things," until in the middle of the hall he thrashed the coat repeatedly against the floor, yelling louder than he had ever done. "That's enough. Jesus, I detest you." And she was silenced as one watching the rerun of an all too familiar catastrophe beyond change. "Don't talk to me about help. Do you really imagine I don't know what you're pretending? That I'm Francis. Why do that, Mrs. Sutherland? Kind of silly, isn't it, when it seems he was such a pain to you? He let you run this place like a fucking doll's house 'cause he loved you. I see it. I see it too. But you remain a cold, remote woman, Mrs. Sutherland. Now let me by."

"Wait. Who said that to you, those things?" He passed her on the stairs. His bedroom door slammed. She did not move.

It would be all right again soon. Later. He didn't mean it. Stand here awhile, calm down and then, and then the rain will have stopped. I'll ask him if he'll walk the dogs with me. He likes to do that. We'll have a drink. Then dinner. We'll do what we always do and everything will be all right.

He returned with an overnight bag in his hand.

"Leon, I wondered if you'd like . . ."

He spoke from the front door. "I can't live like you do with broken tractors and trees lying around, people who can't work properly 'cause I can't afford to let them. And the goddamn government paying me to do sweet nothing with my fields. You're no businesswoman, Mrs. Sutherland, you're lousy at it. This place is moribund. Now, I've got plans, and I hoped I could bring those about while you screwed on with this cockamamy setup. I wouldn't have minded that. I'd have liked it once, Mrs. Sutherland, but you don't care about people at all. I don't find that easy to live with. And I can't live with your abuse. When did you last notice something someone else had done? Or how they felt? I know you enjoy your own company and that's a good thing 'cause it looks like it's the only kind you'll ever get. I'm going away for a while, give you time to pack your things. Maybe that's best. Good-bye."

His voice was subdued and so was hers, "Where are you going?" So subdued that the clock striking four in the dovecote could have drowned it, probably did, because he did not answer her "Don't go, Leon," did not say a word.

I stood at the front door for a long time being soaked by the rain. It was night when I became aware of the dogs whining somewhere and called them. At the sound of my voice they stopped whining so I didn't know where to look. It's often that way with dogs. I tried several places before they tumbled through the ballroom doors. Then I sat down by the letter table. The dogs circled nearby, depressed by my inertia.

Eventually I fed them, shut them in their kennels; didn't go to the dining room where dinner would have been waiting, already cold; instinct walked my weight to Leon's bedroom. The most I'd allowed myself to see of the inside of that room during his three months at Sleet was himself half-naked ruled into a margin of light. Now I was standing at the closed door listening to his absence.

I find myself here and now—at my hotel window, the road below crowded with traffic, the fish market gone until tomorrow, the winter sun lighting the exercise book in which I'm writing these events of nearly three years past—wanting to put down my pen, lean back and wonder at my arrogance, such stubborn obtuseness. But why stop to wonder at the very point where cause for wonder really begins?

Despite Leon's words, despite my certain knowledge that the

spirit of Francis had sailed away after its living son down the drive, out of Sleet to freedom, I entered Leon's room determined to winnow some vestige of that poor ghost, Francis's ghost, from what I would find in there; and, having found it, perhaps my intention was to sit with it awhile uttering such emptinesses as, I'm sorry and, Forgive me.

The blast from a phalanx of heaters struck me on opening the door. There was an electric blower on the dressing table, another on the chest of drawers, two or three bar fires familiar from nursery days; the fumes from three ancient paraffin stoves hovered in such air as was left. Vapors made the light from the bedside lamps unsteady and caused suffering to the roses in vases all around.

Sheet music was open on a stand, "The Isle of Capri"; there was more scattered on the floor. His clarinet lay in its case on the stool at the foot of his bed, the very wide bed Francis bought when we married.

I went to close the curtains and found the windows sealed with silver insulating tape. In the wardrobe his clothes were divided. Pushed to the left were the tweeds and a green three-piece number the texture of a holly bush in a style unseen since the fifties. There was the cashmere jacket he wore every evening. I found my hand on its sleeve, drew it back. On the other side were his own worn clothes, loose, light-colored. With my face in the folds of his jeans I smelled again the salt.

In the chest of drawers were notebooks, some bound in marbled paper, some in kid. There were wooden boxes; bangles made of brass and silver; and more jewelry, bright, semiprecious, some items still wrapped as when they were bought.

Thermal underwear was in another drawer, vests sleeved and buttoned, a pair of long johns. I remembered his amusement about such underwear on his first evening at Sleet, how he subsided into laughter, infectious to everyone but me. Then, alone there in his room, I began to laugh, as I should have laughed at the time. When I touched my face it was wet. This was as surprising as discovering blood from an unsuspected wound. I peered at the photographs on the dressing table. A large studio shot showed Euturpia Kennedy at the age when I first met her, shy hope not yet driven from her eyes. In another frame Leon, about six years old, was embracing his mother from behind and pulling a face, while she stood, hopelessly desirable, in a white dress. A close-up showed the two of them as they were now, toasting each other with mint juleps. The quality of their companionship seemed to me palpable in that colored eight-by-five. There was a large school group with "St. Andrew's College" inscribed on the mount. Leon's features were singular among the rest. He was in the photograph of the baseball team too, looking proud, a giant glove on one hand. There were pictures of him fooling on a mono-ski; triumphant beside a huge fish hauled tail-up by a rope, his arms flung around the necks of two fellows.

I picked up one photograph only: Leon in profile, back to the camera, dancing formally with a girl, his hand raised with hers, his head solicitously inclined to her young, upturned, joyful face.

On the bureau among the pencils, ink, writing paper, was a list:

Toothpaste
Reeds from Mitchell's
Order Johnny Dodds album (get number from Curtis)

14 March: Mrs. S birthday. What? What?

How had he discovered my birthday?

Sticky bottles of cough medicine lined his bathroom shelf. Yes, when I came to think of it, he'd had a cough for some time.

I turned off the heaters. It seemed the safe thing to do. Straightaway the walls, the solid furniture, the dreary curtains took possession, leaving his belongings with the bereft, hastily gathered air of a refugee's luggage.

No need to pack trunks this time. That sort of thing could be seen to. Anyone who says, as I did, leaving isn't simple, is lying. What you do is go. Only one thing struck me as essential: the dogs' bowls from the kennels. They'd be too unhappy without their own battered bowls to settle them in Scotland.

The dogs were surprised when I disturbed them in the middle of the night and they chased in their runs when I left again, strained to see me departing through the rain, and hear the car door opening, their bowls clanking as I threw them inside. The dogs themselves I'd collect at the last minute.

Wet through again I wandered about inside the house touching pictures, clocks, trying to feel loss for these things, but it wouldn't come this time—that sense that had been with me since the reading of Francis's will had vanished. What had it all been about, then?

159

I took the pins from my hair to dry it a bit and it sprang free. Those tears. Those damned tears.

The curtains were open in the morning room, no lights on; the objects insubstantial, abstract, in the varying depths of gray. I sat in my armchair; the fire was cold and so was I, my head shrouded in damp hair.

How do you start to notice people after a lifetime of indifference? If I could take away with me the beginning of such an understanding it would be enough. How's it done? Do you say, "How are you?" to everyone you meet? Do you actually stay to listen when they tell you? How did he come by Mrs. Files's first name? And be invited into Curtis's flat? If I'd been kinder to Leon would he have done those things? Needed to?

He'd be with friends by now. They'd have welcomed him because he is as he is while I was remote, cold. What words; what things to be. Who do you go to to unlearn them? My mother might have taught me. She was another who was loved because she was as she was. There was no one else anymore. My conscience, unmoved by this self-pity, kept asking: Why did you stay, Delia? And I answered aloud, "Because I didn't want to leave him." Who didn't you want to leave? "It could've been a life," I said. "I would've learned." And Conscience said: No, you wouldn't.

The door opened and I covered the terrible state of my face with hair. "Sorry, Curtis. Did you think I was a burglar? Nothing to worry about. Back to bed." And I thought then that maybe I should ask him how he was. It'd be a start. But not now. He must go away so I could too.

"Mrs. Sutherland?"

"Leon. I thought you were Curtis."

"Ah." He hesitated. "Your hair. It's, it's huge."

"Yes. Yes. It does that when it's free and a bit damp, you know, rain and all." I was standing, although couldn't remember getting up and, unable to think what to say, sat down again. I nearly said, What are you doing here? Rubbed the words off my mouth in time. "How are you?"

"Very well, thank you." He came quite close. "Can I touch it?"

"My hair? Oh heavens. Well, yes. Why not? Gosh. Who'd want to?"

He rubbed it between his fingers, staring with admiration, then

160

sank, cross-legged, near my chair, the way he'd done on his first night.

"Fire's dead," he said.

"Yes."

"Went to my room. They're off in there too."

"I didn't know when you were returning. Thought it was dangerous to leave them on. Don't think I'm hanging around. I'm not. You haven't given me enough time."

"No. I know."

"So."

"Do you want to know where I went?"

"To see friends?" He shook his head so I said, "Well, it doesn't matter. Not my business."

"I went to find a hooker, Mrs. Sutherland."

He watched my face while I touched the top of my head, patted the arms of the chair, folded my hands away in my lap. "Well, people do, don't they? Men. 'Men have needs,' that's what Francis used to say. 'Needs.' 'So have I,' I used to say. But I don't think we were understanding each other."

"So I checked into Park West, had dinner, got talking to the barman, said what I was after. He asked what I liked, dark, fair, black, white. It was like ordering in; which I guess it was. He was serving other people all the while and making out we were talking about the Superbowl. Experience, I guess.

"I went back to my room and soon a girl came with flat blond hair, sickly-looking. Very young. She was real brisk. I could tell she was a user. I've never had a hooker before so I didn't know the form. It's just the kind of situation where a man feels he's the only guy in the world who doesn't know the form and it's embarrassing. She was very young. Did I tell you that already?"

"Yes."

"She asked me what I wanted. Do you know what I said? Jesus, it's pathetic, but I'd had a few bourbons . . ."

"They have it in the Park West, then?"

Pinching his lower lip he studied me sideways. "That's right. That's right. Do you mind me telling you all of this, Mrs. Sutherland? Was your joke to stop me?"

"No. What did you tell her you wanted?"

"I said I wanted . . ." His hand distorted the word.

"What? I didn't hear."

161

"Never mind. If I could've chosen I would've got a girl more sophisticated, talk awhile, have a few drinks, then screw. She wasn't that. She was in a hurry to get the money for her fix. She started undressing. I've never seen anything so fast; then she began on me and I said to wait. Why? she said. Was I shy? Did I want something special? I only had to ask. I said I wanted time. She looked kind of disgusted and then, like, eased me back into a chair. She had real strength in her. She sort of collapsed me at the knees and I was down there. Then she unzipped me and sucked me off. Just like that. She tried undressing me again and I said no, she'd better go, that I'd changed my mind. She said the price'd be the same. She didn't know it but I'd have paid her double to get her ass out. I can't believe I'm telling you all this."

"Why?"

"Why can't I believe it? Christ, Mrs. Sutherland."

"No. Why did you take a whore? You must have friends, contacts in London. You're so, so . . . There'd be someone in no time."

"There's no one, really. Yes, I have some numbers. But you know how it is, answerphones and stuff. It takes time, all that. I needed it then."

"Sex?"

"Maybe. Sure, why not? But mostly what goes with it, like warmth. I don't know."

"I see."

"I miss her, you know."

His eyes filled, but he did not know it was happening, this over-flowing, until I reached down, wiped his face, showed him my wet fingers which he dried with his own.

"Who? Who do you miss?"

"Mamma. She'd say to me you fight on, Leon. Fight on, boy. You're gonna be okay. There's nothing for you here, she'd say, nothing here that you can't come back and buy. Take your place there."

"You can ring, surely, and have her visit? Is it me here that's stopped you? Well, I'm gone now. Call her today."

"I can't do that."

"It'd be kind." Me, all of a sudden, a connoisseur of kindness.

"She died before I came over, Mrs. Sutherland. I would've thought you knew that."

"No one told me."

"David could have. He knew. But you saw her, you must've known she was sick. Crack, that's what it was. She was into it when I got back from college. I lied to you, Mrs. Sutherland. She didn't want me as a kid. She was a kid herself, making good. I could've found her. I knew where she was, the fancy house in Delaporte, any night at the Big Bamboo. But I wanted to be the Somebody when I came back to her. Corny, right? But, you know, in those months we had together she really tried to make up. When we heard about the will she put her arms around me and said, "You go there and fight on, boy. Fight on." That made me feel good, having those words from her. She didn't want me around 'cause she was sure I'd get hooked too. She was wrong, but it's easy when it's everywhere like it is there. There's a lot she knew about the danger. I couldn't leave her, not after so long finding her. And I couldn't bring her either, she wouldn't have it, and she wouldn't have made it anyway. So I waited while she died, and she wasn't slow. She'd had enough.

"So anyway, Mrs. Sutherland, she can't come, can she? And I don't hear those words, "Fight on, boy," or feel those long arms around me like I dreamed about for years and years. Sometimes it's okay. And other times it's not." He dug his face into his knees.

The cold in the room was awful. I turned over the ashes, found the glow within the crust, added some kindling and a log, then stood to stretch with my hands in the small of my back because it was aching. I lifted my hair, let it fall, and the weight of it brought my head down to see that Leon hadn't moved.

Outside, Mike was calling the cows through the dark to morning milking. Bung was howling; Ho joined him intermittently. The dovecote clock struck five; the clock on the mantelpiece behind me struck fourteen, mad as ever.

I rolled up my sleeves, those tartan sleeves, still damp, closed my forearms together and saw arms which, the same as the rest of me, had received no care.

"Leon?" I said, still looking at my arms. When he didn't answer I crouched in front of him. "Leon?" But he wouldn't lift his head so I put my hand to his cheek, which startled him, slid it under his chin and lifted his face. I drew my arms together again in front of him, doubtful about my offering. "Would these arms do?"

He drew my arms around him; he kissed the palms of my hands and drew my arms around him without speaking. I stayed wooden, afraid of the power that let me say those words; afraid to hold him too hard or too close. To move would be to give myself away and frighten him as much as I was frightened.

He knelt up in front of me, our bodies touching from shoulder to knee, his hands in my hair, his mouth at the side of mine. The temperature of his skin was so much the same as mine I hardly knew we touched, yet I remained very still, my hands laid on his shoulders with the exaggerated formality of one learning to dance. Which, of course, I was.

He whispered something but so close to my ear the sound was distorted and I said, suppressing my voice to no more than a breath because it can be so harsh, "Say it again. I didn't hear."

So he said it again, "Help me."

I can't say touch for touch how we became lovers because, really, we had been ever since he came into the room and found me still there, waiting and pretending. I don't know, either, how I left the room later. I've no pictures in my head to describe, can't make them up. It was cold, though, I remember that, on moving away from him. No doubt the fire had died again. But was I still wearing some of my clothes or carrying them all bundled in my arms? He was watching me. Or was he with his arms over his head on the floor?

Yes, one picture does come to mind: before I broke away we lay facing, learning each other's features in this new light. I touched a hair away from his lower lip, kissed the place where it had been, then I left him.

I went into my bed and slept free of any kind of consciousness. Maybe it lasted half an hour, that sleep, it couldn't have been longer because there was still no daylight when I was woken, although he didn't mean to wake me.

I was on my side, facing away from the door, the covers had been drawn from me. I turned my head and, partially blinded by my chaos of hair, saw Leon kneeling naked at my back. His hands covered his face until he brought them into fists in front of him, in the way he often did, then he opened his arms along the length of me; his palms warm, close, without touching, cruised first my shoulder, then the weight of my breast under my hair, my hip, my stomach. This body of mine in which I had taken no pleasure or pride, he was honoring, saying to it, "I love you, I love you, I love you," believing me to be asleep, and I let him go on believing. "I love you, I love you . . ."

He didn't leave me but brought the covers over us both and closed his body around mine in a grip that was painful, miraculous, unceasing. He bent his head into the hollow at the back of my neck. His fingertips traveled until they found my own and, with the lightest returning pressure, I let him know it was all right.

Twelve

IN THE MORNING I woke alone and that was all right too. Were anyone alive to be framework to the relationship, I thought, he'd be my stepson, and, yes, even that was all right. I dressed slowly to preserve as long as possible the space between love and tomorrow. Last night had been a gift, a lesson, complete and over. I'd confronted what I'd come to fear most during the past three months, the power of his need for me, and, yet again, it was all right. In fact it had been glorious. I pulled on my Sunday church skirt, buttoned my blouse to the neck. It had been fine to be the woman he made me, one whose body was beautiful, and to wrap him in my limbs with all the strength of my life. But that was that. Had to be.

I was about to knock on his door when I heard him: footsteps, a cough, hangers scratching the wardrobe rail, a tap running in the bathroom. Inexplicably those sounds prevented me from entering. His room exuded the same exclusive privacy I'd felt those nights I prowled, listening to his music. I attributed it then to the guilt of the eavesdropper. Now, this morning, even after my dancing lesson, I still could not make myself go in there.

There was movement in the shabby silver of the mirror opposite, someone in it was turning away from Leon's door towards me, furtive, alarmed at having been caught. I leaned across an azalea. The same one Curtis had placed there so long ago, blossoming on into the gloom in such an unlikely fashion? Coming close to the mirror, I saw, peering back at me, the Bony Lady.

I freed the dogs from their kennels and tried to enjoy their greeting me with particular enthusiasm, as though they'd guessed change had been in the air but not arrived and were grateful. They bounded around me while I said to them, "Silly boys, get on, now."

When, eventually, I returned to the house, there was no trace of breakfast in the dining room, no sign of Curtis at all. Through the kitchen doorway I saw Leon standing by the window, tilting a newspaper to the light, and yes, yes, yes. But it was only Leon I saw. Not Francis. He inclined his head to me, followed with his eyes; he smiled. "Morning, Mrs. Sutherland."

I stepped back into the passage. Mrs. Sutherland? Is this how it's to be? Pretend nothing's happened? I can't do that. If there had been the least hint of facetiousness I might have believed he was joking. Call me Delia—was I to say that? How, after all this time, was I going to wrap up the intimacy of my name and pass it to him, if he wasn't going to accept it as his own, the way he'd done with my body? Could it be he didn't like my name any more than Francis had?

From the shadow of the passage, where he couldn't see my face, I said, "There's no sign of Curtis. I think I'd better check on him."

"He'll be fine. I gave him the day off. It's crazy him working weekends at his age."

"He doesn't have to. He just does."

"Well, I told him not to."

"You mean, without consulting me you just . . ."

He dropped the newspaper and came to me, wrestling my arms into his while I tried to get away. "Stop this. It's me, for Christ's sake. Don't do it anymore."

"I saw me just now in the mirror, Leon."

"Just you don't. Come on. See what I've done? Coffee, which I have to tell you Margaret doesn't know how to make, and I squeezed oranges. Sit down here."

So I did as I was told, sat at my own kitchen table. He was right, the coffee was good. There was a small package beside my plate. "Open it," he said, "it's for you." Inside was a notebook bound in marbled paper with a long cord through its spine so it could be worn round the neck. He reached across to show me how. "You're always taking notes, making lists then losing them. I've noticed that. This way you won't lose them."

I showed delight, I think. It was one of the many similar ones I'd seen in his drawer, among the jewelry and the scented wooden boxes, things of whose existence I shouldn't have been aware; gifts bought in advance of acquaintance or occasion, as though giving were part of a stratagem, his stratagem. I felt ashamed, knowing his implication, that his gift had been selected just for me, was a lie. The shame for myself was mixed with pity for him.

He reached across the table taking pins from my hair, rifling his fingers through to help it fall, stopping my protests with his hand over my mouth. His arms were around my neck, our foreheads pressed together, when Curtis cleared his throat.

I rerolled my hair and Leon swung himself onto the table, banging it with his fist. "Jesus, Curtis. Didn't we agree you're off?"

"Yes, Mr. Kennedy, only I came to empty the churn, put the milk in the fridge. Such a waste otherwise."

Greater than my confusion, embarrassment, was my astonishment. Curtis was wearing no jacket, not even a shirt, only a long-sleeved vest with the buttons undone; his usual striped trousers had the top fastener lolling open and his belly was something remarkable, a wobbling, low-slung edifice pulling the braces taut. His trousers had been let out on the back seam, leaving a deep V of fresher cloth from waist to mid-hip. His hair framed his head in stiff unbrushed tufts. He was aged, slowed, reduced by the slacking of formality. I did not want to see.

He hauled the gallon churn from the step of the yard door, tipped the two pints it contained into a jug, stored the jug in the refrigerator, washed the churn, returned it to the step. Never had time passed so slowly and we could think of nothing to say. When he'd retreated to the passage, and it was too late for me to answer without raising my voice, he called, "Morning, Miss Delia."

We listened to the brushing of his slippers dying away along the flagstones.

"No corset," Leon said.

"He wears one?"

"Yeah. Seen it in his flat and . . ."

"Don't tell me more. It was ugly, what just passed."

"His belly?"

"You know very well. Him seeing me. Me seeing him. It's not right, or fair."

"You're human beings, Mrs. Sutherland, not archetypes."

I thought: Playing archetypes is what makes false relationships possible, especially in a place like Sleet, but you'll learn. You'll learn things the way I've had to. Besides, what was he making me with his "Mrs. Sutherland," if not an archetype?

"Look, Leon, I'm going upstairs now and when I come down—" There must have been something in my voice because he linked his fingers over the side of my shoulder, his forehead lowered against it as though at a prie-dieu.

"Don't. I know what you're planning to say, Mrs. Sutherland. But please don't. Not yet."

With my eyes closed I took a breath to speak and felt his fingers tighten. I summoned Delia Sutherland the authoritative. "Very well. I'm going to church now but when I get back perhaps you'd like to show me where you're going to put your dreary little cabins?"

So Delia Sutherland, the respected matron, went to church. I sat alone in the Caldwell pew, as usual. Little of it meant anything to me, as usual. The difference was my elation. I'd never felt elation in church before until, sweeping from the pages of the hymnal, came a vision of Euturpia Kennedy naked in the shadow of the sea-grape tree. Francis was with her, holding her close. Her leg lifted high around his waist, she was leaning back over his arm, right back, laughing.

My singing mouth remained open, silent. Dead now, I told myself, both dead. Another vision superimposed the first. Euturpia, the raddled addict, in her office with a universe of suffering blowing through her eyes.

I inched out of the church with the rest of the congregation, all of us slowed by having to greet the vicar. Seeing me, he bent his head into his surplice, a preening pigeon with pale eye cocked. "Not gone yet, then, Delia? That's nice. Will we be meeting Mr. Kennedy soon?"

At first prepared for rejection, Leon came to my room only after I had turned off the light. Soon he would arrive while I was reading before settling. Not long after that he was wandering between my bedroom and his, half-dressed, brushing his teeth, impatient to deliver every thought that entered his head.

His use of my name, always without the least trace of irony, transformed "Mrs. Sutherland" into a term of endearment. Nothing matters, I told myself. For a while longer let nothing matter.

Soon people were avoiding me. Mrs. May, when I visited Forester's Cottage to discuss a new thatch, pretended she was out. I saw her, behind the curtain, waiting for me to leave. The younger men on the farm still spoke to me, only there was an edge to their attention that made me uncomfortable. Of course everyone was wondering why I hadn't left; of course they thought they knew the reason. And they did.

I doubt if two weeks passed before our new relationship was common knowledge. However discreet we tried to be, Mrs. Files's knowing eye and lusty networking had the better of us. What could I do about that except tell myself that people treasure their prejudices? Denied one, they'll replace it with another. With fascinating ease Leon had made himself liked, accepted. No resignations had been received on account of his taking over. Not even from Frank Grimwood. Perhaps this was because he couldn't find employment elsewhere, or because his son had been employed by Leon in connection with the holiday cabins. Any residual prejudice towards Leon was offset against outright condemnation of me. I avoided the farm.

Standing with Holland May in New Hope, a forty-acre plantation of beech, ash and oak, he said to me, "Staying a bit, then?"

"Yes. A bit. Did so many have to go?"

"Seems so, Mrs. Sutherland. Those Happyhol men aren't even sure we've cleared enough yet."

"You've worked so fast."

"Mr. Kennedy had me bring in contractors."

"I see, of course."

"They're starting to put up the cabins tomorrow." Holland pointed to stacks of prefabricated log walls covered in black sheeting at the side of the wood that was the same age as me, planted to celebrate my birth, and he'd been one of those to set the scores of saplings.

My father used to carry me there when I was a baby. When I was old enough to walk, my arm would ache from reaching to keep hold of his hand while he told me why they'd been planted, how there'd been a party when the last one was dug in. He'd tell me this every time we went there and I never tired of hearing it. If it seemed he was going to forget this litany I prompted him, asked, "And how long will my trees live, Daddy?"

"Long past your day, old girl. Friends for life."

Nearly a third had been felled to make way for the cabins; felled and dragged away one after another by chains at the back of a tractor leaving behind great ruts in the ground and the vivid sores of their amber stumps among the standing trees. Violet smoke from the heaps of burning branches roamed so thick it was hard to breathe.

Holland said, "Smarts, doesn't it?" And I tried to look into his faraway eyes (like those of a sailor, they all have them, the foresters) so he could see that my smarting eyes were only due to the fires, and that I could bear it, all this.

"It's good business, Holland. It'll make the forestry pay properly. Amenity woodland, that sort of thing." And listen to me, I thought.

He scanned the scene, pushed his cap back, scratched his head. "Still. Smarts the eyes, though." He wouldn't face me.

I'd avoid New Hope after that and on leaving turned for a last view. Holland was watching me. I raised my arm to him. He didn't return the gesture and the scene was erased by smoke.

How could I possibly expect him to understand?

Leon continued to enthuse about his project, talked about a profit. I didn't try to make him see sense about the capital outlay, the seventy-five thousand due on the fertilizer, because, of course, I'd pay. I'd make it all right. It excited me that I could do that. But would I pretend to let him sail down that stream to bankruptcy, bailing him out all the time so he never arrived? No, I wanted him to understand I'd pay. So what was my scheme? To support financially his wild ideas, because I did still consider them wild? My way to make him need me more?

The luxury was rising most noticeably in the food we ate: quail, fillet steak, turbot, wild rice, champagne sauces, all cooked to a standard of which I had believed Mrs. Files incapable.

In the kitchen one morning Mrs. Files's Auntie Megan set up a racket the minute I entered, drumming her feet on the cupboard doors. When Mrs. Files brought her to work, Megan's day would be passed in a corner of the kitchen, imprisoned in a chair with a tray fixed to the front of it. Most annoying of all was that she was usually half-dressed. This seemed to me unnecessary, unkind and somewhat unhygienic.

Mrs. Files reached a floury hand to switch off the radio, saying,

"Now, now, Auntie, that's enough of that," and Mrs. Files pulled her away from the cupboard leaving her to stamp ineffectually on the stone floor. "Sorry about the nightie, Mrs. S, I know you don't like it, but tantrums this morning and there was no time to dress her"—raising her voice—"was there, Auntie, eh? Who was a naughty girl, then?" Mrs. Files returned to rolling pastry on a marble, her back to the window, the light all on me. "You look well, Mrs. S, if you don't mind my saying. Very well."

"You look well too, Mrs. Files." And she did.

"Well, he keeps me on the go, Mr. Kennedy. Livens me up, and that's not such a bad thing, is it? And he's appreciative," tending her pastry with a sealed smile.

When I told her what I had come for, to see the receipts from the fishmonger, the butcher, the new suppliers we must have been using, she paused to wipe her hands on her chest, flat, white-aproned. I waited, only she took up her rolling pin again without a word, continued to work. A mute and fleeting defiance because she said, "Very well, Mrs. S. I'll have to see where I've put them," but it was enough to show she regarded her compliance as a favor, that, in her view, I wasn't the one in charge.

From deep in the dresser drawer she produced a book; a book bound in marbled paper, with a leather spine, the receipts tucked into it, fluttering around its edges. Involuntarily I covered my own marbled notebook hanging at my breast. She saw the movement and held hers towards me. "Nice, aren't they?"

Megan screeched, "Lemme out, lemme out. You've no right to keep me here. I'll tell the authorities . . ." and continued over Mrs. Files's "Later, Auntie, love. Cup of tea in a minute, pet." Fury unassuaged, the old lady worked herself low into the chair until her head was on the seat, her nightdress a ruff about her neck, her naked lower-half thrust forward, legs splayed and kicking.

Leon peered around the door, "Hey, Margaret, what's the racket?"

Seeing for himself what it was, he went to stand in front of Megan, hands on hips, head inclined in a critical fashion. He might have been at an art gallery, stating dispassionately, "You know, Megan, that's not a pretty sight."

She froze, legs in the air; her face still invisible. "Are you the authorities?"

We knocked shoulders in our hurry to leave and fell through the

172

open door of the silver vault, so as not to be heard laughing, as we were, like a couple of drunks. Simultaneously we became aware we were not alone in that windowless space, with green baize shelves, where the silver was stored in bags. Perched on a stool at a high pine table, sharp knees bent at right angles, pink cloth in hand rubbing at a fork, was Curtis. He let us gape at him while he held the fork to the light above his head, examining his work, before saying, "I've told Mrs. Files before that if she has to bring Auntie in it's knickers on. She never listens."

Bunching his withered lips he blew fastidiously, rubbed again before his eyes met ours. Very green, they were, I'd never noticed quite the depth of it, and sharp with humor.

No receipts from Mrs. Files. Didn't ask again.

Only later in the afternoon, the notebook knocking against me as I walked the dogs, did the memory of a certain kind of distress come back to me. I put the notebook away in a place where I wouldn't see it anymore.

Thirteen

NOW THIS IS INTERESTING: I haven't been back to the New York for some days, not since they took the tables in—as I've mentioned, I shall do so when I'm in the mood to buy the silk flowers for her lapel. Having selected the New York, I don't want to frequent another café. I walk past each morning and I've noticed that the waiter, the supercilious young waiter who brought my postcard back at the old lady's instruction, comes out when I pass. He nodded to me the other day, yesterday he smiled as well. It's taken four months and my lost custom to earn that smile. I think I rather like the French. Here's the interesting thing: this morning, a fine clear morning, there was one table and a single chair outside the New York. I couldn't pass on, could I?

"I'm sorry. I guess you want to sit here, only it's got the light. I'll only be a minute," Leon said.

"No, no, that's all right. Carry on."

He was in my chair in the morning room, that chair into which I'd shoved a cushion between seat and back to make it just right for me; the one beside which there used always to be a bundle of files awaiting my attention. Not anymore, though. "I'll sit over here."

His head was hung so close to papers on his lap I worried for his eyesight. He reached for the brass angle-lamp behind him, centering its beam.

We had been lovers for over two months and there was ease between us. I could have disturbed him, settled myself on the floor between his legs, hugging them. I often did. Then I would have leaned my head back and we would have kissed and kissed before he returned to his work and I opened my book. We would have

174

done that; it was the way we liked to be. But that evening, watching him struggle with what I knew were sums that wouldn't balance, I had something to say.

"What are you doing?" although I knew.

He answered, distracted, "These, these goddamn figures. The cabins. You know."

Reaching down the neck of his pullover, he produced a calculator from his shirt pocket and sank back into the chair, tapping it, glowering from time to time at the pages.

I spread the fire with the poker and, shoulder to the mantelpiece, watched him. If my expression then could have been kept, bottled, we would see, suspended in formaldehyde, smug, upper-hand love, relishing itself. And it would have been worth keeping, a collector's item, because it was the last time I'd ever look that way.

"Do the figures balance, Leon?"

He scratched his ankle, shook his head. "The little suckers don't say what I want, but I'll make 'em. Just you wait." He looked up. "I'm sorry, Mrs. Sutherland, I'll be there in a minute. I hate screwing around this way of an evening. It's not civilized."

"Have you thought at all about the fertilizer bill?"

"They're just going to have to wait. Only a couple of weeks now."

"Then what, Leon?"

"Then I'll make it okay. All right? So don't worry. You can buy all the shit you want soon."

"Due to the cabins?"

"And such," his mind back on the papers.

"Listen to me, Leon." My tone was intended to make him put down his papers and he did. "I've paid the fertilizer bill. All right? And it's not a loan. It's to keep things going until, well, until the cabins pay. If they do."

He stared at me until my smile became an embarrassment. Placing his work aside he walked to the Chinese boys, my Chinese boys. With his hands in his pockets and his back to me he said, "Why did you do that?"

"Because you needed help. It had to be paid, Leon. You don't understand yet but . . ."

He swung round. The table with my boys shuddered and I said, "Careful," very quickly, not very loudly, misunderstanding his force, mistaking it for carelessness.

"No," he shouted. "You're the one who doesn't understand. I talked to those guys, the fertilizer people. They knew they were getting paid. It was agreed, the timing. I don't want your money, Mrs. Sutherland. Hear me? I told you that. You had no business paying any debt of mine, of Sleet, behind my back."

Still I hadn't caught up with him and was, maybe, good heavens, shaking my head, features squeezed to indulgent exasperation. "Leon, please. I want to. I can't simply stand by and see you struggle. Look at you with your figures. Do you really believe you can make them work? Come on. Seriously?"

The quiet lasted so long I picked specks of mud caked on my black knitted dress; that one with the wide sash to make me look less tall. His expression was a version of my own, my collector's item, but his wasn't smug, it was compassionate.

"Listen, Mrs. Sutherland, thank you, because I know you didn't want to lend me money. You said so. I can see what a decision it must have been for you." This was all very measured, controlled. "But you should know now that I don't need your money because I have my own."

"You have something, yes, presumably from your mother. She told me she'd made money. But, seriously, Leon, how much can it be?"

"Why do you do that?"

"What?"

"Why do you always scratch at your palm when you talk about my mom?"

"Do I?"

"Yeah. Every time."

"Oh."

"You're right. There was money from her but not serious money like I need to get Sleet up and running, so I'm selling thirty acres. Ragge Down, in fact. It's prime development land. We put in for planning a couple of weeks back."

"We? We?" Yes, oh yes, I was screaming. He wasn't.

"David Rosen and me."

I'd regained my own chair at last. "David hasn't been here for months. Not since you came."

"We meet in London, we talk on the phone. Come on, Mrs. Sutherland. He's embarrassed to come here for me when he's spent all those years coming for you. I appreciate that. Don't you?"

Ragge Down, where my mother used to course her lurchers? Where we used to hold Harvest Festival parties? Where Daddy raced Valentine Harbroke on Arab ponies because he got drunk and bet any fool could ride a horse and Daddy fell off at full gallop, was blinded for ten minutes, leg broken in three places? Ragge Down where I sowed wheat last year? And where that old badger has emerged? That Ragge Down? "I know Ragge Down."

"I guess you do."

"You're destroying Sleet. Breaking it up. It's finished. You don't understand: you must never, never sell land. Once you've begun there's no end to it. It's not too late. Don't do it."

"I must. It's four miles from this house, Mrs. Sutherland. We'll never know the difference and they need more homes that way; it's an expansion area. The planners are pleased. And I'm not destroying the place. This is how to make it work. It's only thirty acres and it gives me the capital I need."

I don't know what I looked like but whatever it was made him come over, kneel with his head in my lap, his arms stretched along my thighs, and say, "Don't look that way. I hate it."

I wanted to touch his hair, of course I wanted to. I didn't. I only stared at his head there in my knees.

"That's why I didn't tell you," he was saying. "I couldn't think how. I didn't want to see you like this."

"I'd give you all the capital you need for your, well, your projects. Francis left me a great deal. What's wrong with taking it from me instead of selling Sleet?"

"Please don't ask. Please. If I can't make you see, then just, just . . . I don't know." He was rocking himself and me. "You'll be so pleased when it all works. I know you will."

He fell aside when I got up. "Here we are again," I said. "More loss for me, more outrage for me to accept. Well, no, Leon. I can't do it, stay watching all this."

I'd nearly reached the door when he wrenched me around and I remember his eyes for two things, first the anger but beyond that, far beyond, the fear. "No. You're not doing this to me again. Don't say you're leaving me 'cause you're not. You can't. You mustn't. Every time something comes up you don't like you try to leave me. You say you love me but—" His voice was different, higher, uncontrolled.

"Leon."

177

"Stay to talk things through. Come on, come on," bringing me back into the room.

"Leon."

"Yes, yes. Talk. Explain. We can understand each other. I know we can."

"I never said I loved you."

He let go of me; regained his normal voice. "But you do. I know you do."

"Maybe, but don't tell me I've said something I haven't."

"Then don't say you're going."

"Then take my money. Don't sell Sleet."

"I'm not selling Sleet, only thirty acres to save the rest. Why can't you accept that? I don't want your money. I want to do it myself."

"Then what is it you want of me? Sit and knit while you wreck the place? What in God's name is it you want? Well?"

He rounded his shoulders, brought his fists to his temples carefully, tentatively speaking out the vision from his cradled brain. "I want you to be. Just *be*, Mrs. Sutherland. Why can't you relax in my love? I just want you to be there. Here. Like that. Like you are."

I closed the door; left him in there. Went to my room. The Bony Lady sneered at me from inside the mirror on the kidney-shaped dressing table. Vanity, that's what they say, isn't it, of those who study themselves in mirrors? But I was seeking confirmation or, at least, a reminder of existence. I was also confronting a face I'd disliked, regarded as unlovable, taking stock of its features and the minute degrees of change, the softening, the setting free. Equally I was conducting a futile search for what was there to make him watch me, in moments when he thought I didn't see, with such penetrating tenderness. I wanted to find that and so, perhaps, preserve it.

"What are you doing?" His face appeared beside mine.

"Looking for myself."

He hunched beside me on the stool, his back reflected in the mirror, shirttail hanging. We were close without touching, facing our different ways.

"So you won't go, then?"

I watched the Bony Lady's image until it wavered, fused with one I recognized as my own. "No. Not yet."

He left me, returned with his clarinet.

I put a match to the fire in the grate that I had been using since he had been spending his nights with me—found it made up one day, when it never had been in the past, presumably by Curtis. Of course by Curtis.

Couched in the armchair I waited while Leon walked around sucking on a new reed to moisten it, and frowning, considering what to play. "Okay, listen. See if you remember what this one's called."

His complete absorption was beguiling. There was a great deal in life, beyond his music, from which he drew pleasure. His plans for the garden, choosing what to grow in the greenhouses once they had been restored, business projects for Sleet. To all of this, and to those associated, he brought the same concentrated enjoyment. Now, as his hands with which I was so familiar worked over the silver keys, he was submerged in his music, in a safe place.

My background was being dismantled by him, only I was coming to wonder if there might not be greater disciplines than those I had previously served. Wasn't he inviting me with him into that safe place, one which had less to do with possession than acceptance and relinquishment? He laid aside the clarinet. "Right, what was it called?"

"That's . . . don't tell me, I know it. It's, it's 'Saturday Night Blues.' Bechet."

"Very good, Mrs. Sutherland. You've been studying."

"I've had time."

"Now listen to this one. You don't know it yet. Sit down. Be comfortable." He returned the clarinet to his full, pale lips.

I knew I was trapped. The cycle of row, attempted departure, only to remain, always remain, had been set up from the night he arrived. Each time I conceded more, accepted that what I had to teach was not required; what I had to give already taken. All the time we were coming closer; without explanation or understanding.

When he leaped into my bed, lean, agile, eager, I'd be reminded of one of my mother's lurchers who, after she died and before they were given away, had taken to leaping, just like that, into my bed at dawn. The memory made me smile. He smiled too in my night-bright bedroom, no doubt at some recollection of his own. Sometimes I think the closer the bodies the further the minds. He sat astride my legs, drew me up, close to him. In a voice rough from its journey through feeling, he would say, "Thank you. Thank you."

"What for?"

"Just, thank you."

And I'd try to drink from his mouth the sincerity with which he gave his love, so that I, defensive, cynical, hidebound Delia Sutherland, could return the same; as I had once, for five minutes, a thousand years ago to his father.

In the morning I'd leave him in a lavish sleep, just conscious enough to grasp my wrist as I bent to kiss whatever showed of his head in a whirlpool of pillows, sheet, blanket. "No. Come back. Too early. Much too early." By the time I'd breakfasted and walked the dogs he'd be in his own bed where Curtis would bring his tray.

What nurture he found in me I'd no idea. But he did, and was strengthened. He planned projects he couldn't share with me, and those spawned into further appalling projects, rubbing out meaning to my existence at Sleet, the only environment in which I'd ever flourished.

I was counting, never costing, every minute we spent together because there had to be an end. There had to be an end. I dared not acknowledge there could be something as remarkable as to-morrow-still-together.

Leon curtained anything from his mind, anything but the present we shared. He was content, busy and becoming fulfilled: the holiday cabins, a livery stable, riding school and worst of all (even now I find it hard to write the words) a two-hundred-acre golf club. Agriculture as an expanding business was dead, he believed, the future was in leisure. I'm ashamed to say I wasn't sufficiently greathearted to admit highly paid professionals had been advising me that for some years. No doubt he had the same advisers.

I had all the time in the world to watch the inevitable being set on track around me and so fast.

Relaxing in a deck chair at the foot of the morning-room steps, I was struck by something written by André Maurois: "The dangerous age afflicts those women who have been cheated of a woman's life. It is they who, when signs show that the body is aging, are obsessed by regrets which turn to manias."

Perhaps I should have panicked then. After all, I hadn't had children. Was that what Maurois meant by "a woman's life?" Was Leon my mania? Was it recognition of imbalance in the order of things that had provoked me to try to leave so often? But I hadn't invented Leon's need for me, nor the form that that need took. Nor had I invented my necessity to supply it. It was only going to require the slightest hint that there was indeed selfishness on my part, or greed for him, for what he gave me, to make me run, to cut, to go. Right then, at that time, such a course had become inconceivable because he was as familiar to my spirit as I was to his.

All right, I'd lost my work, my position. My only remaining responsibility was as a governor at St. Mary's. Hardly onerous. Yet I was tranquil and he was strong. Should I mention the life which, sometimes, I would remind him was waiting for me—the small-holding in Scotland, the flock of sheep—he would shout, "Stop it," or just, "No." After that he would appear disappointed in himself, as though he were failing some standard only he under-stood. He might slam the palm of his hand against anything that was near, a wall, a chair, a tree.

Then, frustration relieved, he would return with even greater tenderness and some plan. A visit to a tree nursery, restoration of the neglected folly by the lake, an evening in London at Ronnie Scott's.

Anything shared bound us closer. Waiting for me to agree he watched my face, smiling beyond the panic in my eyes and his. He believed I had the capacity, when it came to it, to go, just go. He was right. That was my sadness.

Curtis found me in the house at hours when he had had the run of it, caring for the things he loved best. "Can't be bothered with dailies," he had said. "Too much trouble, better off doing it my-self, then I know it's done." Which it wasn't.

Sitting, in my deck chair again, at the bottom of the morning-room steps, I heard movement behind me. Curtis had arrived with a stepladder to polish the books in the glass-fronted bookcase. I didn't move from my place in the sun. "Still at it, then, Curtis," I called over my shoulder, "the books?"

"Forth Bridge, Miss Delia. No sooner finished than you start again. I'll be back on Vertue soon. I do enjoy him. *Sculptures par G. Vertue*. Such a lovely tone of red and he responds so well to a little rubbing. Quite worth the effort."

He positioned his ladder before coming to stand beside me, a sweep of gray apron by my eye, his chest dubiously hoisted. Why had I never guessed a corset? The engraved copper bangle was on his wrist.

"Look," I said, "I've been watching those spider threads—can you see them? They don't seem to begin or end, just sway about in nowhere."

"Can't say I can, Miss."

"Well, of course you can't if you don't bend down. Bend down, Curtis, this way. If you get the angle right the sun catches them."

Duster clutched between knees, he stooped, head angled beside mine, eyes diligently screwed. "So it does. Got them now. Yards long, they must be, if they come from that tree or that bush even." He speculated about other starting points before concluding, "Fancy that."

In order not to face him directly I waited until he was lodged on top of his ladder with a book before standing below him. "So. Here we are, Curtis."

"Yes, Miss."

"I mean, still here."

"Yes, Miss."

"We haven't retired, you, me or even Mrs. Files."

"No, Miss. Thought I'd hang on a bit, so long as Mr. Kennedy's satisfied. Get him on his feet, like."

"Quite. That's what I thought too."

"Yes, Miss."

And, oh, I was listening for all that might have been in those two words but there was nothing beyond accord, understanding. Especially understanding. "Actually, though, Curtis, he *is* on his feet, isn't he?"

He ceased the rhythmical hand over hand, one empty, the other with duster, across the book. He told me once that the grease from a human hand was the best nourishment he knew for fine bindings. He turned the copper bracelet in his fingers, and answered without looking at me, "It would seem so, Miss Delia," and his eyes met mine on their way from him.

So, having known him all my life, at last I understood Curtis cared for me. It was not that I thought he hadn't cared, only that I'd never thought. In his "It would seem so, Miss Delia," I heard the untethered, selective love of friendship without judgment or demand.

How many years had it mattered to him that I shouldn't be hurt or ridiculed? When had he started to mind about the loud-voiced, insular woman who grew from the sullen little bush head he ferried back and forth from school, helped with her homework, nursed through both measles and meningitis in the year after her mother's death? And what did I know of him? Nothing, except that his adored brother with whom he shared a tied cottage died when I was eighteen, which was why he moved into the flat in the house. I'd retained my child's perspective on him; he was a player in my existence not I in his. I knew his foibles, moods, had learned, lately, that he wore a corset and, now, that he was on my side.

He closed his arm against himself, turning Leon's bangle.

"Looks nice on you." It did, there against his skin, good color.

Flushed, holding his hand out for a better view, he was extremely pleased. "I thought so too, Miss. He has good taste," drawing his wrist close again as though the bangle had whispered to him.

I left him aloft with *Stephani Thesaurus*.

After dinner that night Leon disappeared upstairs and came back with a clutch of papers, which he spread on the desk to examine and take notes from. I didn't say anything because the papers looked to me dreadfully like maps. I assumed, of course, they were maps of Sleet. More parcels of land to be sold off. But I couldn't keep my mouth shut. "Maps, Leon?"

"Yeah."

"Thought so. Sleet, of course?" Because he didn't answer I was sure it was so bad even he, despite his uncontainable enthusiasm, knew it was better kept from me. "How many acres this time?" I couldn't help it.

"What?"

"Of Sleet?"

At first he frowned at the tension in my voice. "Oh, I see, the maps. No, France and North Africa. Routes. It's for our trip. My car wants to go traveling so we've got to go with it. Come here. I'll show you where we're going. See this place, Le Havre? That's where we begin. Okay, then here, then Paris. We have to go to Paris. You ever been there?"

"No."

"Cool. Then we go on here and here, then to Marseille."

"What's wonderful in Marseille?"

"I don't know why Marseille. I've never been there, never even been to Europe. The name excites me, that's all. It feels like a dream in my mouth, one that's easy to make real just by going there. Marseille's an exit and an entry from one culture to another. Sure it's probably a dump. But who cares? We'll take a boat from there to North Africa. Then anywhere we like. Don't you think it's a good name? Marseille, Marseille. Go on, say it. Try. It feels good."

I laughed and went to shut the curtains but it was still too light. "Would you like a walk?"

"Aren't you interested in our trip?"

So grudgingly I entered his game. "All right, then, when's it to be?"

"Autumn."

"Autumn? Imagine." There's no such thing as autumn, I thought.

He folded the maps. "You see? That's why I didn't show you to begin with. You don't believe it'll happen, I know it will. But that's okay. Sure, let's take a walk."

He didn't hold my hand the way he usually did, including it with his own describing gestures through the air; this time he brought his arm around my shoulders tightly, understanding the unsteadiness inside me.

Walking back Leon said quietly, as though not to disturb unduly the once formal garden surrounding us, "I've got a landscape gardener coming down soon to look at all of this," indicating the broken statuary, helter-skelter clematis, the weed-filled urns, the empty fountain and overgrown boarders. Even I could remember it all being wonderful once. "I thought we'd look out the old pictures in the albums to see how it used to be and make it again. I don't think we could improve on that, do you?"

"No."

"There's something else too."

I'd known there was going to be. His voice always became extraordinarily gentle when there was about to be something for me to handle. "What?"

"I want us to give a dinner party."

"Oh, for God's sake, Leon," and I freed myself from him.

"No, come on. Just hear me out. We don't see anyone, Mrs. Sutherland. This big place, all that stuff to put on the table, the dining room itself. And that aside, it's not right to stay away from people so much. I want to meet them and have them know me, that

I'm here, okay? And if we don't show ourselves they'll misunderstand us and talk."

"Misunderstand? That'd be hard. Do you imagine they're not
talking already?"

"Maybe."

"Certainly."

"All the more reason. Now, who shall we ask?"

"That's up to you. It's your dinner party, nothing to do with me.
You're young, of course you want companionship. Go ahead without me."

"That's not the reason. It's for us together. To make a statement, to show we're proud and happy together."

"I simply can't."

"Because you're not those things with me?"

"No. Because, heavens, I don't know anyone anymore and,
quite frankly, it's too much trouble."

"That's what I thought. It'll be no trouble 'cause I'll fix it. All
you have to do is invite. Certainly you know people; you just don't
want to bother with them. Tell you what, I'll buy you a tree for
every one that accepts. We'll plant a little wood and call it Renewed
Hope."

"Some wood. Some hope."

The dinner was to be on a Saturday night two weeks away and Leon
wanted twenty people, the complement of our dining-room table. I
doubted my raising even ten.

It had been a long time since I'd spoken to Muriel. Shamelessly I
rang, invited her over.

"Why, it's lovely in here," she said on entering the morning
room. "What have you done to it?"

"Nothing."

"I suppose not. Wonder why it feels different. You're looking
pretty wonderful too."

I explained about remaining to settle Leon—talked on through
her noting aloud, "Four months," and explained that I, well, we,
wanted to give a dinner party for him to meet some people. I
assumed what I considered to be an air of detachment. She listened
like an adjudicator with a drama school applicant. My audition was
a failure because when I'd talked myself to a halt she said, "So the
rumor's true?"

"Which one?"

"You and Mr. Kennedy." All I did was resettle a hairpin. "So then, it is," she said, and, "Oh, Delia," as if I had confided a terminal illness.

"I'm happy" was all I could think of to say. All I wanted to say.

"I can see that. Don't think I'm judging. I want to be pleased for you. So, a dinner. I take it that's why I'm here?" She delivered me one of her lopsided smiles.

From among the shops, suppliers, business contacts that filled my address book, she helped me sort twelve possible candidates. This seemed to me an unnecessary miracle.

"They won't come. For one thing, a week's too short notice and, for another, well, why would they bother?"

"Why bother?" Muriel squawked. "Are you mad? They'd kill to come. You're sure you want to do this, Delia?"

"No, I'm not. Leon is."

"And there was me thinking I knew you. Come on, let's get ringing."

Matthew Hurst, an art dealer whom I'd consulted a few times about valuations, Colonel Peters (retired), a fellow governor at St. Mary's Primary School, both accepted immediately. So did Alicia Gross, a monosyllabic vegan dog breeder from whom I'd bought Bung and Ho thirteen years before. She said she'd bring her own food and I said good idea. When I told Leon about that later he called my response unfriendly and unnecessary. I rang her back to say it'd be all right, we'd manage vegan for her. She sounded quite moved. Tricia Lock, the wife of the local MP, thought she had to decline because her husband would be away on some MP thing. She telephoned two hours later to say she'd had it wrong and they'd "love to come." Fred and Angel Grant would "love to come" too, their farm marched with Sleet. And Alan and Mrs. Sending could come; he was Chairman of the County Council.

I was still speaking to Mrs. Sending when Leon rushed into the room; unable to stop her telling me about an international Girl Guides' convention she was helping to organize, I watched him stall at the sight of Muriel and introduce himself. She sank back into the sofa with her hands patiently folded, head inclined to the left, listening to him recounting something or other. She was the drama school adjudicator once more.

"What's so funny?" I asked her when I replaced the receiver.

"Leon's telling me about Mrs. Files's aunt. So you like life here, Leon?"

"Yes, and Mrs. Sutherland's helped me so much."

"Mrs.?" She checked herself. "Well, she would. I'm looking forward to your dinner party. Should be an interesting evening. Let me know if I can help at all. Would it be all right if Melinda came? Only she'll be there that weekend and I don't want to just leave her alone."

"Of course," we said together.

"I'm very glad to have met you at last, Leon. And by the way, you can call *me* Muriel. I must go now, Delia." It was an instruction for me to accompany her alone to her car.

Leon stole her left hand from her side. "I'm really glad you're coming and that I've met you at last. Mrs. Sutherland's talked about you a lot. I see why she's so fond of you."

The smile she let fall on the floor was brief and sad. Whatever she was thinking prevented her from speaking to him again.

Outside the front door she gripped my arm. "You did buy the place in Scotland?"

"Yes. Haven't been there. It's pretty run down. Why?"

"I know you won't ask so I'll tell you what I think of him. I think he's genuine and very, very fine."

"I'm frightened, Muriel." I could not think where the words came from, as though they had been lined in the wings of my thought, longing to be out. They were true. I had not thought it so clearly before, I was frightened.

"Yes," she said, filtering all possible meaning from my eyes. "I would be too."

I walked her to her car, inexplicably unwilling to have her leave. She had switched on the engine when her intensity vanished in that novel smile. "Here, 'Mrs. Sutherland.' What's all that about, you stuck-up old bag?"

She drove away before I could explain, which was just as well because I couldn't.

Leon lay on the floor in the morning room calling names from another address book he was holding above him, the old red one I'd had in use in the days before Francis abandoned Sleet as a scene for social life. Each name was an echo of those times but not to do with Sleet, the neighborhood or the county. When he said, "How about the Muirs, Gaby and Henry? They sound fun," I snatched the book from him.

"Where are you getting these names from, for heaven's sake? These aren't my friends." "Muir," "Gaby," "Henry" was written in Francis's gallant hand, taking two spaces for one entry, whereas mine fitted two into one. Flicking through the pages I found that every name Leon called had been written in by his father. "Why are you picking these names anyway?"

"I don't know, guess they stand out. So what's wrong with the Muirs?"

Should I tell him? Jingling Gaby Muir, tacky Gaby Muir, at the table opposite me in the Italian restaurant, "He's got a little girl out there, you know . . . I thought you ought to know . . ." watching my face to see how humiliation fitted. And here he was, the "little boy" at my feet on the morning-room floor.

The first strike, if that is the word, was made against me at church. I wasn't ready for it because, although I knew people were talking, drawing conclusions about us, they nevertheless seemed removed from any reality of mine. A lifetime lived some miles from the nearest village, within gates locked from dusk until dawn every day, creates a sense of isolation from the community. You need great energy and commitment to overcome the self-sufficiency such separation presses on you. As the years go by it is easier to believe, not that you're alone in the world, but invisible to it. Which, of course, is the opposite of the truth.

I went to church. Leon didn't come. He'd never asked to; I'd never suggested. I was late, the pews were as full as they were going to be and the first hymn was under way, "Love divine all loves excelling . . ." The Caldwell pew was at right angles to the altar, below the marble plaque listing those of the parish who'd fallen during the First and Second World Wars—one of them was my uncle. On reaching the pew I couldn't sit down because it was stacked with old galvanized pipes, boxes of jumble and forsaken prayer books. There was no cloth under all of this to protect the oak of the Caldwell pew, and no way for me to make a space for myself there without disturbing the congregation. Eyes examined me with great interest as I worked my way back down the aisle, found a space and settled.

In the usual shuffle after the service I was ready, when it came to my turn to shake hands with the vicar, to ask him about my pew. I had my hand out when he released that of the woman in front of me, swept his arm wide and high over my head and greeted the couple behind without so much as a catch in his high-octane smile.

I didn't tell Leon.

A few days later I received a letter from the Board of Governors of St. Mary's. It was a church-aided school and I'd been appointed as a foundation governor by the Parochial Church Council when my father, who had been a governor before me, died. We, the Caldwells, had given them the land to build their school in the first place. The letter told me, very formally, that, having reviewed the appointments of the governors, they had decided not to renew mine.

A little longer, just a little longer. Four months isn't long in a life.

Fourteen

W AS THAT the bell already?"
     "But I've told you three times, Leon. It's eight-fifteen now. We said eight for eight-fifteen."

"I know, but you mean people really come at the hour asked them here? That's incredible. I'll have to remember that. Pass a towel, Mrs. Sutherland, would you please?"

Leon was in my bath in my bathroom. He'd come to dress with me because he couldn't stop fueling his information on the dinner guests with any extra detail I could muster, although he already had plenty from the local newspaper and, of course, Mrs. Files.

"Some punctuality would come in handy, just sometimes, don't you think?" I was already out of the door.

"Hey." He opened the towel he had wrapped around himself and pulled me into it. "Don't look so worried. This evening's going to be wonderful, you'll see. You'll be saying to me let's give another one next week. May I add, Mrs. Sutherland, that I've never been so happy? Here, come closer. That's right."

When I finally arrived in the ballroom, where both fires were alight, Alan and Mrs. Sending were there.

The bulk of Alan Sending's appearance and his quiet attentive manner implied wisdom, inspired trust and drew responsibilities that a weariness in his eyes suggested he found hard to discharge. I doubted he had a deep well of imagination but certainly his embarrassment at this moment was depthless. He was so obviously preparing himself for the thing he dreaded even more than my presence that I took pity on him and warned, "Leon'll be here in a minute. He was, well, detained."

"No. No. Fine," he said.

190

"My God, haven't been in this house for years, have we, Alan? Not since your father's day, Delia. Not changed a bit except for the flowers. Quite a display, I must say." Mrs. Sending muscled onto a sofa, guarding her knees with her handbag.

"That's Leon's doing."

"Now is it? I'm not at all surprised," she said, very interested, accepting her sherry between forefinger and thumb. "You see? Didn't I say, Alan, coming in the car, about them being artistic?"

Mrs. Sending was a middle-aged English lady who, outwardly, had subsided into androgyny. Her gestures to femininity and elegance—pink lipstick, floral chiffon—appeared almost as perversion. Even recalling Ethel Sending, now I find her type too easy to ridicule and, ultimately, there's something touching in the ham-fisted goodwill, the gratification from bossing, arranging, interfering. If it weren't for such women the "community show" would soon be off the road.

It was important for Leon to get along with this sort and, I thought, most unlikely that he would.

"Such a good idea of yours," Mrs. Sending said, "to have a little dinner for him, Delia. So where's he hiding, anyway?"

"He'll be along." I was irritated by her but more so by Leon.

"No, but it's right to make him feel at home. One shouldn't be shy of that. After all, his is a long way off."

I was about to tell her that this was his home, when Matthew Hurst and Alicia Gross arrived together. She was driving so he could drink.

Behind her back, people would pay Alicia, in her late-fifties, that last-ditch compliment, "She was supposed to have been beautiful once." Conversing with humans, she was timid, unless there was a dog's head close by to fondle. Bung and Ho obliged quickly and, having crackled Ho's ear for a minute, while he succumbed to paroxysms of undirected scratching with his back leg on the parquet, she said, "He needs some Oterna in that ear, Delia. I'll get some over to you tomorrow."

And Mrs. Sending said, "Eerchh, not before dinner, Alicia, please."

"Well, sorry, but he does. It's important, it could be a burst boil."

Matthew Hurst, a bachelor with dark, pained features, looking younger than his fifty years, and who was rumored to have had affairs with a few local wives, went directly to stand before the oil painting beside the fireplace. Arms crossed, head lowered, he reminded me of Leon who arrived, finally, at the same time as the Grants and the Locks.

There was a minute hitch in the chatter when Leon kissed me on the cheek before going to Matthew. They reached for each other's shoulders like old friends. Leon had visited his shop and had him in search of certain paintings. I followed him round the room with rather ineffectual introductions because each name he knew straight off and quickly gave his own with a warm familiarity.

Mrs. Sending held out not one hand but two. "Welcome to our country," she said with the careful enunciation the English employ with foreigners and imbeciles.

Leon grasped both her hands in his, taking them to his chest, which brought the two of them quite close. "Thank you, Mrs. Sending. That really is so kind of you."

Mrs. Sending was androgynous no longer. She was smiling, hardly able to look him in the eye. "No, I, well, I mean it . . ."

"You're doing that fête, aren't you? The big one in the village. I read about it in the *Echo*. We must talk about that later, I want to hear all your ideas."

"You bet, Leon. You bet." He gave her back her hands and it was a while before she could think what to do with them.

To Alan Sending he said, "It's good to meet you at last. It's Pocock, isn't it, who's Head of Planning on the District Council? He told me how much you're in favor of me getting permission for the development on Ragge Down."

Scratching his neck as an excuse to face away from Leon, Alan said, "Mmm, yes, well, I'm not Planning or District, you know. Can't influence or anything like that."

"I realize it but I'm pleased that, unofficially at least, you're in favor."

Sending, coming to terms with some indeterminable danger, looked at Leon, but with his head back and eyes directed to his hairline. "No, no. Good thing, developing Ragge Down. They need it there."

Leon steered Angel Grant away from her husband with, "You have to meet Matthew Hurst. He went to your seminar at the Courtauld? He says you're a genius. We've got pictures here that need restoration. Would you advise me sometime?" Then he re-

192

turned to her husband. "It's good to meet my neighbor. How do you do? Mrs. Sutherland says your farm 'marches' with Sleet. Such a cool expression, don't you think? So positive and reassuring. Military."

"Golly, I suppose it is. Never thought of it like that before. So that makes us, what, soldiers-in-arms? Eh?" The tips of his rough, nail-bitten fingers circled one ear before entering his sparse ginger hair.

"That's it, Fred. You've got it, man."

"Jolly good. Jolly good," and Fred looked immensely, if self-consciously, pleased with himself.

So it went on. Leon brought grace and festivity to our fumbling gathering, infusing everyone with a sense of occasion.

He even knew about Colonel Peters's garden and asked if he could visit, touching on the Colonel's sole source of pride. I wanted to be glad to see Colonel Peters. I thought he'd been a friend of sorts, a good colleague, certainly; but I didn't know how much he'd had to do with the cancellation of my post as governor at the school. When he huffed into the room, just the way my father used to, he let me know right away where he stood. "Gotta talk after dinner, Delia; I've heard and it's a rotten business. Down right silly."

That, even more than Leon's reassurance in the bathroom, freed me to make the most of the evening.

The Fullers arrived quite late with apologies and Melinda. Beautiful, beautiful Melinda. Nothing to be said about her beyond that. Seeing her face close to I remembered what her mother had said, "A bad time with a fellow, a bit bruised still," and it was there, the hurt disillusion of the young before they learn how to pretend. Her pale slippery hair was swept into a chignon and she wore black leggings with a gold-embroidered T-shirt. I guessed I was being honored by the formality of her dress.

On the way into dinner I heard Leon say to Alicia, "Bung really likes you. He likes me too. Ho doesn't. I don't understand why because I've tried with him. I expect all dogs like you, though."

"I know how they feel. I empathize with them. That's all. There's no mystery about it." Very crisp she was, twisting a button on her jacket.

"Wouldn't it be something, Alicia, if we could all be like that with one another. Think of all the time we'd save. Look, you're sitting right here." He drew out her chair even though Curtis was waiting to do that, with two young ladies I did not recognize in tow. (Mrs. Files's granddaughters, Curtis informed me between guinea fowl and sorbet.) Alicia's eyes followed Leon as he told Muriel and Tricia where he'd like them to sit, and speaking as though answering an imaginary voice, she said, "You're absolutely right, Leon. I only wish I could."

There was no harsh damask cloth, as had been the custom at Sleet, so the table returned a glow of candlelight that thinned the lower darkness of the room; there was no blockade of candelabra either, just two long lines of candlesticks and Leon's face, celebrated, framed, smiling at me from the end of that brilliant highway.

I was thinking: Oh God, here we go, then, and trying to control the lethargy that had always descended at the beginning of dinner parties in my own home, when, next to me, Tom Fuller whispered, "Hey, Delia, no yawning now."

"Me? Yawning?" making out something was stuck in my tooth.

"You always did that at your own dinner parties, I remember. Muriel does too, actually. Nerves. All the planning that goes into something like this, I suppose."

"Well, this isn't me. Leon's done it all. It comes quite naturally to him."

"We keep saying, Muriel and I, who'd have imagined this? Him here. You too. He was a little chap when we visited Francis out there."

"Muriel told me you visited once."

"Yes, that's right. We stayed friends with him a while after you two were sort of separate. Not for long. But a visit to the Bahamas, all expenses paid, is difficult for a hard-up couple to resist."

"So you knew Leon and Euturpia . . . Jeanne."

"I wouldn't say 'knew' exactly. Not 'knew.' " A nerve twitched the lower lip of his tight-drawn, banker's mouth and I thought I saw another side to his nature. He watched Leon as he spoke. "They were about the place, but background figures. It was embarrassing for us, his guests, the English ones, at least. We were aware of who they were but didn't quite understand the form. You know. She'd sit in silence at the table and if she did speak he'd usually cut her; shout if the little fellow made too much noise, that sort of thing. It's weird to see him tonight, though." The nerve worked at

194

his lip again. "He has the same quality she did, that deadly vulnerability which you find yourself serving even when it's the last thing you intended. And, I suspect, the last thing they require. I mean, look at old Tricia next to him now."

The few times I'd come across Tricia Lock had made me regard her as a woman accustomed to being attractive, even bored with it; not this evening, though, next to Leon. She was drenching him with her allure, leaning, touching, playfully admonishing, and he was responding with more of the same.

"And I always thought she was such an aloof bitch. Hope he talks a bit to my poor Melinda. She's very shy."

There was a natural lull in the talk and Nigel Lock said into it, "Uh-oh, angels passing. Let's see." He looked at his watch. "There you are, everyone, twenty past nine. Twenty to, twenty past. Never fails. Angels."

"God, that man's a bore," Tom said when everyone was speaking again, "and to think I voted for him. The funny thing is a man can like him too. Leon, not Nigel. He's not threatening despite being a flirt."

Yes, I thought, I suppose he is flirting with Tricia, and I waited for the old intoxicant to shrink my skin, swell my blood, impair my concentration for anything that wasn't to do with him, all of which happened when I'd seen Francis flirting. It didn't come. None of it happened and I really believe I was enjoying myself with Tom and Colonel Peters.

Fred Grant was demonstrating something for Alicia with his unused knives and borrowing a fork of hers. "It's a hydraulic, inflatable penile prosthesis . . ." I heard him say and she said, "Jolly handy. Would it work for a dog?"

Muriel and Matthew Hurst were speaking at once to each other. Later on Nigel Lock needed to leave the room and on his way out slapped Leon on the back. "Great party, Leon. Good fun." Leon returned a broad salute.

His leaving made a temporary space between Mrs. Sending and Melinda to whom Leon still hadn't spoken, Tricia wouldn't let him. Mrs. Sending didn't speak to Melinda either; she talked across her to Leon.

"I say, Leon, we were just talking holidays over here. Are you going on one, or is this it, if you see what I mean?"

"No, Mrs. Sending, this isn't holiday, this is home and work but we're planning one."

Silence infiltrated the various conversations, and again it was obvious, despite everything, where the real interest lay. I raised my arms above my head, stretching as sinuously as possible to draw Leon's attention, and I tried discreetly indicating "No" with my hands.

He purposely took his time to decipher my pathetically obvious code and, smiling, leaned towards Mrs. Sending. "I—okay?—*I'm* going to France in the autumn, driving across to Marseille then taking a boat to Africa."

"My dear, how gorgeous. Roots. What? You know that man. What was he called? Cunt something, Cunta, you know."

Matthew Hurst choked and Muriel offered, "Water, Matthew?" which made him worse. *"Kunta Kinte,* I think you mean, Ethel, don't you?" she said to Mrs. Sending whose eyes latched on to her before quarrying out Matthew as an oblique source of ridicule. "Mr. Hurst." She ordered his attention and he pulled himself together.

"Yes, Mrs. Sending."

"I've been to your shop, you know."

He raised his hands. "Then I'm a finished man, Mrs. Sending. I'll come quietly."

Mrs. Sending surveyed the gratefully laughing company before retreating to her handbag to produce a compact and draw reassurance from a reflected fragment of her face.

Nigel Lock returned and Leon talked to Melinda. A while passed before I noticed anything more and when I glanced that way I think I expected Leon to be giving Melinda the treatment as he'd done with Tricia, but no. The two of them, Leon and Melinda, had their chairs turned towards each other; his legs were crossed on her side so, in effect, abandoning Tricia who was looking sour with only Muriel next to her. Matthew and Angel Grant, who was on his right, were engrossed in each other.

With Melinda, Leon's gestures were reserved, contained, as though in the nervous presence of a rare creature. He was letting her talk and it wasn't coming easily; she twisted painfully, eking out every word, and he encouraged with the absolute focus of his attention. Their heads were very close. When she'd finished explaining something using her shoulders and hands, bringing them down with an emphatic finality, she raised her face to his and I remembered the photograph in his room, the one of him dancing with a girl. Melinda was beaming to Leon that same trust, a certainty of understanding.

Slowly he touched her cheek with one finger, tapped it once gently, then the air, in an instructive way, paternal even. Yes, she'd see him like that, as wise. And she'd be right. He was no boy. Never had been. I felt none of that, that swelling of my blood, nothing so meager, so prosaic as jealousy. I simply became entirely, unwillingly aware. It made me feel very faint.

"Are you all right, Delia?" Tom said.

"Bloody hot in here, you know." Colonel Peters fanned his napkin at me.

"I suppose we should go on through," I said.

In the ballroom there was the usual dislocation when a party's moved from one place to another. Mrs. Sending sidled up to me. "Any chance of a loo?"

"Absolutely. Through the gunroom on the right."

"Oh, Delia. Come on." Muriel took my hand. "Let's all go to your room."

I'd forgotten that. That it's customary for the women to troop to the hostess's bedroom after dinner and I thought: Bugger. So up we went with me picturing the trail of Leon's clothing between my bedroom and bathroom, not to mention other signs of his occupation there which I'd no longer notice but they would.

As it happened someone (who but Curtis?) had been there before us. When on earth had he found time to remove every trace of Leon and place a pile of hand towels by the basin?

They sat on our bed, Leon's and mine, Angel, Tricia, Melinda, Mrs. Sending and Alicia, from whom everyone wanted a puppy that evening. Mrs. Sending said, "Well, I don't care what anyone thinks, I think he's a darling."

"Who, Delia, is your cook?" Tricia said quickly, leaning into the mirror. "I've never tasted such delicious food in a private house."

"Mrs. Files."

"I don't believe it. You haven't still got that old gossip?"

"Yes."

"Well, she's a genius." Angel was dodging behind Tricia to gain a view of herself.

"But it's Leon," I said. "Mrs. Files never cooked like that before." All the making-up, hair-combing, talking ceased. "I don't mean he cooks himself but he takes a great interest, plans a lot with her."

"He's rather wonderful, actually, Delia, isn't he?" Angel lifted her short brown hair from her eyes to see me better as she said it.

"Yes." There was restraint among them in case speaking just then might prevent me from embroidering that simple affirmation. So I did say something: "If everyone's been then let's go down."

They filed away through the door except for Muriel and Melinda.

"Go along, darling," Muriel said to her daughter. "I'd love a word with Delia. Are you all right now?" she asked as soon as the door was shut.

"All right?"

"At the end of dinner you were a bit pale, shaky."

"I wish I'd never given in to his idea for a dinner party."

Muriel sat down, pushed off her shoes. "How can it end, you and Leon?" raking in her handbag for cigarettes. "Don't tell Tom, he thinks I've given up."

"That's when I feel the fear I told you about. Thinking about the future. He sees one for us. It doesn't make sense." She said nothing, drew on her cigarette. "Does it, Muriel?"

She would agree with me in her own time. "There were moments during dinner when I could have believed it was Francis sitting at the table, the resemblance was so powerful. It made me remember evenings here. I so admired your pride and dignity. Driving away I'd say, "Don't ever do that to me, Tom, humiliate me like that, because I'm not like Delia. I couldn't take it.""

"The fault wasn't all his, and I was very young."

"And now?"

"Now? With him?" I pointed to the door.

"Yes."

"Very old." We skimmed off some of that laughter that comes to the surface when everything's too much.

"I like these menthol ones. Never see anyone smoking them nowadays. Do you?" Muriel gazed at the tip of her cigarette. "They came here with knives out and tongues wagging, now every woman here is in thrall to Leon. From that clot Ethel to Melinda. Even me, given half a chance. I tried to work out how he sets spinning such affection. It's interesting. It's a compulsion with him, isn't it? He seems to need to know he can have it. And of course, like his mother, he can."

"She's dead, you know."

Muriel continued her staccato puffs, like a furtive schoolgirl. I didn't understand her lack of interest until she said, "That made a bad rift between us for a bit. Tom and Jeanne. His first infidelity. Now I've learned how not to know. Maybe he is, maybe he isn't."

"With her? With Jeanne?"

"Whether Francis knew or not I couldn't tell. He was hurting her, I think, and she wanted to make him jealous. That's all it was."

"There was me thinking you and Tom were so happy."

"Oh, but we are, very." She examined my face, considering where this obtuseness might come from, then slumped back in the chair, elbow in palm. "So it was something in particular that upset you at dinner?"

"Seeing Melinda with Leon, the rightness."

"Not Melinda necessarily. Not Melinda at all, but the rightness, yes. Delia, he's young, he'll want a family. That's natural. People, society, if you like, will help him towards that. They'd see you two together as a threat if only because it doesn't fit. He's the owner of Sleet, good-looking, charming. Never mind blood, he's a catch. He's accepted now, that's obvious. He's in first-class waters and, make no mistake, they'll cut you out. You could be hurt again, the way Francis hurt you."

Muriel searched the dressing table vaguely for an ashtray; failing, she threw her cigarette into the fireplace. "Oh, your poor face, Delia. But how can I not say this and still call myself your friend?"

I was bound with my limbs. Legs crossed at the knee, the ankles, arms folded so tight I could feel the back of my rib cage under my fingers. I rocked and rocked, holding inside me, for as long as I could, the remaining traces of happiness. "It's why I never called you. I'm terrified. Can you understand being terrified of peace, of happiness? I'm loving life, Muriel."

"I can understand if you know, at heart, that that happiness is selfish."

"There. There you are. You've said it, haven't you? There's no unsaying that. This happiness of mine is selfish. I'm blocking his way to fulfilment, whatever that is. You can't imagine how many times I've prepared to leave." I was rubbing my face to nonexistence. "No, don't touch me, please, I'd collapse. If only we'd never had this dinner. One of us has to stop dreaming."

The Grants and the Locks were in the hall on their way out, all rather drunk, effusing over the evening. Outside they called promises to ring, get together, do it again, while bumping into each other and opening the wrong cars. Colonel Peters and the Sendings arrived behind me while I was still on the step.

"Jolly good time, Delia. Now you're sure about the School Board, no intervention on my part? Be happy to, you know."

"Positive, thanks, Colonel."

"Delia. Thank you." Mrs. Sending linked her arm in mine. "What an evening. He played jazz records while you were upstairs. Lovely."

"Yes. He's crazy about jazz. Like my father. Did he tell you he plays the clarinet?"

"Why no. But he would. Rhythm, you see."

"Oh, do come on, Ethel. Night, Delia, thanks."

In the ballroom Matthew Hurst and Leon had been sitting either side of Melinda on the sofa. Leon came to me as soon as I entered.

"What's the matter?" he asked not very quietly, then the Fullers surrounded us with thank-yous so Leon escorted Melinda to the front door.

Alicia and Matthew followed; he brought my hands to his lips. "It was all wonderful, Delia. Thank you for letting me share it."

And Alicia said, "He's right. It is. Yes. Thank you. I'll ring Leon about his puppy. Same line as Bung and Ho, you'll be glad to hear."

I sank into the blasted sofa. Despite voices still in the hall and the pungent aftermath of perfume, cigarettes and cigars, this pompous room was cold again.

"I hate it in here," I said when Leon returned, "and all the furniture in it."

"So we'll change it. But some of this stuff's nice. What's the matter?"

"Nothing," my hands covering my face.

"Did you enjoy yourself?"

"Very much. You?"

"Yeah. It was good," he said, "I liked it," refusing bail to any

200

word, any movement that might smash the fragile surface between us before he'd divined the trouble he knew was below.

"How was Tricia?" I asked.

"Which one was she?"

My hands dropped. "You're joking. Which one was she? After your great show of rapport at dinner?"

"Oh, right. She was saying how she lost this baby some months back. That she hadn't wanted it at first 'cause she thought she was too old but then she was pleased and that it would have given, I think she said, 'a little more meaning' to her life. Then she lost it and had to have a hysterectomy and she's had this big depression. I guess they're not too happy, she and the guy, whatsit, Nigel?"

"She told you all that?"

"She did. Boy, has she some cage around her mouth," indicating the same place on his own face where there were no lines.

"So that's it, is it? The sum of all that intimacy, 'Boy, has she some cage around her mouth?' Well, I've got a cage around mine too. Look. Here. People get that when they grow old."

"I know." He was still guarding himself from a word too many, one too few. "But when your cage opens birds fly out."

Now I was too tired to stay upright and fell back, hiding my face again, this time with my arm.

I felt him come close, stroke my hair. "Tell me what's the matter, Mrs. Sutherland. Has someone said something? They have, haven't they? Why were you upstairs so long? Why were you faint at dinner?"

"You saw."

"Of course."

"And Melinda? How did you find her?"

He couldn't see my eye watching him through the corner of my elbow. He lowered his head, those lines settled between his brows. "She's very sweet. I liked her. She's been with this guy who really screwed her around but she couldn't make a break with him, like find the strength until—"

"All right, all right. So you had her history too. Is that what happens to you with women, they give you their tragedies?"

"I guess. A bit." He tried to laugh.

"I'll give you a warning: women invent wounds for men like you." He stirred, vaguely bored, and I understood he didn't care much one way or the other, that the intimacies were digested and passed along with the food. "Not Melinda, though," I said. "Take her seriously, Leon. It's right you should like her. She's your age."

"She's only twenty. Why are you doing this? Being this way? Trying to make yourself hard? You know how I feel about you and that it's real. So why make it like I'm cheap, like I'd hurt you, like there's anything more to me than you?"

"Don't."

"It's true."

"Well, it's got to stop being true."

Don't let him touch me, not while I'm hurting him this way. Don't let him guess how I want it all to be, not change, how I want to carry on the way we were before the world trudged in.

He did touch me. He knelt beside the sofa with his head on my stomach, a hand on my breast. "It's not a good time to talk," he said. "If I let you go on you'll trap yourself. I know what you'll say. What you're trying to do. But you're wrong. I can't believe that you don't understand yet, that it's all right between us and won't go away. That I won't change."

All the time he was speaking I was pressing his head hard against me and he said, "There, you see, your hands tell the truth even when you try not to."

He stayed very close to me going up the stairs to my bedroom which was, after all, our bedroom. He only undressed when I'd done so, watching me all the time as though I were a valued prisoner.

Whenever we made love he'd speak, things I couldn't always hear, and I'd say little. Something I'd yet to learn. I hoped I was conveying everything with my touch and I think it was so. It was. But this time he was asking me incoherent questions through the darkness. Usually we lit candles to see each other but not that night. It was so late. We were so tired. He breathed out the questions with the movements of his body until at last I heard only one phrase clearly. "It's all right, it doesn't matter," he said. "I'll understand from silence."

Over the weeks that frantic grip of his throughout each night had lessened with custom, security. That night it was back, his instinct to readjust every time I turned, even when he was submerged in sleep, clutching my hand with what in daytime would have been a cruel force. But in the night I understood it; I always had.

I don't think I slept at all; one can't be sure but I didn't want to.

I wanted to count the minutes of the night, hear him, see him, as the light grew and finally be aware of the time of his deepest sleep. That was hard to know because of the vigilance of his body. When I heard Mike calling the cows I withdrew my fingers from his fist and recurled it on itself. Carefully, carefully I extracted each of my limbs from his. He slept on. I took my clothes from the chair and dressed in the passage. Not daring to return for the shoes I'd forgotten I went to the gunroom and found an ancient, cracked pair of my father's walking shoes. The front door I left ajar behind me to prevent the inevitable clatter of its shutting. It was a bright, still morning. Bung and Ho quickly tuned to my stealth and, teeth chattering with excitement, leaped obediently into the car, snuffling their bowls with curiosity.

I reached for the ignition. With the first turn of the engine Leon would wake. I knew that. But all I had to be was fast. Very fast. My fingers felt for the key and it wasn't there. I had to reenter the house. They'd be on the hall table.

The keys were in my hand when I looked back, up the stairs. Leon was naked at the top of the first wide flight. He hurled himself down but without falling, I don't know how, and letting out a scream that was a word as well, "No."

He reached me before I could turn away, crushing my shoulders, his face distorted with hysteria. Only able to shake his head he kept repeating the word, the noise, and pulling me to kneel with him on the floor.

"Please let me go, darling." I whispered it, to be sure he'd hear my pain too.

His arms were around my neck, his face pressed into it making it wet with his tears and saliva. "I won't. You can't. It'll never happen. I want to make you happy. Don't go. Let me make you happy."

"Please, Leon, please, my love." And I listened to my voice unroll into that old hall. So contained, it was. Where do my voices come from? How can the sound of them lie so well when I'm not, by instinct, a liar?

Gripping my wrist with one hand he wiped his face with the other, trying to calm himself inside and out. "You have to listen," and he did face me, and he was calm, severe with sincerity except for kaleidoscopic panic in his eyes. "You have to listen, Delia." He closed his eyes when he'd said my name, my real name, as if it were unbearable; his fingers pressed hard on my mouth. "Delia." A smile crippled his lips. "I love your name. It's the name of a brave woman. I love you, Delia, without power, without guile, without qualification. And it's the best thing I've ever done, ever shall do."

I kissed him and rose like a calf getting to its feet for the first time. Curtis came from nowhere with a blanket which he dropped around Leon. Leon who was still kneeling. Curtis in trousers, vest and braces with his secret belly let loose. He nodded at me and winked, I think, if such an unsubtle cue could be attributed that dear man, and he ushered me to leave. He stood, bending a little to grip the blanket in place over Leon's shoulders, and bunching his lips to kiss the air, blinking, urging: Go. Go. Everything will be all right.

When I was through the front door Leon screamed again, the same sound, the same words, "No, don't go." I ran to the car and then I heard him shout, "You don't understand anything yet, Delia."

The last time I saw him was like that, on the steps of Sleet with Curtis struggling to keep the blanket over him, his cries torn up in the noise of the engine.

PART FOUR

Fifteen

THERE IT IS, THEN. There's no more than that. I was a child when I should have been a wife; a lover when I should have been a mother; a mother when I should have been a friend.

He knew he shouldn't try to find me; that I wouldn't ring, wouldn't write. I'd monitor his life from a long way off, far enough to make him believe I wasn't anywhere at all. Except he had faith, he believed.

The place I drove to was the one I'd bought in the Flow Country, in the far north of Scotland. The one I had bought eight months before, from a photograph, one visit, and an inauspicious surveyor's report. One hundred acres with a small farmhouse and steading comprised of a barn, granary, byre, stable and implement sheds. Uninhabited and unworked for some years, the fifty-odd acres of arable were fallow, the rough grazing ungrazed.

Petrol-blue and white-eyed flows, some no more than a puddle, others an expansive loch, stared from the face of this vast mireland, bearded by conifer, scarfed by snow-sloped mountains. There was no other habitation within sight of my house.

I can't guess whether I'd bought it believing I'd never go there, never require it, or whether an unacknowledged instinct understood that the very dereliction of the dwelling and the harsh demands of the land would be essential to me if I did go there, had to go. The woman I was then did so much lying to herself, even now I can't untangle what she was from what she pretended. But the rudimentary nature of my existence during those first months—a mattress on the floor of one of the three upstairs rooms, no running hot water, a broken lavatory obliging me to dig a pit outside and use that, a break or fault in the electric cable so it was oil lamps if I

207

required light, which I did rarely throughout the long summer of days linked by notional twilight—was so demanding that any possible regret, doubt, analysis was rubbed out by fatigue. I lived as an animal might, addressing only my physical needs, hunger, thirst, security and warmth at night; existing without reflection or anticipation. What I was aware of, and this only at first, was a broadwinged sorrow that had settled on me, fastened itself and become my condition.

A solid fuel stove was installed before too long, a gorgeous, glossy, blood-red one. He would have approved. On this I cooked while it heated enough water in the tank for my uses and provided a base for the dogs. They settled beside it from the first moment it was lit and rarely shifted away, following me with their eyes, heads unmoving, sucking in their gray muzzles, shifting from paw to paw. "Lie down," I'd say. "Lie down, boys," and they'd obey, remaining stiffly alert in case I should abandon them. Their days of ball-licking gusto were gone. They circled the yard when they had to, dubiously sniffing, glancing furtively about as they balanced to lift an arthritic leg. They only accompanied me walking if coaxed. They ate little. They'd been too old to make the move; the water didn't suit them, the air was wrong.

First I attended to the house, buying furniture by mail order and from the shops in Thurso. But whether from a picture, shop or salesroom it was his judgment guiding me: Not that one, Mrs. Sutherland, that one, it's simple and more comfortable, such a beautiful shape. It was the same with the clothes I had to buy, since I'd arrived with nothing. I chose softer fabrics, kinder lines, subtler colors. And one time I found a dress I'd never have bought—Now, that's really something, I heard—and bought it with no earthly reason to wear it.

Possessions weren't sent to me; no one at Sleet knew where I was. I wanted it that way. If Sleet came to mind at all—who knows what was unraveled in dreams too deep to recall—my thoughts zeroed succinctly on the Chinese boys.

After some weeks I was ready to address the wilderness outside. First I repaired the dikes, windbreaks made from Caithness flagstones set sideways one after the other, iceberg-style, with two thirds below the peaty soil. From my bedroom window I could see their dawdling lines making sheets and pockets of the purple-brown land. I cleared out the implement shed and reequipped it. When I'd

208

repaired the slate roofs of the stable and byre I was ready to buy my sheep, fifty Cheviot ewes and a tup from a local livestock sale.

That tup had a splendid autumn. Having smothered his brisket in raddle mixed with engine oil, blue for the first weeks, red for the rest, I could easily mark his progress covering the ewes by the color left on their rumps. Through the *John o'Groat's Journal* I bought an old Ayrshire due to calf in October and a dozen point-of-lay pullets.

My ewes weren't the self-sufficient mountain sheep one associates with the north; they were particularly silly and very dependent, prone to anything at all that troubled sheep, it seemed to me. The worst was an outbreak of twin-lamb disease. I lunged after them with a syringe full of glucose and glycerine, and despite the lethargy brought on by that sickness they still managed, when I was full-tackle midair, a last-minute skip out of range.

I'd given instructions to the lawyers appointed for my own affairs, shortly after Leon arrived at Sleet, not to disclose my whereabouts to anyone, only to forward my mail. Nevertheless, at Christmas I received a card direct from David Rosen with a letter inside. He'd guessed where I was. That wasn't hard since he'd acquired the property on my behalf, his last act for me as my lawyer. He wrote that he'd wished to reaffirm our friendship "or at least my affectionate respect for you." I laughed when I read that, he came so clearly to mind. Such a funny, measured man, he was, even in the written word. But when I read his last line, "Might I visit, I wonder?" I thought: Yes, I'd like that, and invited him by letter.

Early in the New Year, Bung died. A stroke paralyzed his back legs and I spent two nights beside the stove cradling his old head in my lap, willing into myself enough courage to call the vet and have him put down, and Ho watched from my feet. On the third day a second stroke finished him. I took Ho to sleep on my bed after that but he didn't find it the treat he would have done in the old days. After a night or two he chose to remain downstairs by the stove. One morning I arrived in the kitchen and he was stiff, nearly cold, his eyes very slightly open under those expressive tufts that are a dog's eyebrows. It was hard to believe he wasn't alive.

They were old boys, the two of them, brothers from the same litter; they'd had good lives. It was in the order of things that they should die but that didn't make it easier. The only vestige I had left of other times was my father's old walking shoes. They resided by the stove on the opposite side from where the dogs used to be.

I didn't wait long before buying a collie, highly trained and experienced, something I'd wanted as soon as I bought the sheep but never sought out of respect for Bung and Ho.

His name was Pete and he tried to disguise his searing intelligence with a panting laugh and unending smile but I said to him, "I know you, boy; you're a clever one. No point in pretending." Yes, he was a dear brilliant fellow but I was determined ours was to be a working relationship and shut him in the barn at night, never allowed him in the house.

Come April, when lambing began, Pete and I spent many hours under the pale, flat hand of night watching the ewes for signs of trouble, and there were plenty.

Delivery didn't come easily to all of them and rather than let a ewe strain too long stressing, weakening herself, I greased up and, lying behind her, forehead resting on upper arm, eyes shut in concentration, I eased my fingers then my hand through the tight, swollen vulva to plunge, elbow deep, into that viscid mystery, identifying a hoof, tracing it to a head, unlocking twin from twin, or turning a large breeched single so that, cupped in my hand, its nose then body slithered out and slumped into our airy world.

The blue-rumped ewes all began at once, each setting off the other. I had such a time distributing my attention in the open that I partitioned the barn into sixteen stalls and set up a maternity ward. There I could keep a close eye, not only on those in labor, but on some of the unreliable first-time mothers. It was a good way too of preventing the poaching of newborn by one or two of those whose lambs had arrived dead. Twice I fostered successfully by skinning a freshly dead one and jacketing its coat around a triplet from another ewe. All of it was involving, exhausting and utterly, utterly rewarding. Soon, day and night, I was surrounded by the wailing of young ones answered by the reassuring burr of the mothers.

It wasn't until August that David's visit finally came about. He'd suggested April to me which was my busiest time with the sheep; we'd agreed on the end of May but he canceled with some obscure excuse. Waiting at the station I was shocked to calculate that over a year had passed since my arrival in the Flow Country.

When his short, dapper figure stepped towards me holding an old-fashioned leather suitcase he reminded me of a cut-out traveler to stick on a child's cardboard station. He had no briefcase. I'd never seen him without a briefcase before and I thought: Well done, David. He finds it hard to break a mold. He waved from a long way off, which was my cue to prowl a bit, hands in pockets, walk to the car before him, lean across to open the passenger door. We were both seated before the greeting, the kiss on the cheek.

"Your hair, Delia." He leaned back, arms crossed, head cocked, to assess me while I was driving.

"I know."

"When did you do that?"

"Soon after I got here. It was too much trouble, all that folding and such. Should've done it years ago."

"I've always thought long hair was the most feminine but now I'm not so sure. You look great and, if you don't mind me saying so, ten years younger."

"I don't mind. Ten years younger, ten years older, it's all the same to me."

He laughed. "You've not changed, then?"

It made me look at him, his saying that. For a moment our eyes were caught before he turned away to watch the road on my behalf, as it were; then, coloring a little, he pointed at it to redirect my attention. I couldn't speak.

We stayed silent for what seemed a long time and probably wasn't. I was thinking: I shouldn't have done this, had him here; he belongs to the past, the over, the finished. Questions to which I didn't want answers formed without bidding. So life goes on, I thought. Well, of course it does, what did you expect? They're all there, living on, Curtis, Mrs. Files and the rest of them. The rest of them. And Leon. "How is he?" I asked. How is he? I asked and we hadn't even reached home yet.

"All right, Delia. He's all right." Voice gentle, he touched my shoulder to say it and they were our last words until reaching the house.

David placed his case on the kitchen floor. Linking his hands in front of him like a polite child he swiveled without moving his feet. "This is charming."

"Good."

"No, I mean really. Did you have someone, an interior decorator?"

"Seriously, David."

211

"No, well you could have had. It's welcoming and pleasant. Thoroughly inviting. Fancy you creating this."

Yes, it would have been surprising, had it been me alone, but I couldn't explain to him how it wasn't; how there was nothing, from the flagstone floor downstairs to the mountainous duvets on the beds, the soft tweed curtains and the voluptuous armchairs, the choice of which wasn't primed by a sensuality learned from someone to whom such things were elemental.

I showed him his room and returned downstairs while he changed. There was going to be nothing I could get on with so long as he was staying: only one night. I knew from the moment I saw him there wasn't enough between us to protect me from rediscovering a world I imagined I'd eclipsed. He was already proving that what I thought to be walls were only screens.

"Bleak landscape, Delia."

I'd been staring out of the kitchen window past the yard, away to the hills, and he startled me. "Shall we go out, then, walk a bit?"

"Walk the policies?" he said, and something must have happened to my face, to the whole of me, because I heard him speaking beyond my attention. Words, words until I made out, ". . . I don't have to stay, Delia. There's a train back tonight. I'd quite understand."

Yes, that's right. Go away. Don't make me look back along the short road I've traveled. "Don't be silly. You can't possibly go. Come and meet Pete and Deirdre."

"Oh, right. So you're not alone, then?"

In the byre I introduced him to Deirdre and her calf. "He's nearly a year now and I still haven't named him. I just call him Wee Caffy. That's what the children call him."

"Children? Do we mean humans this time?"

"Yes. They bike over occasionally. Miles it is but they like helping out. I'm grateful to them, they do a lot. I hear their laughter and it's nice."

He stroked Pete's head. "Who else?"

"No one."

"Bleak landscape."

"You said that. It's not. I don't find it so."

"Are you ever lonely?"

Years and years ago he'd asked me the same question one night at Sleet. I can't remember my answer but I do remember he choked on his brandy. "I don't know," I told him this time. "Don't know, so it doesn't matter, does it?" I hadn't been lonely in those other days; there was nothing then to be lonely for.

Tutored from his visits to Sleet, David asked questions about the fields I would be preparing and sowing in the coming months. But all the time I was struggling against what felt like his surveillance of me. He was trying to define something he couldn't tell from my appearance. Yet, walking back to the house, I began to wonder if I was wrong, that really he was searching for the moment to deliver what he wanted me to know.

On entering the kitchen he saw me look at the clock above the stove and joked, "Too late, I'm afraid. The train'll have gone by now."

I must have smiled although this known man, who was my friend, was frightening me.

Later in the evening a malt whisky dissolved the self-conscious membrane between us. Having eaten we sprawled in armchairs in the kitchen, separated not, this time, by the fire and mantelpiece of the morning room, but by a window that nearly reached the floor. Through that and the open stable door flowed the evening light.

"I can't believe it's so late and there's still no sign of night," David said.

"It'll shutter a bit in an hour or two, not much, though. One gets used to it."

I watched him watching me. Why this fear? There was nothing I cared about that hadn't already been taken from me; no one I loved whom I hadn't lost or left. So why? Was it simply that this trim and respectful man who, for years, had wanted more from me than I would ever give him, I could now only associate with dispossession? Pity overcame fear.

"Talk about Sleet, if you like," I said. "I'm ready now. Do you see him much?"

He eased forward, frowning into his malt after reading my eyes, tipping it to his lips, hardly parting them. "Yes. Yes I do, regularly. You do understand, Delia, don't you, about my not coming down while you were still there? How could I have talked business with him the way I had with you and especially with all he had in mind to do?"

"Shh. I do understand." I took his hand and I think he was as surprised as I was. "I've never known you not do anything right, David."

He watched me in silence with the reflection of an incarnation in his eyes. Mine. "You're awfully good news," he said, and I wondered if any language offers the shelter that English does.

We let our hands part smoothly, mutually, and sank back into our armchairs. David crossed his legs. "He's being highly successful. Ragge Down's gone through. There's plenty of money and every enterprise he's into makes more. Extraordinary, really."

"So?" Because there was more, I knew it.

"I don't know. He's liked. Very liked. He has an ingenuousness, hasn't he? You want to help him all you can. He's got a battery of advisers, specialists in the leisure industry, accountants. You name it. They distance him, somehow. He's very impatient. If I'm too, in his view, slow or pedantic . . ."

"You? Pedantic? Come, now." I filled his glass from the bottle at our feet.

"It's the way I'm made." He sighed in his pleasure at being teased but felt for his cuffs all the same. "But he won't wait, you see. He'll bring in another who's faster."

"Quit, then." I kept very still to say it.

"You know I can't do that to him."

He waited for me to answer. What did he think I'd say: I did. It's easy? He saw I wasn't going to speak and went on, "I did suggest it once but he made it clear he regarded me as essential. Which I'm not, in any obvious way, any longer, but just the same . . ."

"Curtis?"

"Getting old. Very old. He's devoted to Leon and it's mutual but the fact is his mind's wandering. Worse, to tell the truth."

"Why?"

David shook his head. "I can't." Was this it, then? What he knew would cut me down yet had to tell? It almost certainly was because he raced on. "Well, all right, I will. The last time I went down to stay over, like I used to with you, dear old Curtis served the two of us dinner in full evening dress." He was silent.

I realized he thought he'd finished and that it was my turn to speak. "Nothing wrong with that."

"A lady's evening dress, Delia. A lady's one. Long, blue jeweled bodice and full skirt. Straight out of the fifties. Nothing under it. I

214

mean, bare arms, shoulders and all. In and out he sailed with the courses. I didn't know where to look."

Making out the view from the window was all of a sudden more interesting than what he was saying, I stood close to it.

"It's not funny, Delia. It's pathetic. It's incredibly sad. Curtis is a fine man, he shouldn't be allowed . . . I can't believe you find it so amusing."

I was wiping my eyes. Let him think it's laughter; he's probably right. "What did Leon say?"

"Nothing until dinner was over."

"Then?"

" 'He's better in pink.' "

David at last seemed to guess something about my response because he came over, took my arm. "Come and sit down again."

He hasn't finished, I thought. That wasn't it, the blow. It's still to come. This time he filled my glass. "He doesn't have friends, you know. Leon." He said, "I see any number of invitations lying around and he gives lavish dinners, parties that are the talk of the county, by all accounts, but, like I say, he doesn't have friends."

"Why so sure?"

"Guess."

"Mrs. Files."

"Right. He never leaves Sleet."

Twice I took a breath to ask a question and failed, resorted to the malt, then David answered anyway.

"He does," he said—I brought my face from behind my hand— "ask about you. He does ask about you. That's what you want to know, isn't it? Well, he's given me letters addressed to you once or twice but always taken them back before I left. He lets his question wait, only one it is, until the very last moment and never looks at me to ask it, he'll fiddle with something, pat the dog. He's got a dog now, black Labrador, very like Ho was as a youngster. 'And Mrs. Sutherland?' That's how he asks it. 'Nothing, Leon,' I say. 'Not seen her.' The same every time. He never fails and always at the last moment. But it's there between us until he does. He never changes his question, I never change my answer. It's easier that way."

"And now that you have?"

"Seen you?" He recrossed his legs but it didn't assuage his restlessness. He walked to the stable door, leaned through, came back and stood in the middle of the room delicately scratching his scalp through freshly washed hair. "If I told him anything I'd say you'd changed; that you were a different woman. Warmer, more tender, more worldly, a lot of things. I'd tell him you were all the things I'd imagined, hoped you were, knew you were really but which you hid. Only, Delia, you see, I don't think he'd find those qualities a change, would he? That's how you were with him. Wasn't it?"

I linked his arm into mine. "Come on, old friend, let's walk awhile then it's high time I went to bed."

"I couldn't possibly sleep, not when it's this light."

"Get into bed and make believe. You'll find the night passes."

And the night did pass. So did his visit. The next day was easier. We hardly referred to Sleet. I took him to the station for the evening train, went to the platform where it was waiting. There were ten minutes before its departure but he got in just the same, secured a window seat with his suitcase although there were no other passengers, and came back to talk to me over the door. We chatted until quite suddenly that sensation of an impending blow returned to me. "I'll go now," I said.

"No, wait."

"I don't think so. It can't be long before you're off. I must get back to the—" I couldn't think of what I had to get back to but was already turning.

He grasped my arm. "There's one thing. I couldn't think quite how to put it and it's good news. Or should be." There was no good news in his face. "He's engaged, Delia, to a girl called Melinda Fuller. He told me a while back. That's why I canceled May. I think I hoped you'd have heard by now."

"You misled me, then. You said he didn't have friends."

"He doesn't."

"You only need one." I think I was shouting.

"I wish I'd told you sooner. I was a coward. I've never met her or seen her at Sleet. He just told me one day back in April, then nothing changed. I even asked him recently if he was still engaged and he said, 'Sure.' Nothing else. Oh Lord, it's moving, the train's moving. Where's my case?"

"On your seat, David. Good-bye."

216

Sixteen

YOU'D THINK there'd be some solace in having done the right thing. You'd think there'd be some rill of satisfaction, now that my hideous departure, my abandoning of him and that living thing that was the joy we shared in each other's company had been proved to be the correct move. After all he'd advanced without hesitation into the conventional social channels, hadn't he? And what did I feel? Nothing but parched horror. So fast? As fast as I'd needed to be on driving away from him. That fast he'd been in finding a young wife, as though just waiting to be set free.

I decided to sink back into the timelessness I'd achieved before David's visit; reconvince myself that anything beyond the world I could see with my eyes was unreal. Leon lived, presumably loved and would marry in another dimension. Somehow I'd construct immunity from existence.

Melinda Fuller. Beautiful, vulnerable Melinda Fuller. It was so obvious; so pat. Hadn't I said to him, "Take her seriously, Leon, it's right you should like her?" And he'd done it. I think it would have been easier had David given an unknown name. But who knows?

Throughout the following autumn while I cleaned, plowed and sowed the few fields and while the tup revelled in his second season, images elbowed into my mind, surrealistic scenes of the wedding with our dinner guests identically multiplied, a dozen Ethel Sendings showering pages from *Roots* as confetti, a dozen Matthew Hursts and so on, with Curtis, the only one in the singular, wearing another of my mother's Norman Hartnell evening dresses. I dare say he felt, and with reason, some reward was due from his years of caring for those beautiful clothes.

By the late spring when lambing was nearly over I was picturing Leon with a child of his own and that was easier to support. The rightness of it, that rightness again, assuaged me. The images were no longer so mad, so painful. He was a young married man with his family, the thing I couldn't give him and couldn't give his father. I began to acknowledge a justice in Leon being there at Sleet with his wife. And why just one, why not squads of children? It eased me to think in those terms, to place him in scenes in which I could never have had any part.

I applied my own advice to David, I made believe. I made believe that while I might not be exactly happy I was content. I certainly had the things I'd always valued most: land, work on it and the company of a dog. I purposely didn't consider any change in me brought about by David's late-flung news. It would have been dangerous because although I was using up the days of my life, occupied, concentrated, certainly just beyond my acceptance was emptiness. But if that was the case it meant that all the time since arriving in the Flow Country I'd been hoping. It meant I remained what I'd always been, a woman pretending.

I received Muriel Fuller's letter far into summer when night's only the half-shut eye of day. Having been outside since early morning walking along the dikes, checking for gaps, resetting slipped flag-stones, I returned to find the postman had left on the kitchen table the yellow packet in which, monthly, the lawyers forwarded my statements and business communications. I don't think there'd been anything personal among all that since David's note following his visit a year previously. But then why would there be? I never wrote to anyone.

On seeing Muriel's signature at the end of a number of pages I set them aside, regarding them from a distance while waiting for the kettle to boil. Then I went into the yard with a wooden chair, a mug of tea and her letter. I'll copy it out just as she wrote it:

My dear Delia,
You'll already have looked to see who this is from and I hope that doesn't mean you'll tear up my effort before reading, although I know it could and I'd understand why. I've torn it up a few times myself, I can tell you. Mr. Curtis has given me your lawyer's address but I've no idea when or if you'll receive this

and feel like I'm writing into a vacuum. That might make it easier.

Is it crass to wonder whether you're happy wherever you are? The danger of getting old without being old enough is that you begin to think you know when you don't, and you compound that error by going on to give advice. I remember our talk in your bedroom at Sleet. How much did that have to do with your leaving? That's what I keep asking myself. I was talking conventions then, the deadly order that keeps society on the straight and narrow. But believe me, Delia, I sincerely feared for your happiness too. No matter how I try to rephrase that last sentence it doesn't sound sincere and it should because it's true.

Melinda went round to Sleet the day after your dinner party with flowers from our garden as a thank you. She found Leon— well, she found him. I can't describe what she did but when she came home she cried in my arms for him, for his wretchedness. If I could have found you then and made you return I would have done so because right away I guessed I was holding in my arms all the sorrow of the coming months.

Of course she fell in love with him and he let her. Why should he not? He could barely cope with his own feelings. I saw him enough during the first few months to watch the draining away of all that vitality. The sweetness, that charm of his, remained but I know now it's no effort for him to be like that. He doesn't select then bestow his tender and instant intimacy. It's just how he is and it's nothing to do with him. I've no doubt he'd be astonished to discover the emotion he stirs in men and women alike but women mostly, needless to say, by merely listening in the way he does. And if they expected, these uninvited confidantes, any return from him as a result of their unburdening, which they would, and do (because that's human nature, isn't it, to bear your soul and expect to have it kissed because there's nothing quite so remarkable as your own soul?) they'd be disappointed and, quite likely, humiliated. Because there's lots that's more remarkable than any old soul, especially to Leon who's probably been up to his ears in souls for years.

But Leon's developed his method of defense and survival. He doesn't belong, does he? Not only does he not belong to a country or wholly to a race, he's carried it further and chosen not even to belong to himself. So he feels no responsibility for the reactions he promotes in others; even his own actions he views with ingenuous wonder.

It's all very well me observing, rationalizing, in this way, now that it's all over, but Melinda was the victim of it all, you see. We humans and animals are drawn to warmth; it's natural to move closer expecting the warmth to increase. It seems against nature to find absolute coldness at the source. That's what Melinda found in Leon. He let her come close, he let her fall in love with him and, Delia, despite all the reasoning I do hold him responsible. I do say it's due to him she's been in a clinic for months now. He could have protected her from himself.

Her period of blooming with him was short, that time when she discovered the last heartbreak was nothing and that her feeling for Leon was something far bigger. She mistook his passivity for reciprocation. She could never accept that he didn't really love her, not fully, not in the right way. I can't imagine how the engagement came about. I can only think it was a kind of assumption that grew. After the occasions Tom and I went to dinner at Sleet with Melinda there—neither guest nor host—I'd leave thinking to myself: I've just met the saddest man in the world and my daughter's going to marry him.

Slowly something began to devour her. If it's possible to be devoured by a lack then that's what it was, some missing component in his love. She hung on and tried to make plans, the way girls do, to change this and that in their prospective homes. He wouldn't have it; without actually preventing her he never allowed her. She once said to me, in the early days when she still confided in me, before the unhappiness set in, that talking to him was like trying to grasp a fish. There's no point in detailing her decline but she became anorexic and, you saw her, there wasn't much of her in the first place. It's a horrible condition. We watched her go down very fast. She was admitted to the clinic. It was suggested by her doctors that Leon should stay away until she was stronger, and he seemed to understand, accepted it. Tom and I were appalled that he did. We knew what it meant.

I'll try to write out the exchange between Tom and Leon that settled the matter a while ago. We went to Sleet. Leon was expecting us and led us into the morning room. Same as it ever was, Delia. Still your room. As soon as I was in Leon's company

220

I began to want to change my mind, to think: How could someone so engaging and sincere not be loving my daughter properly, be doing her harm; how could Tom and I risk anything that might mean she loses this rare person? But there, I'm a woman, aren't I? After a drink and a few words about Melinda's improvement or lack of it, Tom asked Leon, "Do you love my daughter?" and Leon said, "Don't ask me that, Tom. She doesn't, although she has the right to." Then Tom said, "If I asked you to leave Melinda alone and never let her come to you again even after she's out of the clinic, what would you say?" He took a little while to answer and when he did it was, "I guess I'd do like you ask." "Then why not do it yourself? Why let all this happen when you can't even say you love her?" And Leon answered, "Why hurt when there's no good reason? People do that too much. She wants to get married and that's all right. Isn't that right? Isn't that the way things should be? I won't hurt her, I'd never do that. And I'd make her safe."

There you are. He values what, no doubt, he's always most desired. We all do. Not to hurt, to make safe. Good grounds for a marriage, all too rare as well. But it's not necessarily what one wants to hear for one's child when it comes without mention of love. And it was lost on Leon that the want of loving, while he was letting Melinda love him, was killing her.

All Tom said was, "All right, Leon, then I'll have to hurt her for you." After that we went.

I'm ashamed to say that I came away with those blessed arms of mine wanting to hold him, as a mother would out of pity for a boy who's nothing but a victim of his own defense. A fellow shut out from the start but for whom the door's been opened and he's been let in on intangible conditions. Of course there was nowhere or anyone safe for him unless, Delia, it was you.

Now I think you'll understand why there's no one other than you for me to express all this to. But I wonder if you can imagine how hard it is for me to write this way? Delia, it's my daughter, it's Melinda, it's our Melinda who's five stone and wasting, who fixed her love in a time of weakness, and that's the hardest kind to withdraw. She is, was, a straightforward middle-class girl, privately but not broadly educated. Her childhood was happy and secure with no dark corners. Yes, she went to Cambridge, yes, was doing well in her job in a publishing house but there was nothing in her experience or nature to prepare her for Leon's, brewed as it is with rejection and complexities that don't bear thinking about. I'm not blaming. I'm just desperately, desperately grieved.

It wouldn't be possible for her to return here, visit us, to have this be her home the way it's always been, and not see Leon's picture in the local paper, hear his name everywhere. His success runs throughout the county. So we're moving away. We've found a nice place, not as beautiful, though, and without the memories, of course.

This letter is to ask you to forgive my vanity. I should never have interfered. And I don't really know why I've told you all of this except that I thought you ought to know.

With my love and deep regret at the loss of our friendship.

Muriel

I wasn't shocked, disappointed, and no, there wasn't satisfaction for me either from that letter. But it did arrest me in a profound way. Back among these pages I described my condition during the early days in the Flow Country as having a broad-winged sorrow attached to me. Well, with the receipt of that letter those broad wings closed, enfolded me, obscuring my ordered days, making me forgetful and tired. My reservoir of physical strength emptied and tasks that once I'd not given a thought to tackling were out of the question: patch-repairing a roof, changing a wheel on a tractor. The old tup did his stuff during the autumn but by New Year I knew I wouldn't have the strength to handle lambing. I sold the whole flock, and Pete with it, to my neighbor. It was, in fact, to gain that remarkable dog that he bought it, he told me. I leased the grazing, along with the sheep, and I sold Deirdre and Wee Caffy, who was no longer wee nor a calf, through the same newspaper in which I'd found her.

There was little for me to do anymore and what had to be done wasn't. If the weather was fine I sat on a chair in the yard watching shadows of clouds on the hills. Otherwise I lived mainly in the kitchen the way the dogs had done at the end of their days.

I wasn't reflecting, questioning or planning although I have to admit that almost by sleight of hand I'd freed myself. With no creature to take care of, and through its dependence have my existence beamed back on me, I became almost unconscious of living.

It was a time of distillation and recuperation with my mind as incapable as my body—for once the one wasn't using the other to forget. My being was in unison, a slow vacant unison.

I allowed six of my lawyer's monthly yellow packets to arrive before I troubled to open them, and when I did it wasn't systematically. I pooled the contents of all six on the kitchen table and was outfaced by the dullness of the heap. But I did find, among the usual communications, a printed card. On this, under the word "OLD" was written Sleet Park's address, and under the word "NEW" was printed "The Old Manor," following with an address in the Savernake Forest. Handwritten along a dotted line at the top was "Digby Curtis, Esq." The postmark showed it had been sent four months previously.

I spread the heap of papers to see if there might be a letter from Curtis among them, which there wasn't. That was when I found the postcard of the fish market here in Marseille with your handwriting on the back.

Marseille. It's where you said we were going when you spread out the maps, "My car wants to go traveling," you said. Marseille was to be our first stop after Paris. "There you are, Mrs. Sutherland." From that moment the card's handling began, turning it into this tattered thing. I read uncountable meanings into those five words. Then I heard your voice saying them. When that happened I laughed; there in my kitchen I laughed and laughed with not so much as a chicken to witness me through the open stable door.

One day in the springtime after I'd spent the morning in the sunshine of the yard, I took my chair indoors, damped down the stove which had been continuously alight for nearly three years, turned off the water at the mains, and closed the front door behind me. Walking to my car I was flooded with the familiarity of leaving.

It took me six hours to reach the border and I spent the night in Carlisle. I only mention that because when I'd left Sleet three years before I'd reached the Flow Country without stopping other than to refill with petrol.

I found The Old Manor easily and telephoned from a nearby village to arrange a visit that afternoon. It was a large Victorian house set in several acres of rhododendron. The front door was open. There were a dozen elderly people in the sitting room, playing cards, talking, watching television. The atmosphere was not institutional, except for the number of chairs. A grand piano occupied the space in front of a bay window.

When I asked the room in general where I might find Digby Curtis, a frail-looking woman teetered towards me. Reaching up for my elbow she guided me back to the hall where she pointed to the stairs, with a charming smile but not a word.

Mounting the stairs I heard someone else come into the hall. "Who's that, Mrs. Price? I say, excuse me, who are you?" A young, brisk individual raced after me. When I told her who I was she said, "I'm so glad you've come. He's spoken to me about you. He's so fond of you. I wonder if you could help us with a small problem?"

"If I can."

"He won't socialize, Mrs. Sutherland. He remains in his flat, which is, of course, quite self-contained. All the flats here are. But we do like everyone to, at least, have supper together in the dining room once a week. It's not good for the elderly to become too reclusive. In six months he's only been down once. And I'm afraid, that time, I couldn't let him into the dining room."

"Why?"

She chewed the pad of her thumb, route-marching her eyes along the floor, up the walls, back to my face. "It sounds so silly. But he came down dressed most oddly. As a woman, actually. No makeup or wig. Nothing silly like that but wearing a dress. In fact it was the most lovely ball dress I've ever seen."

"Hartnell," I informed her.

"Thought so." She worked her thumb some more. "Please don't think me unreasonable or narrow-minded, Mrs. Sutherland, but I simply can't encourage cross-dressing. Some of our residents are confused enough as it is. Could you possibly have a word, say how we'd love to see him, only in something more conventional?"

"Come in, Miss Delia. I heard your step in the passage and knew it was you."

A large room with a bay window and a fireplace—it was the one above the sitting room. Curtis was attending to a table laid for tea. I clasped his hands and they held mine tight.

"Cup of tea, Miss Delia?" He handed me a cup. I stepped backwards towards a chair. "Let's move the cat off first, shall we? Come along, Bully, shove off for Miss Delia." He scooped a Persian Blue kitten into his armpit. "Always wanted one of these. But what with Mr. Grimwood shooting every cat in sight, then the dogs, well, I didn't embark."

"You've been here six months, then?"

"That's right. Mr. Kennedy bought me the lease on this little place. It'll see me out. There are five others but we had the pick. All newly converted. Full up now, all elderly people like myself, and it's supervised, you understand. Help at hand if we want it."

"I'm told you don't socialize."

His lips pursed in amusement. "Spoken to you, has she?"

"Just a little word in the friendliest way. I think it's your dress sense they don't appreciate."

"Thought that would keep them at bay. Just the one gesture. They haven't troubled me again. I never was one to enjoy a crowd. Lot of silly talk. I've kept just the best of the dresses, Miss. They were too lovely to leave behind. I hope you don't mind. They're in the cupboard over there if you'd like to take a look . . ."

"No, thank you. I know you take splendid care of them."

The fly-following spasms of his head had worsened; all of his movements were unsteady. He must have been wearing his corset under the same black jacket and pin-striped trousers he used to wear on duty. I knew he'd dressed that way to diminish the changes between us, have everything, as far as possible, as it used to be.

"Scotland, after all, was it?" he asked.

"Yes. But I've left now."

"Ah."

"He's left too, hasn't he, Curtis? I think he's left too."

"He has. Sold up four months ago. Gone traveling, he told me. That's all. He gave me some of the books, let me choose. It's pleasant to have them. Now and again I get down old G. Vertue and give him a bit of a rub."

We sat without speaking, our thoughts ranging over our shared past. Mine were of his brother, of how, before Curtis moved into the flat in Sleet House, even I had been able to feel all his energy and involvement directed towards the cottage where Maurice lay ill for so long, just as my mother had lain ill. "I can't remember his face, you know. I'm not even sure I ever met him."

"Who's that, Miss?"

"Your brother."

"Brother, Miss?"

225

"Maurice."

"He wasn't my brother," he spluttered. "He was my friend. My very great friend."

My features must have looked rudely enlightened because he chuckled and bowed over his lap to bring his face close to mine. "You never did have much ear, did you?"

"It's developing, Curtis, I'm growing one."

"Is that so?" He was skeptical. I drew out the postcard, showed him. He turned it in his fingers and smiled at the message.

"I'm taking the ferry to Le Havre tonight."

"So you are, then." Skepticism gone.

"It's been a while, hasn't it, since the card was sent?"

He didn't bother to look at the date but tugged his lobe. "Learn to trust it."

He drifted into thought again, raising his eyes to inspect the window, the cat in his lap, and seeing altogether different things. His eyes had changed. There had been a time when they held disappointment, disillusion, but no longer. He said, "Funny you should mention Maurice. He's with me from time to time, in this room. Now, he hasn't done that for years." After a while he said, "You'd better be getting along, Miss, if you want to catch that ferry."

On my way out I touched the keys of the piano. "Did you play a lot together, you and Leon?"

"We did. We had some pleasant times." He clasped the copper bangle on his wrist.

"I heard you both once. I was outside your flat and the two of you were playing in there, him on the clarinet, you on the piano. You were awfully good."

Curtis shook his head at me, tutting, pulling on that lobe again. "No, Miss. We couldn't play at all."

I've bought a flower, a large silk flower. Not violets with their connotation of dotage, but a shaggy-headed, dust-pink peony. I came in here half an hour ago. Yes, in. I've moved inside despite the courtesy table and chair outside. There's too much rain. I hadn't counted on rain. The old lady was in her place with that bit of a dog on her lap as usual. We come early, you see, she and I, we're the first to arrive. I handed her the flower in its box, with the lid off so she could see straightaway what it was. *"Pour moi? Vraiment? Pour moi* . . . ?" she repeated with enchanting delight while removing that greasy bunch from her lapel to replace it with the peony, and I stood beside her watching, encouraging.

She didn't ask me to join her. She understood this to be my offering in acknowledgment of her respect for my unsociability. And, of course, above all for saving your card.

I'm at my new chosen table, right by the glass partition, and there's the pavement, the traffic-thick road, the fish market. Yes, I'm here. I can be seen by anyone who's looking.

I think of Francis. He's returned to me twice. The first time was in the early morning on the Boulevard Charles Livon where the pavements under the mulberry trees are stained blackish-red from fallen fruits. There he was next to me, that's all. Nothing to see, to touch. No message. The second time I was in my bathroom here in the hotel. I was brushing my hair, still glad about it being short. Over a space of minutes I grew certain Francis was stretched on the bed next door, hands behind his head, the heel of one foot balanced on the toe of the other. I didn't go through to see, I've learned enough not to do that. My impression, soundless, you understand, was that he chatted to me. Trivialities delivered in the unemphatic manner couples share when dressing and at ease with each other.

About all of this—these numerous exercise books filled with my words—I've finished. There's nothing more to say. Everything else is ahead. Before long I'll rise, leave, circle and, perhaps, return. You may be with me; you may not. I prefer to believe you will be.

A NOTE ON THE AUTHOR

The Possession of Delia Sutherland is Barbara Neil's third novel, following *As We Forgive* and *Someone Wonderful,* which has been translated into six languages. She lives in Wiltshire with her husband and her five children.